TURNING

TURNING

JOY L. SMITH

A Denene Millner Book

SIMON & SCHUSTER BFYR

NEW YORK LONDON TORONTO SYDNEY NEW DELHI

SIMON & SCHUSTER BFYR

An imprint of Simon & Schuster Children's Publishing Division
1230 Avenue of the Americas, New York, New York 10020

Text © 2022 by Joy L. Smith
Jacket illustration © 2022 by Talia Skyles
Jacket design by Krista Vossen © 2022 by Simon & Schuster, Inc.

For information about special discounts for bulk purchases, please contact
Simon & Schuster Special Sales at 1-866-506-1949 or business@simonandschuster.com.
The Simon & Schuster Speakers Bureau can bring authors to your live event.
For more information or to book an event, contact the Simon & Schuster Speakers Bureau
at 1-866-248-3049 or visit our website at www.simonspeakers.com.
Interior design by Hilary Zarycky
The text for this book was set in Adobe Jenson Pro.
Manufactured in the United States of America
First Edition
2 4 6 8 10 9 7 5 3 1
CIP data for this book is available from the Library of Congress.
ISBN 9781534495821
ISBN 9781534495845 (ebook)

For Lettie, the "L" in my name.
Miss you, Grandmother.
Wish you could hold this book in your hands.
And for Cherish. You know why.

TURNING

CHAPTER ONE

The Barre

M iss Kuznetsova was right; I don't know what hard work is. I'm ghost-knuckling the barre, doing the opposite of what I was taught in ballet—clinging for dear life, trying to hold myself up. I want to tilt my head to reroute the highway of sweat working its way down my face, but dare I tempt the balance gods and risk eating the floor? On the other hand, I'm hungry. I'm afraid to move my eyes anywhere but in front of me. I've been staring at the corny LET'S GET PHYSICAL poster for ages now. It brings a new definition of spotting.

I remember my first-year training under Miss Kuznetsova. I knew I was great, everyone told me I was. Miss Kuznetsova worked that attitude right out of me with my first pirouette. *Trash. You call that spotting? I'm surprised you aren't picking yourself off the floor. Come back to that spot or leave my class.* That was her being nice.

God, I miss her.

"You got this, Genie," Logan tells me. He sounds so sure, loosening his grip around my waist.

"I can't do this." My elbows shake in sync with my voice, I

swear. Is the ground getting closer? Logan tightens his grip on me, and I fall back into him. "Dammit!"

"None of that. Come on. Straighten up. You can do this," Logan says.

He's so close behind me, it reminds me of partnering class. The way his hands round to the curves of my waist. I close my eyes. I want so bad to be back. I want to be lifted. To feel as if I'm soaring through the sky, then put down, ever so gently. But it's not pointe shoes skimming the surface, or boys landing out of jumps that I hear. No. It's the sound of a walker scraping and a metal leg stomping across the room somewhere.

"I'm done with this." My hands start to slide, and I have nothing left in me to straighten myself up. Danny, Logan's assistant, sits on a rolling stool; he holds my ankles, the only thing keeping me weight bearing.

"Okay, hold on." There's subtle defeat in his tone. "Bring me her chair," he orders Danny.

I hate this place.

I'm mad at myself. Scratch that. Mad doesn't begin to describe how I feel now that I can't stand on my own and the only place I want to be is at my summer dance intensive. I had so many new dances I wanted show Kuznetsova. This was the stepping-stone to my last year of being a student. Logan lowers me onto the floor, because everything in this place is a test. I'll have to work to get into my chair. "Don't be so hard on yourself." He kneels down and looks at me, but I turn my head.

"You said I'd be able to walk again."

"No, I said you could work toward standing with supports and *maybe* taking some steps, but I didn't say it would be today." He takes off the ugly ankle-to-knee braces I wear in therapy and stretches each of my legs out. "You okay?"

Just this morning, Miss Kuznetsova asked me the same thing. She's been checking up on me since the day after my accident. It's been nearly three months of daily emails filled with her life affirmations, well wishes, and the same question: *When will I see you again?* I love her too much to reply. But every morning, despite my silence, there's her email asking me if I am okay. She doesn't need my answer to figure it out.

I glare at him. "I'm at Disneyland."

"That's the spirit." He smiles and gets up to write some session notes.

I take the time to feel him up with my eyes. Given his long, lean build, he would be a perfect pas de deux partner. Whenever he's spotting me, I sometimes imagine he's Chris, my ex-partner and best boy in our level. Naturally, he'd fit me in skill and height for partnering. If I squint enough, Logan's shaggy brown hair could be Chris's.

Finally, I'm able to wipe some of the sweat off my face with my T-shirt, which reads VAGANOVA AMERICAN BALLET in the boldest, most sparkliest red letters the school store offered. Pink has never done it for me. The black shirt makes the red pop more anyhow. I should be there now, throwing Black Girl Magic pixie dust in their faces. Funny, right? Now all there is to throw is salt in my wounds.

I watch Kyle, the guy who's usually here with me, shuffling along the length of the room with a walker. Slow but steady, he's making it. Not just his exercise, but this whole rehabilitation thing. Just two weeks ago he could only stand with that walker. Before that he needed all hands on deck to kick a ball. His eyes bulge out of his face, and his patchy head mimics a water slide as droplets make their way down his neck. Not even the railroad-track-like scars lining his head can stop them. Standing. Walking. That will never be me, though. Not as an L1-L3 incomplete paraplegic. We exchange a fuck-this-shit glance and a small, friendly smile. While we're on different sides of the boat, it's still the same boat, so despite the fact that it took me a month to smile back, I can return the nice manners now.

"You should really think about going to group therapy sometime. Kyle goes."

Logan lowers himself onto the floor, and I scoot backwards into my chair. "I won't go."

"Did you miss what I said about Kyle going?" Logan whispers. "You'd be surprised to know you're not alone in this whole recovery thing."

"I heard you loud and clear. Can't see what that has to do with anything."

"If you go, you could actually talk to him instead of secretly wondering what his deal is," Logan reasons.

"Why do that when you could just tell me? Actually, don't." I would hate if Logan told anyone anything about me. Especially my injury.

"It wouldn't hurt to check it out."

"Kyle or the QUEST group?"

Logan crosses his arms and smiles that Realtor-ad grin. "Both."

I use what strength I have left to lift myself into my chair and push off. Pretty sure Logan could've picked me up by his pinky.

"Great transfer! Maybe I should get you angry more often." He follows me out into the hall. "Think you'll stay the full session next time?" Logan asks.

And watch Kyle pass all his tests? I think not. I keep rolling away, pretending not to hear him.

"Try to have a good day, Genie," he says behind me. "Buckle up!"

Too late.

I follow no hallway etiquette as I rush by everyone and every room on my way out. It feels like I slam directly into the beaming sun, finally out of that maze. How can anyone move in this heat? If a power chair didn't cost college tuition, I'd look into one for summer purposes alone. At least there was air-conditioning inside. Now I'm rethinking my signature dramatic exits. As Miss Kuznetsova would say, *Come in with presence. Leave a legend.* Logan would argue I'm not on the stage, and I'm not doing myself any favors, but once prima, always prima. Yep, that's how I roll now—twenty-four-inch rims.

The good thing is, I still have my amazingly flexible arms to fish around for my bookbag hanging in the back. My hands swim around inside the bag, pushing away Vaseline and a pack of gum, until I pull out my shades and slide them on my face. I readjust my feet on my footplate. Good. Now I can go.

Starbucks's mermaid logo on the corner taunts me. The calories alone used to be deadly to this ballerina. Now the distance is the killer. I make my way down the block. It's slightly uphill, which is why I try to talk myself out of needing a chilled drink. The mermaid won't get to win this round. Double caramel drizzle *will* coat my thick lips like fancy lipstick. Starbucks lipstick. Makes me think of Hannah, my best friend. The girl who would rather wipe her bright lipstick off before class than not wear it at all. I can hear her voice now: *Genie, which one? Selena or Salsa red?* I'd shrug because they look the same to me.

Before I know it, I'm halfway up the block. Just three weeks ago I didn't have the strength or the willpower to make it up a block, let alone up an incline. Logan would be pleased.

How's that for needing a full session?

"You got this, Genie," I chant. "Two more pushes and you've earned yourself a venti iced caramel Frappuccino." Logan's rubbing off on me.

The door is closed.

I'd rather do thirty-two fouettés on pointe any day than open a door now. Before my accident, there'd be someone on their way in or out. All I'd do was slide in. Now people sympathetically open the door for me, but no such sympathy today. Damn, I pushed myself all this way, too. I'm starting to feel like I'm peeling off a Band-Aid every time I lift my arms.

Don't let this mermaid bitch win, Genie. I take a deep breath and align myself to pull the door open. Success. *Take that, you scaly bitch!* With my right hand I hold it open for as long as I can, but it's heavy and my palms are sweaty—the door closes too early and sandwiches me between it and the frame. Touché. We're both being bitches to each other. I've been known to be competitive.

The barista's mouth opens and closes like a fish. She doesn't know what to say. What do you say? Sorry you suck at navigating the world? Sorry you spend too much time leaving therapy early and angry to properly learn how to get through doors?

Trapped, I rock side to side in my seat, trying to squeeze by. Relief hits me as the door opens behind me, and I'm able to wheel myself to the other side of it.

"Thank you. You'd think they'd have automated doors," I say loudly, so the barista hears.

The woman who opened the door gives me a quick nod and smile, making her way to the register. The cool air calms me, and I take in the famous coffee smell. It's not often I get to have these high-calorie frozen treats. I never starved myself, but I did have to diet. Being a little curvier than most, I had lines to maintain. As dancers, our bodies are not just a form of entertainment. They're living art; we have to take care of them. My art died along with my nerves.

After the woman places her order, I'm next. I can see the unease on the barista's face. She's trying to be professional, but my chair makes her uncomfortable. At least it feels that way. I can't tell if I'm being sensitive. It's a turn of events from the glowing looks I could conjure before by just walking in a room. Yes, I'm that gorgeous, but it's like I can't be pretty *and* in a wheelchair. The computer monitor blocks her name tag. Being low is a pain in the ass.

"One venti iced caramel Frap, please," I order.

"Whip?" she asks.

"Yes, extra drizzle, too," I add.

"Name?"

"Cripple," spills out my mouth like a slippery ice cube.

Her eyebrows rise in question or shock. Both? But I'm not in the mood to apologize.

"I'm sorry?" she asks again, probably hoping she heard wrong.

"Genie. Just Genie."

The space is tight. I survey the room for a spot to wait that won't be in the way of the line that has formed out of thin air. *Just great.* I swivel behind me, looking for another door to exit out of when I'm done here. Nothing but tables and a bathroom. *What happened to our truce, mermaid?*

People tend to part like the Red Sea around me. No one wants to get rolled over by a person in a wheelchair. The funny thing is, even if it isn't their fault, they usually apologize. I guess they figure I have it bad enough. Actually, I don't really know what they're thinking. "Genie?" The man behind the counter places my Frap on the bar top. He looks out at average height, not even noticing me approach the counter.

The counter's a bit high, but I push up on my arms to reach it. I grab a straw and place my drink between my legs. If I didn't watch myself place my drink there, I wouldn't even know it was there. I have no sensation in my legs, but if you bang my knees hard enough, there's some reflex capability. The perks of my low-level paralysis. In common terms, it means my back broke just close enough to my ass that my top half works, while my hips and lower are equivalent to a wet noodle. "Perks" and "paralysis" shouldn't be in the same sentence.

Out the same way I came in, I make my way to the nearby park and find a shady area to sit under. I need two hands to push myself. Drinking and driving is not an option for me. *Ba dum tssh. Thank you, I'll be here all week.* I'll be an artifact before I laugh at that joke.

I'm not doing myself any favors taking out my phone to scroll through social media, but I do it anyway. It's a struggle to see all the dancers I follow, yet I can't bring myself to kill my own profile. Scrolling down the page, I hover over a picture of Hannah. Black leotard, arch to die for, 180 degrees of perfect penché, posted just fifteen minutes ago. Hannah smiles, making it look easy. Just fifteen minutes ago I was at a barre, and I didn't look beautiful. I didn't look effortless.

Why would Kuznetsova want to see me again when she can look at that? Even though I want to hate the picture, I bring myself to like it. Hannah and I were two of the few minorities at our studio. We connected the minute we started at VAB when we were twelve. Between my caramel and her mahogany skin, we stood out in our black leotards among the girls who looked like they were taken right off a music box. Five years later, Hannah's living out the dream we planned together on train rides home from class.

Come fall she'll be auditioning for top ballet companies all around the world. And she's good, too. Some company will want her. Wouldn't be surprised if she got a few offers. I figured we'd drift apart from being busy working our way through our respective companies . . . but I never imagined it'd happen like this. Hannah always wanted to dance in Paris at the super-exclusive Opéra National de Paris, but I fancied Germany. Specifically, Semperoper in Dresden. I haven't spoken to her since my accident. All my doing. I don't want my bitterness to rub off on her.

I look down at my legs, covered in sweatpants. I had plans to wear the shortest shorts possible this summer. Now I don't feel comfortable showing my legs. To me they look misshapen already. Like my bones have forgotten so quick they're supposed to be lithe and muscular and gorgeous like everyone says they are. But they know they're useless, so they're starting to look like it.

My phone rings, and Mom's picture engulfs the screen.

"Yeah, Mo—"

"Where are you? Why aren't you at the therapy center?"

I roll my eyes so far back I can see my brain. "Relax, I'm up the block at the park."

"You need to stop leaving your sessions early because you find them hard." She pauses. "And if you're going to leave the center, at least have some decency and text me, Genie."

She can't see that I'm giving her the speed-it-up hand.

"Leaving." I end the call and shove the phone back into my pocket.

Not in a rush to get back, I sit tight and finish my drink. She can wait if she insists on coming to pick me up every time I have a session. I can take the bus home, but she's too busy suffocating me to allow it.

"Genie?"

The voice sends me to a time of sneaking kisses between classes. Hershey's and real ones. Being serenaded with improvised songs about pretty brown girls and the promise of never being left. Freshman year was sweet in every sense. Junior year was beyond rotten. A squirrel squeaking brings me back to the real Nolan. The one in front of me with the water bottle dripping sweat down his arm. Speaking of arms, he's got his muscles and a few new ones on display in the Looney Tunes tank top I got him from Six Flags the first summer we spent together. It makes me sick to see him looking so healthy.

I turn my head, hoping he'll take the hint. He doesn't. He sits down on the bench so close to me, I have to remember we aren't in calculus, let alone dating anymore. Feeling safe with him is no longer a thing. And now the smell of chlorine is attacking my nostrils.

Mowing him down comes to mind, but so does guilt and shame. I hate how he makes me feel. I'm a knot around him, twisted and hopeless to untie. That wasn't always the case.

He hums. That's what Nolan does when he thinks. What is he thinking about? Us? The last time we spoke? What to say next?

"I miss you," he says finally. "You went ghost on me. I was mad close to talking to your mom. And you know how we feel about each other."

That's what he says. No *Wow* or *Are you okay?* I'm not surprised.

"Ghost would mean I died, though. What are you even doing over here?"

"Lifeguarding at the Y up the block. Getting back into

11

swimming. I work for training." His earring catches the light. Against his dark skin it's like a flashlight in a tunnel.

He's getting his life back while I get to work on not killing myself if I fall out my chair. And only two blocks away.

"I didn't know you were so bad," he says, voice low. "Is it permanent?" There's an uncomfortable hopefulness in his voice.

Maybe it's the milk from the Frap, but my stomach boils with fury. "Don't do that."

He inhales sharply, sucking back anger. "You still look the same to me, Genie. Beautiful." He licks his lips. "I can come by later and show you what I mean. We got to catch up anyway," he suggests.

Sweat drips down my forehead like rain on a window. The last time I saw Nolan, he proposed the same thing. And just like before, I'm not having it. He can keep all of that to himself.

I sense him staring at the chair. I don't want to look, but I can tell he is. Everyone does. Intentional or not. He swallows loudly, and my attention turns to his Adam's apple. What is he feeling? Guilt? Shame? Disgust? Fear? Everything I feel when I transfer into this aluminum hunk of transportation.

"What's up with Hannah?" he asks. I know he doesn't care. He's just trying to get a reaction.

I think of the picture she posted, stretching against the barre. "She's fine."

"Good . . . good." He nods. Nolan does that when he's nervous.

His hand lingers over my thigh. I don't blink. If I do, I won't know if he touches me. Reminds me of calculus, when his hands would slide up my thigh.

I finally look at him. "Are you going to leave, or do I have to?"

He squints from the sun moving out from behind the clouds. "Something told me to wear this shirt to—"

"My mom's waiting for me. So . . ." I place my hands on my push rims, ready to go, when he grabs the back of my chair.

Where were those reflexes that night? "Let go!" I yell.

He jerks his hands away quickly. "Sorry! Please. Don't go yet."

"What do you want, Nolan?"

"I just want to—"

"I have to go."

I throw my cup into the trash and work my way out of the park. Pretty sure I just made wheelchair drifting a thing. And Nolan better not follow me, but I don't look back, either. By the time I cross the street, I'm sure he isn't. There's nothing like hearing your heart as the soundtrack to the insanity that just played out.

Mom's waiting for me outside the center as if she thought I might pass her and the blinking hazards on the car. She looks like she's about to melt. Her twists hang down in front of her face as if she's started to already. Why not wait in the car?

"You overworked yourself," she starts. "If only you took direction from me like you did from your dance teachers." She realizes what she just said and tries to backtrack. "I just mean you're so stubborn sometimes. Guess you get that from me."

I dismiss her. "Whatever."

She opens the car door and tries to help me get in. I push her away.

"Let me help, Genie."

"No. I can do it myself."

"What's wrong with you today?"

"Let's see, my legs—useless. Bladder—useless. My bowels are like—screw it. It's hot out here, and instead of you just letting me hurry up and get into the air-conditioned car, you're asking me what's wrong."

That shuts her up for now. What I really want to say is the boy who let me fall off a three-story building showed up today.

But I can't say that, because she thinks I just lost my balance, which isn't a total lie, but it's not the whole truth, either.

CHAPTER TWO

On the Mag

O n this episode of The Breaking Pointe: *No. Just no.*

Mom wants me to sleep with chucks under me like some elderly dog. It's not until I pull my covers off that I see the stain on my bed. I touch it—still wet. I feel my face contorting. This just happened and I didn't feel it—couldn't stop it. Even though no one's here, I still look around, embarrassed. If I tell Mom I wet the bed, she'll give me the I-told-you-so speech, feel bad, and then give me pity eyes. The eyes that stared at me when I woke up out of surgery. She knew my life was over before I did.

I think back to Nolan yesterday. What if it happened in front of him? As if seeing Nolan again wasn't hard enough. There would've been no hiding it. Oh God, what if it were my bowels? No, I can't—won't think about it.

Remember the dream, Genie.

Last night, I had my first dream in a month. It all felt so real. So real that I thought I could walk again. My legs felt real. I could feel the coolness of the lotion that I put on my legs before class, so my knees wouldn't be ashy.

It's all been nightmares since my accident. Flashes of the seconds it took to fall through the sky. The moment I knew there was nothing I could do. My heart drums so fast that I wake up, my sheets clenched between my fingers, mirroring the way I held on to the edge. Sometimes it's just dark and my screams play over and over.

But not last night. This was a dream, a show, a reminder of who I used to be. I didn't want to wake up. I was back in class. Hannah and I stood in our favorite spots at the barre, right in front of the large window, open to the public and the restaurants across the street. We chatted about auditions. The school was putting on a production of *Giselle*, and we both wanted to be her.

Other girls fit the bill of Giselle more. Maya comes to mind. Her long, lanky limbs and small head are the definition of a perfect ballerina body. Clean technique and blue doe eyes say Giselle belongs to her. But Hannah and I wanted to stir the pot. We would force a new way of dancing Giselle that fit us.

Miss Kuznetsova entered and everyone stood tall. She bowed and we all bowed back, signaling class was beginning. The piano started slow and precise and I closed my eyes. I like to hear only the music sometimes. We've done the exercises so much, it's muscle memory. Grands battements. Ronds de jambe. The sound of pointe shoes lightly rapping the floors is comforting. Nothing else matters when I dance.

There I was onstage—flying, my white tulle tutu catching the air in time with the music, my brown peasant top telling me I got Giselle. I performed the whole show. The audience cheered on their feet when I took my bow. Miss Kuznetsova applauded from the wings, a smile on her face. A former Giselle herself, her smile told me I was where I belonged. My music-blasting neighbor woke me up before I could accept my flowers.

I transfer into my chair. The smell confirms that I definitely peed myself. Great, I'm going to have to do some sanitizing when I clean up. I do my best to take my covers off the bed myself. Despite pushing myself on stealth mode, I roll over every creak and groan in this apartment. I throw the sheets into the washing machine and squeeze myself into the bathroom. Hopefully Mom won't barge in so I can keep this to myself.

After getting myself clean as can be, I roll down the hallway to the kitchen. I scrape my elbow going around the corner. Technically, we need to move to a more accessible space. My occupational therapist, Kelly, described moving a wheelchair through here as "constipation." The sad thing is she isn't wrong. Shortly after that talk she went on vacation, and when she comes back, I guess we'll pick up where she left off. She'll be back in August refreshed and I'll be here still constipated.

"How about we go out for breakfast?" Mom asks when she sees me.

"No."

"Pastrami omelets," she sings. "It'll be like girlfriends and brunch."

"I said no." We're not girlfriends.

"Genie, let's go out. I don't feel like making breakfast."

"Don't. I'll make it." And it's not like she ever feels like making breakfast.

"You can't reach the stove."

She immediately covers her mouth. I'm annoyed with her, but mad at myself for even forgetting that I can't properly cook in this kitchen. I can barely open the fridge without hitting my knee.

"Mom, one. Genie, zero."

"I didn't mean that," she says, sticking up for herself, obviously hurt.

"Yes, you did."

"Why can't you ever just believe me or listen to me just once?"

"Oh boy, here we go again."

"Here." She holds a magazine reluctantly out to me. "This came for you today. I debated showing it to you, but I think you should see it."

I look down and see *Relevé* magazine, the most popular ballet magazine ever, featuring me! I'm doing a grand jeté across the cover in a bright red leotard. My name is in big bold black letters. My throat gets dry, as I swallow repeatedly to keep it from snapping shut.

With everything going on, I forgot. How could I forget that I did a cover? It's the "Dance and Diversity" edition. They scouted across so many schools for new talent and stopped at me. Before I knew it, I was in front of a camera, told to just dance while the camera followed. They wouldn't let me see any of the magic they captured. I had no idea what image they would pick for the cover.

I turn to page twenty and read the headline:

GENIE AND THREE WISHES: WHY SHE
WISHES MORE GIRLS OF COLOR WOULD
DANCE BALLET

Marie, the journalist, told me I was creating quite a buzz in the dance world. Just reading the headline makes my face hot. I remember when she told me. We were in studio four. I could see everyone from class peeking through the paned door. Hannah gave me the thumbs-up, a smile plastered on her face. She herself was a little bummed at first, but I won't be the last brown girl to grace the cover. That I'm sure of.

"You're very popular. I would expect your talent to deter most of your classmates. Quite the opposite. Talking to them, I can easily see they admire you," Marie said, looking behind her at the gawking girls from the studio.

For the most part, me and the girls got along, but there will always be someone intimidated by greatness. I can't change who I am. But that day, the girls were happy for me. Genuinely so. I guess they didn't forget who helped them out with steps. Sometimes I withhold my feelings, but I never did with ballet. I spread it like butter. If you're dancing next to me, you have to look great too.

There's nothing admirable about me now. How can you admire someone whose life is done? I'm not Stephen Hawking. At least he still had his mind. I'm losing the little bit of wits I have left. Without dance, I'm nobody.

I skim through the text and some more poses of me, scanning over questions like, *When did you start dancing?* and *What's your favorite song to dance to when not in the studio?* As I make my way to the end, it's Marie's finals words that upset me the most: *Can't wait to see what happens next for you.*

Follow-up story: WETS BED LIKE ELDERLY DOG.

"You're upsetting yourself," Mom says.

She can't talk to me about being upset. This is the woman who has her therapist on speed dial. She'd suck up all of the Atlantic Ocean to avoid having a drink, or going someplace where they serve them. Seven years ago, she said she was done drinking, but clearly, she's still so upset about it, she goes two, sometimes three times a week to AA to keep from swallowing alcohol again.

The magazine scrunches between my fists. I will my fingers to loosen up and not rip it apart.

"Of course I'm upset! Hey, remember when I was supposed to be somebody?" I wave the magazine at her.

"I thought taking you out to eat first . . ." I can see the guilt on her face.

Great plan.

"You should've thrown it out."

She gives me her heartbroken look, all sad and hopeless. I wish she would think first. What good would seeing this magazine do? How could seeing what I can never have be good for me?

"Give it to me, then." She holds her hands out.

"No, I don't want it in the house at all."

I roll to the window and shove it out. She shakes her head at me, her eyes filling with tears. But I can't comfort her. I can't even comfort myself.

"Maybe I keep giving you the impression we're friends, but watch your tone with me. That was all uncalled for. If you won't talk to me, you need to talk to someone else," she says before leaving the kitchen.

That won't happen either. I will not sit in a circle and explain how I felt falling off a roof. Not even with a hundred-foot pole will I touch how it happened. That leads to Nolan, and I want to forget him.

What would I say? My mom keeps my cereal knee height now so I can reach it? Falling off that roof was the worst day of my life? That's obvious. No one ever just showed up to physical therapy because they want to be agitated by a physical terrorist.

Mom keeps some of the silverware on a short serving tray in the kitchen. It's how she keeps my "independence." Today I'd rather get a bowl that's in the dish rack. I align myself parallel to the sink. The rack's too high and far back, so I have to leave some space to tip on the wheel. I lock my elbows and try to remember what it's like to have balance.

I reach for the rack with my right hand and feel around. I'm hitting a lot of glasses. Where are the bowls? I drag it closer to the edge, seeing a bowl just beyond my fingertip, and I stretch more, reaching it. Just as I'm lifting the bowl, my chair tips back on both wheels and my elbow brings the whole rack down. Glass shatters everywhere. All four glasses and three bowls in pieces.

"Dammit!"

I can hear Mom barreling down the hallway before the last fork hits the gray laminate tile.

"Jesus, Genie! Be careful!"

"I can't step on any of it."

She grabs the broom from the corner and begins to sweep up the shards. "I don't want you getting hurt."

"I'm aware!" I snap.

Her hands press against her temples, trapping all the anger. What does she really want to say? If she knew why we were truly up on the roof, she'd absolutely be pissed. Madder than watching me have to figure out a new excuse for a life. She can't pine about me being a dancer anymore.

"You're frustrated. I know you just want things to go back to the way they were, but quit taking it out on me." She stops sweeping. "I'll ask Anne for recommendations."

"You don't understand. Let me figure it out myself." I turn my wheels backward, creating distance between us. "Leave me alone." I don't need her asking her therapist for special help for me.

"Use that pretty little head of yours, Genie. I'm not keeping things low to embarrass you. It's for your safety. You could've hurt yourself."

"Already got hurt." It's a low blow, but I sit low.

"Go to your room."

I can't believe she's banishing me to my room. Complete with the angry point and hand on her waist.

"And if I don't want to?"

"I didn't ask what you wanted. I know you're not talking to me like that!" Her hands clasp together, and she brings them to her mouth like she's praying for the strength *not* to send me flying through these walls. She lets out a heavy sigh and says more quietly, gently, "You clearly need some air, but I'm going to clean this mess up and you're going to wait for me to *help* you down the stairs."

Ugh. There're only two steps, but it's enough to keep me stuck inside. The makeshift ramp the landlord put out isn't very safe, and some stupid kids keep stealing it for skateboard tricks. I can see them from my window having fun at my expense. We're having a legit ramp installed, but the super moves slower than a geriatric adagio. I don't even want the ramp. That's just something to alert people that some disabled person lives here.

"Genie," Mom snaps when she sees I'm not moving. "I don't care where you go, just get out of the kitchen."

"There's not enough space to go around you!"

She backs out into the hallway and I push myself as hard as I can. I don't even care that I almost roll over her foot. "Watch it, Genie!" She moves out of the way just in time.

I choose not to respond. As soon as I think that next time I won't miss, I scrape my elbow going around the corner. I remember the days I could kick the door behind me, making all the pictures rattle with a slam. I have to settle for a two-handed slam once I face the door.

How can such fire become a flower onstage? Miss Kuznetsova often asked me. That flower is dead. I'm just a pit of burning ashes now.

You need to relax, Genie. Well, as much as I can. I ready myself to transfer to my bed even without any sheets on it. I need to take a nap. Yes, I basically just got up, but I don't want to do today anymore. If I can sleep, maybe the dream will happen again.

Just added napping to the list of things I can't even do right. I fooled Mom into thinking I was asleep while she left a delicious pastrami sandwich from David's on Nostrand on my nightstand. As much as I wanted to get my chin dirty with mustard, I decided to just smell it until it went cold because I have to keep a united front here. Me, myself, and I have to show her that we can feed ourselves without her.

I flip onto my back, checking the time on my phone. It's two o'clock. My collage of photos featuring Raven Wilkinson, Janet Collins, Delores Browne, Joan Myers Brown, Lauren Anderson, Aesha Ash, Michaela DePrince, and Precious Adams poses back at me. Wasn't so long ago I thought maybe I could be on some other little girl's ceiling.

Three hasty knocks turn my head. I see a crouched Nolan on my fire escape. I don't do a good job of hiding my fear. He knocks harder, like I went deaf instead of paralyzed. My eyes shoot toward my cracked door. Now is not the time. Never would be more like it.

"Genie, let me in, please," he says, his voice muffled by the closed window.

Just to see a look of hope on his face, I transfer into my chair and roll out of his line of vision. *Genie, one. Nolan, zero.*

Nolan knocks some more. "Word, Genie? Don't do me like that. Five minutes."

I come back into view. "Why?"

"To talk."

"Talk, then."

His nose spreads wider than it is already. "Let me in."

"Or what, Nolan?"

"I'll tell your mom about the abortion. I got the receipts." He pulls out his phone. "Don't make me knock on the front door."

He gives me a look that says, *You know I'll do it*. We know each other well. I have a good ten seconds before he plants himself in front of Mom, spouting the very thing that might actually break her heart more than me not dancing.

"You're an asshole, you know that?" I open the window. "Keep your voice down. I can't exactly hide you in the dark." Like I would've done if this was old times when he came over in the dead of night.

"There was a time you used to wait for me by the window."

"Yeah, well, there was a time I used to like you too, so . . ."

There's still the lingering smell of chlorine on him like yesterday. He must've gotten out of work and skipped the shower. An ice bag is taped to his left shoulder, so he keeps his backpack on the other shoulder, reminding me of how he walked around school. I thought it was the cutest thing, too. Sneaking kisses in the stairwell, letting our fingers touch as we scraped by each other to our classes before everything changed between us.

"I would've called first, but we both know you blocked my number."

My eyes follow his gaze down to my legs. I knew I should've put on pants.

"Damn, those legs could still be on a magazine."

"Get to it, Nolan." I roll back to the door and shut it. "Mom's going to check on me soon."

"That's never scared me before."

I wonder if I tell Nolan to go to hell, would he reappear on the other side of my bedroom? This is hell. "Nolan, again, what do you want?"

"Do you know how hard it's been for me?"

There's got to be a better word than "insane." It's too nice for Nolan. "More than most, less than me?"

"I'm being serious—"

"I know you are. Excuse me for not wanting to be talked to like this in my own room."

"I haven't seen you in forever. My mom keeps asking for you and I had to lie. You can't just block me and that's it."

"That's how blocking works."

Nolan brings his hands behind his head like he's being talked to by the cops. "I'm trying to tell you—how was I supposed to know what was up with you? For weeks I called here and I just kept getting your mom. Hannah didn't reply to none of my texts or calls."

"You weren't supposed to know what I was up to. That's why I blocked you. I can't speak for Hannah."

"I got more than just baby talk on my phone, Genie." He could choke on his confidence. "I don't wanna straight embarrass you, but I will."

Oh, how kind.

"You wouldn't even ring the buzzer to talk to my mom, so actually I don't believe you."

He lets out a tire-flattening sound and shakes his head. "She hates me, and I never have anything nice to say about her, so I was doing *us* a favor. I was thinking space might be good for us, but it's too hard. I'm so stressed. You're the only one that gets me, Genie."

I wish he were just being dramatic. So easy my mind plays a reel of all the time I made for Nolan here at night. Time I should've been sleeping, rehearsing, or working on my own choreography. He would come over if he was happy, sad, bored, angry, stressed, or just because. Nolan always called to say good morning or good night.

Genie, one. Nolan, one.

"We're not together, nor are we friends. You need to find someone else to do *this* with. You can't pop up to see me anymore. Not without a good reason."

Everything on his face is getting tight. For someone so honest, he gets upset easily when told the truth.

"There you go making decisions without me again." He wanted that to hurt and it does, but my tolerance for pain is at an all-time high.

"There you go stalling like always because you can't take a no."

"Let me ask you this: You really think after everything that you can just end it? That I'm supposed to go away 'cause you got an attitude with me?"

"Shit I'm Not Answering" for four hundred, Alex.

"This is just what we do," he continues, dropping down to his knees. "We're going to figure this out like always. But first you're going to unblock me."

Sometimes he has a way of looking at me like I'm some sort of fish in a tank. He's doing it now, even tapping my arm as he would the glass.

"No. No way."

He stands up. "I know you want me out of here, and I cannot sleep unless I text you good night later on, so please stop thinking about yourself and just unblock me. You owe me."

I hear Mom's slippers shuffling in this direction. If she opens this door, I'm dead.

"Fine," I say too fast. I just want him out of my room.

Nolan watches me as I unblock his number. "I feel better already."

I wish I never agreed to see him that night either. Should've ignored his texts and what-ifs. Then I wouldn't be stuck in this chair. I'd be re-creating my *Relevé* cover all summer.

CHAPTER THREE

Pas de Hell Nah

After my day off yesterday, Mom signs me into therapy like it's a kindergarten dance class, killing any chance of my famous exits. She takes a seat and pulls out her Nintendo Switch. I sit on the other side of the waiting room, away from her, next to a little girl with sparkly pink AFO braces and forearm crutches to match. An adorable high-pitched giggle escapes from her mouth as I stick my tongue out and point to my mom.

When her mom gets up to go to the water cooler, the girl whispers to me, cupping the side of her mouth, "Don't you like your big sister? I have a yucky brother."

I lean in closer to her. "I don't have a yucky brother or a big sister. That's my mom."

"I wish my mom played games."

"Hey, Genie, ready?" Logan has perfect timing. I have to check the wall clock to see how he can be so damn happy this early. It's barely ten o'clock and he's in his superhero stance: hands on his hips and a smile on his face. Superhero name: the P.T.Q.T. "Hey, Tasha." He waves to Mom. "Our girl is doing good."

Mom puts down her Switch. "She gets that from me," Mom laughs.

"But of course," he says, patting my shoulder as I wheel to the back. "We'll see you later," he adds before turning to me and breaking down my day. "Today we're going to start with chair-to-floor and back-to-chair transfers. It needs to be second nature if we're going to let you out of here. Safety is number one."

I literally bite my tongue not to say anything. Today I will comply, because I don't want to lie about how I've been moving around, between the glass incident and only putting on my belt when I reach those front doors. "Always keep this on," Logan said when I sat in this chair for the first time, as he buckled me in. I refuse to wear my seat belt on the off chance I'll fly out of my chair and somehow reconnect my nerves. Meanwhile, a few blocks up, Nolan is perfecting his breaststroke and trying to beat his best time.

Genie, one. Nolan, two.

Chair to floor is a lot easier for me. I scoot forward on my chair—safely unbuckling first. I press the little square of freedom. My arms still have enough strength to lower myself like I'm entering a pool. Logan compliments my transfer to the floor, and for a small moment, I feel the corners of my mouth upturn, but I quickly kill it. Can't have him seeing me smile. He might think I like him or something.

Kyle lies on the floor a few feet away, close enough for me to smell the sweat streaming out of every pore. Looks like he's doing some version of a push-up, or maybe he's kneeling. Who knows with this place? Everyone looks like they're in some horror version of the game Twister. *Right arm ouch, left leg agony.* He turns his head in my direction, and a smile breaks out across his face. "G-G-Genie, right?"

"Yeah, and you're Kyle?" I look down to see Logan tinkering with my left leg. He mumbles about my braces looking too tight. Like I would know.

"I f-f-feel . . . like we've seen each other . . . f-for months, but have never . . . talked." His voice is slow, like his walking.

"It would seem so."

What would we talk about? How every day he gets stronger? Better? Why everyone's so in love with him? I suppose I could've asked where he got the cupcakes he brought for his therapist Lisa's birthday. Cupcakes hit different when you're not expecting them. As if he wasn't perfect enough, he made sure they were vegan and gluten- and nut-free so everyone could try one. The sheer audacity of him to be so thoughtful. To be *here* and think about someone other than yourself or progress—how?

"S-s -so what . . . b-b-brings you here?" Kyle asks.

Apple picking. Cider. The usual.

Logan and I both look at Kyle. Except Logan smiles like a proud father, and I squint, wondering if he's serious. I fight the urge to laugh. I can't believe he just said that.

"S-s-sorry, I w-w-wish I could blame that on m-my TBI, but . . . unfortunately, that's all me," Kyle apologizes.

TBI? Traumatic brain injury? At least that's what some of the "Fun Facts" posters spread around say it stands for. I always thought it was weird that they used "fun" to describe the facts.

There's nothing fun leading to a severe head injury—though, per the facts, some can be mild. I look Kyle over, focusing on his unevenly shaved head. A curly Gumby. I'm sure he had loads of fun waking up to that.

"I hear guys here like to show some skin. Thought I'd check it out." I nod at the amount of thigh he is showing from his warped game of Twister.

That makes us all laugh. I actually find I don't want to stop. It feels good to let some of it out.

"She laughs," Logan says.

"Maybe if you were funny like Kyle, I would laugh more."

"Yeah, yeah," Logan says, giving me an approving wink.

Kyle has to walk himself to his next task. More like dragging his lower half, but his top half seems very strong. He gives me our secret fuck-this-shit look before moving on. I find myself following him with my eyes. Take out the discomfort of pushing your body to remember how to work and the equipment around, and it almost felt normal. I *almost* felt normal, and not like the girl in the wheelchair.

I prepare to transfer back into my chair. Left arm on my seat and my right hand in a fist. I push down on my fist and lift up, but I don't use enough force, plopping back down on the floor.

"Let's go, Genie. You got this, Genie," Logan chants.

I try again. I dig my fist down into the mat harder and pull my top half up on my cushion. From there I use my arms to lift the rest of me onto my chair. Situating my feet back on the footplate, I let out a sigh.

"Good job, Genie. You're doing great."

"Oh goody."

"All right, give me a few more. Back on the floor again."

Kyle and I finish at the same time. We head back to the waiting room together. I usually plow through the hall here, but walking—rolling—with Kyle slows me down. I'm not sure when it happened, but somewhere around three weeks ago, I started looking past the grimacing and stumbling about and noticed that Kyle is fine as hell. And when a cute-ass boy and you have a chance to just look at each other, you take it. That's when the fuck-this-shit glance was born. Besides, he's the first person here I've talked with around my age who's in a similar predicament.

We pass several other "torture rooms," as I call them. A sign leads the way to the pool. It reminds me of Nolan, and I shudder. Some staff push equipment around us and others give supporting smiles as we make our way. The clanking of Kyle's walker on the squeaky tiles fills the silence. He smiles so nicely at me; it feels weird to take off. Now I don't know what to say.

"Heading home?" I ask.

I can see the words form on his lips before he says anything. "N-n-no, actually."

"Oh." I give myself short, soft pushes. I notice the logo on his shorts, a red *S* with a tree in the middle. "In college?"

"H-h-heading. Fall I will be a-a-a . . ." There's a long pause as he stops walking and thinks. His eyes look up to the ceiling, reaching and searching.

"Freshman?"

"Yes." He seems relieved yet embarrassed. "Stanford gymnastics," he pushes out. "S-s-supposed . . . but."

That explains his insanely good upper-body strength. "I was wondering where you got those abs from." They're all hard and ripped, just like I like them.

"I c-can eat what I want now. No more f-f-flying through the air for me."

He jokes it off, but I can feel his pain as if I said it. Once our bodies did amazing things. Now we struggle to do the basics. Kyle fights to get words out. Everyday words. His legs used to send him flying down a mat like an airplane on a runway. I don't think he could pass a toddler learning to walk now.

Part of me wants to ask him if he has nightmares about his accident. Does he wish for dreams, so he can have a moment's happiness? I want to tell him all about what happened, because I feel like he would get it. He used to fly. Kyle knows what that felt like. Maybe I'm reaching, though. He probably hears enough sob stories in group therapy.

"Word. I never knew how much I liked food until I could have it whenever I wanted," I say instead.

"Dancer, right?"

"How'd you know?"

"A-a-arms and . . . l-l-legs for days," he chuckles. "A-a-and the shirts."

I look down at my lifeless legs. I guess they still hold some shape, though I know it's only a matter of time before they'll atrophy. For now, they have no memories of chaînés across the floor, turning my body instead of these wheels.

"Thanks."

He stops at the elevator and presses the up button. I notice he's leaning a little hard on his walker. "One d-d-day I'll make it here ... without f-f-feeling like ... I'm about to die," he gasps.

"I would offer you my chair, but I wouldn't wish it on my worst enemy."

Exceptions could be made for Nolan.

"Th-th-thanks, friend."

Say what? A croaky noise of confusion comes out my mouth.

"I-I-I'm going ... to the s-s-support group, if you'd l-l-like to come." He moves the conversation along.

With that, I wish the elevator were here so I could go. What if Logan put him up to it? That's unlike Logan, though. He's pushy, but not *pushy*. I cancel the thought and linger at the elevator as a possibility. Mom would eat this up if I asked her to wait so I could go to QUEST. I know from the signs around the building it's a Friday meeting around this time. Speaking to Kyle again would be nice. I can't remember the last time I spoke to someone about something that wasn't my bladder, recovery, or what happened.

"No, thank you."

The elevator dings and the door opens.

"Sure?"

"Positive."

He positions himself between the doors so they don't close. "I—I—I know you got a lot going on, b-but in case you don't make it there ..." He pulls a napkin out of his pocket. There's a small chocolate stain on the corner, and it's wrinkled like it's been in a lot of different pockets. "B-been holding on t-t-to this." Kyle holds it out to me.

When I take it, I finally see it's his number, and also that the napkin is from the French bakery he got the cupcakes from. It's been a little over a month since the small party happened. Is that really how long he's been holding on to this? I look past the bakery logo to see *for whenever* in script and underlined. Finally, he backs into the elevator. He gives me a smile after a struggle with the terrain change, even though I can see the disappointment in his eyes.

"Hey, wait!" I stick my hand through the door before it closes. It opens back up. "Next session. I'll be there." Why not? It's my last day of therapy next week anyway.

His eyes search for the words again, but there's a bigger smile on his face. I want to tell him I'm a flake acting on impulse who he won't see after we graduate. I numb my tongue instead. I don't need him to know I've been eavesdropping on his rehab timeline.

"S-s-see you . . . then!" he finally says, the excitement letting loose a bit of spit. "S-s-sorry!"

I take my hand off the door. "Bye."

"B-b-bye."

He gives a smile I would run to tell Hannah about if she hadn't telepathically figured it out. We used to be that close. Once the rest of his hair grows back, Kyle would totally be Hannah's type: cute. He's not tall, but neither is she, so that's perfect. Puppy-dog brown eyes with labradoodle-like wavy hair growing in thick. Being a gymnast, he could keep up with her competitive side. Hannah's sweet, but she'd slap her mother if it meant she would win. To think I even thought about setting her up with Nolan when he and

I first talked. She was so guy shy, I thought Nolan could be good for her. Ultimately, that plan bit the dust when Nolan and I kissed the next day. Strange to think our places could've been reversed.

The door closes. I coast to the waiting room. This is the first time I've slowed down in this place. The hallway never seemed so long.

Mom sits, legs crossed, still playing her game. I slow, tightening my grip on my rims to stop short of her. When she sees me, she checks her watch.

"I thought you slipped away somehow." She puts her Switch in her bag, but I detect the distrust in her voice.

"Walked a friend to the elevator." Is it thirsty to call Kyle a friend? It's not that crazy. Friends have things in common. Like wishing we were someplace else but here. We've both been through something traumatic. We're practically a friendship recipe.

"Friend? I'd like to hear more about this friend."

"Let's just go, please." If I mention Kyle, she'll bring up Nolan.

We take a left instead of the right where we parked.

I stop to rub my shoulder. "We parked over there."

"There's this cute café over here. Seeing how you stayed the whole session, I thought I'd treat you."

I grumble. "I'm sore and tired."

I've only been in this thing for close to a month, and it's only three months post-injury. Cute cafés usually translate to pain in the ass for a wheelchair. Tiny with barely enough chairs to make you think they want you to sit there.

"Come on, it'll be fun."

"For you, maybe."

"What happened to trying new things?"

Has she seriously forgotten that for years my life has been the same routine? Wake up. Go to school. Proceed to dance. Come home. The only thing that changed was switching to VAB from my little storefront school to give myself the best chance ever of becoming a professional.

"If I go, will you please leave me alone until we get there?"

"Fine, Genie."

We reach a café on a corner after ten minutes of pushing. There's outdoor seating when all I want is air-conditioning. I pull up to an empty table, push one of the chairs to the side, making room for my chair. Even out here there's barely space. The chair makes an awful screech as I wrestle it to the side. Mom could do this easier, but of course I give her the *back off* look as she tries to help.

I don't want her helping me in public. It's bad enough that people stare anyway. As I yank the chair, a man with his laptop open shoots me an icy glare.

"What? Am I disrupting you from blogging?"

He lowers his glare and goes back to typing. Figures Mom would know about the most hipster place around here. Two girls drink tea out of a mason jar. Singular! Nolan used to try the same thing. I check my watch. Ten to one. Ten minutes and I'll need to catheter myself. As if I didn't feel out of place enough, I have to drain my bladder with a tube. I could barely weasel into this spot. Now I'll have to do it again.

Mom comes back with her hands full of food and drinks. She smiles as she places it all down on the too-small table. "I got us iced macchiatos. I know you like these Italian calories. No Twinkies, but will tiramisu do?" Finally, she sits down, spreading napkins along the table.

I drag the macchiato closer to me and stare at her. This isn't her real happy face. Something's up. "Why are we here?"

"So you can have fresh air, and we can talk." Her fork has tiramisu on it, but she doesn't eat it, just holds it in the air.

By "talk," she doesn't mean what happened that night. There's comfort in knowing she won't ask, too. She's never inquired past the "I lost my balance" spiel, and I won't give up any more details. It's an understanding we have. Like how I don't ask about my grandmother or what she talks to her therapist about.

"What's there to talk about?"

Her smile fades. "Anything. Want to see any movies? Back-to-school shopping? We can go to the outlets if you want. If we wait until August, I'll have to set up my classroom and stuff. It'll be busy."

"Mom, come on. You're only offering because I got hurt and you're trying to make me feel better or something."

"Is that a bad thing? It's your senior year at a new school over something you have no control over like accessibility. That's a big deal and change. I think a new wardrobe is needed, no?" I take too long to answer because she adds, "You know, at your age I would've done anything for my mother to take me shopping. Should we talk about that friend instead?"

"No. I'd love to spend your money." I feel something of a smile move my face, but it disappears.

Mom, however, gives her variation of a smile too. Still, she doesn't take a bite or a sip. She might not want to eat, but I dig into my dessert. This conversation is going so well. So well that Mom gives me her slice of cake to eat, and I finish off her macchiato she hasn't touched. Meanwhile she checks her watch, then her phone. Something's up.

It's been twenty minutes now. Not wanting to risk an accident, I do end up heading to the bathroom, which is surprisingly bigger than expected. When I get back to the table Mom looks markedly more stressed.

I know it's hot as Satan's balls out here, but Mom's sweating like she's getting a Dominican blowout. More than the temperature is bothering her.

"What's the real reason we're here?" There's nothing else to eat, and I've shut down her fourth attempt at getting something else to snack on. Because, really?

For a minute, she opens her mouth to lie. I can tell by how quick her response was about to be. Instead, she sighs and continues with the truth. "Your father should be stopping by."

I slow blink. "My father?" Now I can't stop blinking.

As in the dude that hit her for years until the night he beat her so bad, she practically became part of the carpet. He never came back. That's how I remember it, at least. He abandons, and she suffocates me. She never talks about him ever, not even to acknowledge that it wasn't the first time he hit her, only the first time I saw it with my own eyes. "He's gone, I assume, since you never bring him up, and he's certainly never tried to call me or see me since I was eight."

"He asked to see you. Called you Orchid and everything."

"So he knows."

"Yes."

"So what is there to see?" I've thought about this meeting for years, to be honest. I always thought he'd make his way back to me somehow. But he never showed up. He always sent orchids for my middle name, and he's the only one who calls me by it. Mom hates my middle name. She said she wanted it to be more common, like Nicole or Grace, after my grandmother, who she also never talks about, but he insisted on Orchid. Because when your parents are kids when they have you, you're named Genie Orchid.

"Genie, he said he wants to see you. That's all."

"Because you told him about my accident."

She checks her watch again but doesn't have to bother with her phone, because it rings. "Bryan, you should've been here—what? No, no, do not do this to her." Her eyes flick over to me before she gets up and walks out of the sitting area. She tries to talk low and cover her mouth, but it's too loud for her to do so. I hear everything. "I know we had a deal—she's your daughter too."

Deal? Daughter? Now I'm getting a dance idea. A pas de trois featuring Mom, Dad, and me. Title? "Pas de Hell Nah." Because we'll never be in the same air space again.

"Mom?" I try to push my way through the tables but get stuck. The blogging man shushes me like I was talking to him.

She gives me the "one minute" finger. "Forget about it. I'm not putting her through this again." With that, she hangs up the phone. "Genie, let's go."

"No, what was that about?" I lock my brakes.

"He isn't coming," Mom whispers, like it'll keep it from stinging.

"Why?" I hate that I ask. It doesn't matter. It's not like I really wanted to see him anyway.

"His daughter . . . your sister is in the hospital. Come on, let's go home."

My *sister*?

Funny, I also was in the hospital and also his daughter and I got nothing. Not even his stupid orchids. "You can't just drop this and say let's go home. But hey, the next time you want to ruin my day some more, can you at least be up-front about it? I know he doesn't care about me, but you, Mom . . . you set me up."

"Genie, I didn't know. I wouldn't have if I'd known he'd not show up."

"What's this deal, anyway? And why not tell me he has a new family?"

"Because it happened around your accident. Her birth. I didn't want you to stress even more. You would've hated me—"

"I hate you now."

I hate the look she's giving me, because I said it. I hate that I don't even know if I mean it or not. I hate that I have no one to talk to about it.

CHAPTER FOUR

Magic

O n this episode of The Breaking Pointe: *Hold on to your blood pressure.*

I was being saltier than McDonald's fries when I made "Kitri" from *Don Quixote* the ringtone for Hannah. Some call it being a sore loser. I call it healthy professionalism. I wanted that variation. Now she's calling me, and I'm wondering if the phone will blow up when I answer it. If I answer. Hannah? Calling me? No way. She has no reason to. I've ignored her, pushed her away, basically telling her to leave me alone. I made that clear when she tried to visit me a few days after my fall. I actually screamed. No words. I hurled all my hurt at her.

Should I flick the answer button? My finger hovers over it. What if she's calling to tell me to get all my things from her room, so she can put her new best friend's things there? Maya, perhaps? She's always been waiting in the wings. I'd rather not answer if that's the case.

Get a grip, Genie. Answer the phone. At least you don't have to look her in the eyes. I flick the green icon. "Hey" is the only word that comes out.

"Is that all you can say?"

"Clearly."

"Same stank 'tude," she says, a small laugh escaping her mouth. I'm reaching a lot lately, but she sounds relieved. Maybe she thought I would sound changed somehow.

All I want to do is ask about classes. How is Miss Kuznetsova? What are the summer intensive girls like? Does she still stand at our favorite spot at the barre? I wonder if Kuznetsova used her connections to up Hannah's buzz for companies. Of course she has—she's amazing. Hannah deserves it. Just hearing her voice transports me back to better times, and yet I'm still reminded that those times are gone for good. How I've missed our conversations. I press the phone to my ear, anxious to hear more.

"I know you've been stalking me on all my handles. Do your hair, because I'm coming over."

"Please don't." My stomach churns at the thought of her seeing me. I've barely been doing my hair. Leaving it in French braids days at a time. I didn't even bother today to spruce them up. I yank on a braid, twisting my face.

"I've given you your space long enough."

"Han—"

"It's done. I'll be there."

"Fine," I groan.

A small smile spreads across my face, even though I'm scared of seeing her. Hannah, Maya, and I were supposed to go to the movies the day of my accident, but I blew them off to deal with Nolan. He left so many messages during class about needing to see me. I'd been avoiding him, his calls, spending the night at Hannah's,

telling him I had to do things for dance when really, I only needed
to be away from him. "Later for Nolan," Hannah said, but I didn't
listen. I'd still be dancing if I had.

I haven't spoken to Mom since we left the café yesterday, but I
should let her know Hannah is coming by. She's in the living room,
her Switch connected to the TV. Her eyes are red. Despite the
sounds of digital happiness, she looks sad. Plain sad. And I know
I had a hand in it.

I lower my gaze. Sucks seeing her like this. It takes me back
to when I was still in the hospital. I wanted to be left alone, not
talking to anybody, not eating, avoiding eye contact. Only turning
my head away when someone's eyes met mine. Mom pleaded with
those same red eyes. They wanted to send me to psych, speaking in
front of me as if I couldn't hear. I did a good job pretending to be
dead.

"There's nothing more we can do for her medically. Her spine
is healing. She needs to be in physical therapy," the doctor told her.

"But she's not well," Mom cried.

"Depression is common with spinal injuries."

"We've tried antidepressants, but she won't eat, she won't move.
She's always moving, she's . . . she's a dancer."

I kept my eyes trained to the ceiling. I wasn't a dancer anymore.

"I'm sorry, but we can't keep her down here for much longer."
He left.

Mom grabbed my face, making me look at her, only I wasn't
looking at her, just seeing her eyes, attracted to the red. "Genie,
please, please," she pleaded.

The sound of her dropping the controller brings me back to the room. "Hannah's stopping by today."

"When?"

Good question. "I don't know."

She sighs. "You need me to make something? I can go to the store."

I shrug. "Wanted to let you know." I needed an excuse to see how she was doing. Hannah provided a good one.

"Mhm."

She goes back to playing her game. "I didn't mean it," I force out. It's like she doesn't hear me. "I don't hate you."

"I'm going to the store," she says, pausing the game, grabbing her purse on the cushion next to her.

She storms out so quick, the words in my throat sound like a toad trying to sing. I get it—how it feels to be rushed out on. Logan is way nicer than I deserve.

I head back to my room to see how best I can fix it up. Maybe if I cross my arms and nod, it'll look more like a bedroom than a cave of someone who gave up on life.

I can hear the knock from my bedroom. I've been staring at the pictures of me and Hannah tacked to my corkboard: us at the beach doing arabesques on pointe, feeding each other frozen yogurt, even me in the middle of a kiss sandwich on my birthday from her and Nolan. Wonder if she still has her matching copies in her room. I'm glad I haven't ripped up the pictures.

"I'll get it!" Mom shouts—the first words she's spoken since coming back from the store.

"Okay," I call out—barely.

I'm glad she's answering the door. It's not like we can skip back to my room like old times. How should I position myself? In front of the door, hands folded in my lap like I'm waiting on her? I could sit on my bed and push the chair aside, to make it feel more normal for her. But that would mean transferring out of my chair, and I can hear her voice coming up the hall.

"Look at you, Hannah." Mom's voice follows behind Hannah's laugh. "You know where to go," she adds.

I get the dumbest idea to hide behind the door, but I talk myself out of it. Chill out, Genie. Most people would think being caught naked would be embarrassing. Not for me. Being seen like this, unable to just hop up and hug her while turning in dramatic slow circles like I want to, is way worse. Maybe that's why when Hannah crosses through my threshold, I can't help but drop my head. I didn't even feel it happening. Every bit of shame weighs down my neck.

"Hey, Genie," she says. I can hear the hesitation in her voice. Knowing her, she probably told herself she wouldn't be nervous or taken aback by me, but seeing me wasn't as easy as she thought it'd be. "Don't worry, I didn't tell any of the girls I was coming by."

"Thank you," I let out, although I still can't look up. All I can see is her feet in brown leather sandals as they sweep the spot she's standing in. I have the same pair, though the straps make it take longer for me to put them on, and these days if I can't simply slide my foot in, it's not happening. "Have a seat." Just an hour ago, this bed was not fit for human life. She'd get lost in a dump of blankets and other things I keep on my bed. Sometimes once I'm on it, I don't feel like transferring back into my chair to get something. I threw everything under my bed or in my nightstand.

Like old times, she sits on my bed, more bougie than ballerina, with her purse held tightly to her. I'm making her feel unwanted, but I can't look up. If I do, I'll tell her everything about Nolan, the fall, the magazine, Kyle, my dad and his stupid new baby girl. How Mom knew and didn't say anything to me.

Once upon a time, the only cure for feeling this way was to dance it out. We'd blast salsa music and spin circles around each other, switching our hips side to side until we couldn't breathe. If we couldn't remember what troubled us—job well done.

Hannah shoots up from the bed. "Genie, you suck."

Record scratch.

My head pops up. "I suck?"

"Yes, you suck, Genie. You're my girl and all, and the best dancer I've ever known, and you may be upset about everything, but you suck."

"Where's this coming from?" We haven't seen each other or spoken in months. Is she still mad I went to see Nolan instead of going to the movies?

"I didn't forget about you howling at me when I tried to visit. I've wanted nothing but to come and see you, and you just up and quit on everything. On us. You don't get to follow my life and cut me out of yours."

"I don't have a life, Hannah. Look at me." I turn a circle in my chair.

She shakes her head in disbelief or maybe realization. "I can't believe you."

"What's so hard to believe?"

"You're a boss, Genie. The most focused and talented, and yeah, maybe you can't dance, but your life isn't over. What about your dream of choreographing? Huh? What about Germany? You love ballet more than life itself, and you're giving up on it like dancing is all there is to ballet." She can turn a nail with her screw-face.

All I can think about is Kuznetsova's email this morning. The usual, but today she's telling me to keep my mind sharp. Keep dreaming up dances. *Come home*, it read, before she signed off.

"But—"

"But nothing. Everyone still talks about you! Not about the accident—you. Your lines, musicality, style, and talent. We talk about how you made all of us want to be better. We miss you. Even the ones who never met you. Miss Kuznetsova tells everyone to aspire to be like you. You're her best student." Her voice quivers a bit in that last line.

"I didn't know" is all I can say. Dancers come and go. Some good ones get bored and quit. Others are pushed back by new talent. I thought my injury nailed my coffin. No one would miss me when there is always someone else. Someone like Hannah.

"No clapback?" She plops down on my bed. Her earrings, a cross between the Dominican Republic and Honduras flags, jingle.

I roll up closer to the bed, my eyes trained on her feet, the bandages on her toes, the bruises and a missing toenail. My feet are healing, and soon there'll be no trace of hours standing on toes.

Even though her feet are ugly, they're beautiful to me. I miss getting hurt for my art. I miss being able to put on those sandals.

"Do you want my sandals? They're a pain to put on now."

She gives me a look that doesn't know if she should be angry or laugh. "Sandals? Really?"

"Yes, they're the biggest pain. Even getting Starbucks is a lot now." I unintentionally load my frustrations on her, but she's not fazed.

"Who's taking you to get these coffees? Nolan?"

I look toward the fire escape. It's bad enough he brought himself up, I don't need her bringing him up too. "You know we broke up. He told me you're giving him the silent treatment too." I suddenly feel like I'm back at the barre, trying to hold myself up again.

"He's just been going crazy wondering where you are and how you've been. I didn't feel it was a good idea to tell him anything, and besides, I didn't know anything!"

I roll my eyes. It's clear I suck at breaking up. "What did he say specifically?" I try to disguise my wariness as genuine curiosity.

"That he misses you and wishes that you'd stop being so childish or something like that. He's cute and all but intense as hell."

"Wishes, wishes, wishes, that is all he talks about when it comes to me. Never mind what I want." Hannah has heard many a rant about Nolan, but they were all petty, minor things. I never really told her how he could be. Some things I thought it would be better if nobody knew.

"I have to agree with him, Genie. The weeks before you . . . hurt yourself, you did shut off a bit. It's understandable with the bab—"

"Shhhh, Hannah . . . Mom still doesn't know. Don't repeat this to anyone." I roll back to the door and shut it in case Mom comes by. "You know how Mom gets."

Hannah knows everything except why I'm in this chair. You'd think telling people would help with the guilt, but it doesn't. I learned that the hard way with the abortion. Hannah goes to Quantico High School, basically, and I have to tell her something. Or Nolan will—I can't let that happen.

"Yeah, go on."

I take a deep breath. "Nolan didn't just find me that night."

She tilts her head in confusion. "I thought you fell waiting for him. Freak accident."

"He was there."

"What happened?"

I debate whether or not to tell it fully. She doesn't need to know. I didn't plan on telling her anyway, even before the accident. "We got into a fight."

Not a lie.

"About what?"

"Doesn't matter." Lie. I'm good at keeping secrets. Mom must've passed it on. "Anyway, I slipped, and he couldn't catch me." I try to avoid her eyes, because I'm playing myself and making Nolan look innocent. If I tell her what really happened, I'd look like a bigger idiot. The one that stupidly got pregnant, deep into a relationship that wasn't working. Hannah always told me I didn't need Nolan the way he needed me, and by then it was all so complicated, I . . . still am protecting him.

"Ay Dios mío, Genie." Hannah uses her Spanish to swear and insult. "That's ... messed up." She gives me a hug, and I feel like the worst person alive. "He must feel so horrible."

"Sure. Look, I'd rather not talk about that night."

"We don't have to." She adjusts herself on the bed and fidgets with one of the million hair clips on her head.

"The end-of-summer gala, since I can't do the pas de deux with you anymore, is 'Magic' over?"

Kuznetsova knows how much I love to choreograph. She told me I could spotlight a piece of my own at VAB's end-of-summer gala. It's an explosive deal, because: (a) Kuznetsova believes in me; (b) Not even a senior gets to do this; (c) Ballet-world people will see it; (d) All of the above. I would've made history with Hannah, but I fell.

I've been dying to know about this. But again, I told myself not to care. That dance didn't concern me anymore.

"That's what I wanted to talk to you about. Maya wants to do it. I told her that since you choreographed it, I'd only do it if you allowed it." She smooths down the hair, or "kitchen" as we call it, in the back of her head with her hands.

"How's her mom, by the way?"

"Not any better." Maya's mom was a dancer too before multiple sclerosis killed her career. "We've gotten closer since you've been away. I think it would make Maya happy if she could dance it." Hannah looks at me. Her hands nervously rub her bronze legs.

It never occurred to me that Hannah would do the dance without me, let alone with someone else. When I dreamed it, created it, showed it to Hannah, it was our dance. She called it "Magic." The dance follows our friendship, how we became friends instantly. The only way we can describe our meeting is just that. We moved so effortlessly together, it looked like an illusion. Feels unfair to let her do it. And it feels unfair not to let her do it. She did name it, after all.

The dance is amazing. Hannah is amazing in it. She has to perform it. Without me. Even if that means with Maya.

"Go for it. No use of it staying with me." It's like giving away a piece of myself. I don't feel like I have much of me to myself anymore. I'm determined to not hurt Hannah again, though.

"You have to come see it. It's only three weeks away. Everyone would love it if you came. I'd love it."

"I don't know, Hannah."

"Please?"

"If I come, the night isn't about you all anymore."

"What are you, a legend or something?"

"Just magic."

She laughs like she always does when I make a pun.

More comfortable, she sits farther back on my bed, stretching her right leg as if nothing ever happened. Like I never tried to rid her from my memory. Even when I transfer onto my bed, Hannah doesn't stop talking to see if she can help. Nor does she stop and stare to watch me wrangle my legs into a position that won't cramp them up. Unlike Mom, Hannah doesn't treat me like a broken toy of a beloved child that she must mend. Any pity she might have had went away when she told me I sucked.

As she tells me about a film crew wanting to make a series about the school, Kyle pops into my head. He was the last person to make me feel this way. Normal. I thought that would be the final time. Having Hannah over changes that.

"What's that smile?" Hannah asks, smiling back at me.

"Not a smile. Grimace. Miss Kuznetsova would never allow cameras in her school."

"What or who are you thinking about?" she asks.

"If I tell you, promise never to tell Nolan."

She kisses her hand and touches it to her heart, bun, and feet. It's our promise swear we made our second week of VAB. We decided we were going to stick together when one of the girls, so irrelevant I forgot her name, told us our hair was too unruly for us to be ballerinas.

"But he's not the jealous type." She quickly swallows her words. "Besides that one time at Broadway Junction."

Nolan is the King of Butt Hurt. That was the one time I told her about. There were countless others, they just didn't get as intense.

He's very jealous and very needy, though he's charming and he's good at showing it. There's a lot to say about someone who doesn't want you to live your life, but insists you stay in theirs.

"There's this boy . . . Kyle. We have therapy at the same time." Hannah squeals as she kicks her long legs. "It's not like that."

"Kylito! Of course it's like that."

"No, only talking. Sorta. I like following his progress. He's a gymnast and is getting better every day. It's nice to see. Yesterday we finally talked, and he invited me to this support group and gave me this." I show her the napkin. "What am I supposed to do with this? I can't use it."

"He gave you his number? For whenever? Kylito means business. Drop the at. I need to see him," Hannah demands.

"I don't have one. We just said words to each other. How can I follow him if I haven't even texted him? He's going to college anyway. It's not like I'll see him after we're done with therapy." As I say it, it makes me sad.

Hopping off the bed, Hannah drops to the floor, and one leg extends as she falls over like she came across royalty. "All-powerful Genie, I wish for your ways with men!" She hails me, throwing her arms up and down.

"Get up!" I laugh. How I kept myself without her I don't know. "Can I tell you something?" I change moods.

"Of course." She plops back on the bed.

"My dad stood me up yesterday."

"As in the one who left you flowers like some ghetto opera ghost?" Hannah looks like she was the one stood up. "For what reason?"

"A two-month-old daughter."

Hannah crosses her arms and shakes her head. "You took it out on your mom, didn't you?" She sighs. "Lucky for you my schedule is clear today."

I nod. This is why we're friends. More than magic is at work here.

CHAPTER FIVE

Deal

L ater for sitting on top of the world. Hannah is walking on it. She struts down the block, legs stretching for miles. I pretend to be paparazzi, making camera noises and snapping invisible photos as she walks toward me. Her purple lips blow me kisses as she twirls and poses for me.

"I thought you were my friend. Out here making me look like a runaway slave," I say as she bends over for a hug.

Before coming here, I made a deal with myself. Just to try. Try to be kinder, less bitter, more open.

"You look sporty chic. That's a thing." She puts her sunglasses on top of her head. "What's up, mamacita?"

"You tell me. You're the one who made time in your busy schedule so we could meet up. I'm here for the food you promised me." It's my Wednesday off and a burst pipe has given Hannah an impromptu day off too.

"Shake Shack?"

"Don't tease me! You know there's never any seats in that place." I laugh. "Oh wait. I have mine already."

Hannah pouts at me. "Hey, Genie, thanks for showing up."

"I couldn't resist that."

"Yeah, I know. How about this? We straight-up old-school this. The pizza shop and go sit in a park?"

"I'm down."

That's what we do. We sit in the park at one of those chess-table-bench combinations. I transfer onto the bench because my chair is too low. It's summer in Brooklyn. Of course, the park is loud. I'm grateful for it. The sprinklers, the children screaming, and the buses pulling in and out. This way I fit in more. Hannah stares at me, her wide eyes full of questions.

Folding my slice, I open the floor. "Ask what you need to, Hannah."

"Sorry. It's just . . . back at your place, it was easier. Seeing you wasn't—I didn't realize how different it is for you to get around."

When we ordered our pizza at the window opening, it was too high for me to tell them what I wanted. Hannah ordered for me, carried the slices, and went the long way around the block because the street was chopped up like a beanstalk broke through it.

"That's not a question," I say.

"What can you feel?" she asks, her purple lips rubbing oddly together. I can tell she's scratching her legs.

"Besides the eyes of people looking at me? Below my waist—nothing. With time I may feel other things." I take a bite into my cheese slice and get a taste of hell on my tongue. I juggle the bite from side to side in my mouth. Never spit it out.

"You felt that," Hannah laughs.

I feel a lot of things. Some make not feeling my legs seem like a paper cut. "I wish I could do one more turn, though. If I'd known when my last one was going to be, I would've done it ten times better."

Hannah folds her slice and takes a huge bite out of it. She shakes her head. "Do you remember the last step you ever did?"

I tap my chin. "Oh gosh . . . I think . . . I went up in relevé and then Miss Kuznetsova told us to stop and that we were done for the day." In a way, it doesn't matter now.

"If it makes you feel better, Kuznetsova is missing her star-child."

"I'm a hippie now?"

I'm glad it seems Hannah doesn't know that Kuznetsova has been reaching out.

Kuznetsova should focus on the students that have a chance now. I will never forget all she has taught me, but it doesn't make me feel better. Makes me feel worse. She should be reminding me to land quietly out of a jump. *You not gymnast, Genie.*

"You're too rigid to be a hippie. I'm just saying. How's your mom taking it all?"

I purposely stuff my mouth so that I don't have to answer.

"Genie, I taught you that trick. I can wait."

I swallow. "She's taking it like a champ," I offer. "I don't know what to say."

"Is she drinking? I know stress can bring out . . ."

"No, but I need her to take a pottery class or something, so she can stop hounding me about therapy and talking to someone. Actually, she needs a good club to dance it out somewhere."

"Well, that I can get behind. There's a party tonight. I'm in need of a date."

"No."

"Because?"

"Because is the place even accessible? Will VAB students be there? And I got other things to do."

"Like what, Genie?"

Our attention follows a little boy running after a plastic ball.

"Like practicing transfers so I don't fall out of my chair and get stuck on the floor. Learning how to care for myself so I'm not a burden. A party can't teach me that." Saying that seems nicer than letting me wallow in my guilt and sorrow.

"You're absolutely crazy. You know that, right, Genie? What's wrong?"

"I don't like parties anymore. Besides, my mom won't want to take me."

"So take the bus or train or something."

I cock my head at her. There's like all of five wheelchair-accessible train stations in the city. I'm not going around the world to get to some party.

"Hannah, it's not going to happen. I can't go anywhere by myself. Mom drove me here; she'll pick me back up. I can barely go forward; I certainly can't dance at a party where everyone is standing and I have to look up at them. Not trying to push you away again, but things have changed."

"Okay, so come to my house, bring Kylito. We can play Monopoly or whatever."

"No way. I'm not bringing a guy I barely know to your house, and you know it's Jumanji or bust. Besides, you'll just be mad if I take all your money."

"Ugggh, Genie."

"*Ugggh*, Hannah."

"I think you're punishing yourself. There's something you're mum about."

"I told you everything."

"You can't play me, Genie."

"Oh darn, thought I had you. Seriously? Punishing myself? You know I'm not into BDSM."

"Stop making a joke out of this, Genie."

"I've spoke-en. Get it?"

Hannah stands up. "I could've been with Maya, practicing 'Magic' and wishing you were with me, but I chose to actually be with you and you're shitting around on me. Maybe we haven't been friends forever, but we've been friends long enough. I know when something is up, and there is, but fine, don't tell me. Just know when you're done punishing yourself, I'll be there for you, but don't take too long."

Her arms hug around herself as she awaits some response from me. The wrong thing will have her walking across the world away from me. Feels like she's a world away already.

"Don't go, Hannah. I'm sorry. I'm not hiding anything. It's really hot out here, and I'm in sweats when I want to be in shorts and a crop top. Since my accident, I haven't been out much. You know I have no behavior anyway."

"No, you don't."

"Can we talk about you now? Please?"

"Go ahead." She sits back down. "Ask away."

"What's up with you?"

"Nothing, really. I've been keeping a low profile."

For the first time I'm really looking at her face. She looks tired. The bags under her eyes are taking over. Hannah's birthday is next week, and even a month before she's turned up and ready to celebrate. But not now, it seems. This isn't like her at all.

"Are you having a party for your birthday?" I ask, hoping to see a good change in her face.

"Not a party," Hannah corrects me, "a get-together. There's a difference. Dim lights, food, and Netflix with you, Maya if she can make it, and Dez."

"Who's Dez?" I swat a fly away from my slice.

"My Kylito. He's a summer intensive kid from Michigan," she says nonchalantly, as she scrolls through her phone. Her face lights up at a *ding*. "Yes! He's coming to the party tonight! You're off the hook."

Hannah does her signature celebratory shoulder bounce. Just like that, her spirits are lifted by some temporary boy. I used to be the one who could change her mood and not the secondary choice of company. "Great, now you don't need my company."

Her eyes don't leave the screen as she types. "Ay Dios mío, Genie. I'm choosing my battles, which is why I gave up on you coming to the party so easy. I need you for 'Magic.'" She finally looks up. "You can still come to the party, too."

"No—can't. I think Nolan might come over. He's not grasping the breakup thing."

Hannah's phone slams on the table. "Genie, this is the stuff you need to tell me!"

"I didn't know how to say it. He showed up to my room, threatening to tell Mom about the abortion if I didn't, like, talk to him. I just—" Now I can't finish the crust on my pizza.

"Does he think you're gonna change your mind?"

It wouldn't surprise me if Nolan thinks not being able to dance makes more room for him. "I can't pretend to know what Nolan thinks is going to happen."

"Tell him you got a new man."

"So lie?" That won't do any good.

Hannah taps her chin. "Then ballet again. If you help me with 'Magic,' you have a reason he can't just pop up. You'll be at VAB. Easy peasy."

"Can't do that, either. Support group and stuff." I pull cheese off my slice, letting it slide that I'm in my last two days of physical therapy. "Anyway, he probably wants to get me out of his system. If he needs to tell me how he's feeling one last time, then so be it. . . ."

"Genie, that's not your problem and you know it. Again, why are you punishing yourself?" Her shades come back down, and I know she's close to tears. Hannah's a crier. "Do you need me to be there? You two shouldn't be alone with all y'all feelings." Her voice quivers.

"Hannah, don't cry. Look, give me a few days to think about 'Magic.' Maybe I can get rid of Nolan." I lean across the table. "Please, don't cry here."

I can make a sweater with the lies I've been spinning. It's not even a good sweater, but scratchy and tight in some areas and loose in others. Really, I don't want to do either. Going back to VAB would make it too real about everyone I let down there. Deep down, part of me feels like I owe Nolan. Hopefully I can help him and put everything behind me. He owes me, too.

"Hey, girlies!" Maya shouts. She's on track to reach us in thirty seconds.

"What's Maya doing here?" I talk with a smile on my face.

"Would you have come if I said she was coming?" Hannah speaks with her own smile.

"Long time no see, Maya." Unlike Hannah, Maya never tried to see me in the hospital. The last time I saw her was on the way out of the dressing room at VAB when I told her and Hannah I wasn't joining them at the movies.

Maya kind of flaps her hand at me. "It's been too long! You look great. Love the hair."

"Chill on the compliments, Maya, but thank you. What's up?"

"Just glad to get out of the studio for a bit. I've never been over here." She looks around. "My brothers are doing the literal lifting today with Mom, so, yay to girl time. No MS BS for a few hours."

"Yay," Hannah jumps in.

"Is Dez coming to the party later?" Maya asks Hannah.

"You're going to the party too, Maya?" I ask.

"Yeah, I have a day off and it's in a warehouse. A warehouse party!"

So it is accessible. Still no.

Maya bumbles on and on about the party and Dez, and Hannah looks almost embarrassed. We're still besties, but my absence is marked.

"Have you told her about—" Maya starts to speak.

Before Hannah can respond, three boys whistle at us, drawing our attention to the basketball courts. The sound of the tall one bouncing his basketball gets closer and closer, until they're hovering over us. Hannah wipes her eyes quickly before smiling at each of them. The short one has an Icee in his hand. Cherry.

"What's up, ma?" the short one asks Hannah. His fitted is backward and he wears an overstretched tank top. "My man over there wants to know if you wanna kick it with him." He nods to a boy in a gray T-shirt by the Icee cart. "But fuck him, can we sit with you?" It's phrased like a question, but he sits down before Hannah can answer.

Maya politely smiles at the one who's just-right height. They begin talking. From what I remember about Maya, she likes her guys rich in melanin, and it shows all over her face now that he's macking on her.

The tall one, who has a small soul patch filtering in on his chin, stares down at me. His lips are so thick, they don't touch but go in opposite directions. He's definitely not a talker, but his friends are. The short one gives Hannah the hundredth compliment since sitting down. Meanwhile Big Guy here hasn't so much as apologized for memorizing my face.

"You cute for a girl in a wheelchair. I saw you rolling in. You got shot or something? My boy got shot and he can't walk, but like he repeats things now and stuff," he finally says. His words roll into each other.

"Excuse me?"

"My bad, you was born like that or something?"

"Hannah, let's go."

I say it, but she isn't listening or moving. The short one is whispering something in her ear, and Hannah looks like a blushing thirteen-year-old. Her shoulders are high, and she has the slightest smile on her face, like whatever he's saying will teach her the secrets to becoming the youngest prima ever.

"Maya?"

"I kinda just got here . . . ," Maya says guiltily.

My anger dances in front of me. Taunting me. Daring me to get mad at Hannah, when it isn't her fault that all everyone can see is this stupid chair. Suddenly I'm not just cute, but cute for a girl in a wheelchair. Before my accident, guys would cross the street to holla at me. Hannah was the one usually off to the side, hesitant to take the attention. Maybe I should do "Magic." I wonder how else Hannah's changed.

So many things are wrong with this picture. Mom smiles as I head to the car. The smile she'd give as she picked me up from ballet class. "You need a ride, Hannah? Maya?" Mom asks, shouting as a bus pulls into the stop in front of us.

Hannah's close enough that I hear her digging in her purse. "No thanks, Ms. Davis. I'm not heading home."

I turn to look at Hannah, standing tall, redoing her purple

lipstick. "Have fun," I tell her, sounding pettier than I meant. I really do want her to have fun. This is exactly why I pushed her away. I'm no fun anymore.

She half-ass blows a kiss to me before turning away and heading up the block, leaving Maya in the dust. I transfer into the car while Mom pops my chair into the backseat. Somehow, we'll figure out this rift between us.

Maya leans into my open window. "Hey, it was good seeing you, Genie."

I nod at her, before she takes off to catch up to Hannah.

Mom immediately starts to talk as she pulls out. My handicap sticker swings from the mirror as she picks up speed. "Things okay with you and Hannah?"

"Yep."

"How's VAB? Did you two talk about what's going on there?" She knows we did, but she's fishing. Looking to catch a glimpse of the old way before my fall. The one where it didn't hurt to talk ballet for even just a minute. "Hopefully she's getting you to open up your choreography books."

"Sort of. She wants me to help her and Maya with the pas de deux."

"You will, right? Think about it. It'll look good for college apps if they see that even after such trauma you can push through. That's how I got to college after having you."

It's childish, but I lean my seat back and out of her peripheral vision, ignoring her comparison of my accident to the birth of me.

"Genie," she asserts.

"I don't want to talk about VAB or Hannah right now. Is that okay?"

"Something happened at the park? You can tell me."

There's nothing to tell. Just like she never told me that Dad suddenly stopped showing up because of a deal. I assume. What else could it be? Well, I made a deal too. To try to be better, and if that means helping Nolan move on, then so be it. If she's feeling some sort of way about me not saying anything about Hannah, she'd be gutted if she found out about the abortion.

CHAPTER SIX
Hail of Genie

leep?

One word. One character. This is what Nolan texts. Sleep? I don't know her. How can I sleep when I keep checking Hannah's socials wondering how great this party is? She must know I'm stalking her because she's posting nothing but face shots of her and Maya. I adjust the pillow behind my back, feeling myself slouch more than I want.

Yeah, I lie. Was until you woke me up.

Liar. I'm looking at you right now.

Just like that I'm tasting my heart. My head snaps to the window. I expect to see a grim look on his face, but he smiles. Hands on the glass like a kid looking at puppies for sale. My room is all bright and lit up like a puppy shop too.

My door creaks open. Mom yawns while scratching her scarf-covered head. "I'm going to bed. Need anything?"

Nolan repellant. A sniper to take him out. A time machine!

I scoot to the edge of my bed and transfer to my chair. If she steps in any farther, she'll see him. "I was just heading to the bathroom. Need to soak, I think."

"I guess I can play another level." She powers her Switch back on, but I can see in the way she rubs her eyes that she's tired.

"Don't stay up for me."

From the corner of my eye, I can still see Nolan's body. Though this late he's more like a shadow, and I'm glad he's a vampire and waiting for my invitation in. I don't know what he's thinking about or is about to do. Maybe he doesn't want any smoke from Mom or he needs something to fight about. I guess I'll have to wait to see what game he's playing. Right now, he's being gargoyle-like still. That makes one of us. I can't keep my chair parked.

"It'll make me feel better. Just in case," she says, stepping back so she can lean against the doorframe. "Is that okay with you?"

"Forget it. I'll just do it tomorrow." I do my best fake-yawn into my arm.

She huffs. "I swear I don't know what to say or do for you."

I know I should make an attempt at going to bed without this dark energy and bad vibes between us, but Nolan just outside the window is giving me this stage-fright-like feeling. I'm afraid to say the wrong thing or make the wrong move.

"Since when am I not allowed to change my mind? I'm doing you a favor. No need to stay up for me."

Mom holds her hands up in truce. "Take some melatonin. You'll sleep through the night, hopefully. And tie your hair down, then you won't have such a hard time combing it. You didn't inherit these beautiful edges for you to ruin them. See you tomorrow."

"Night."

At the sound of the door clicking shut, I flip Nolan the finger.

I can hear him laughing through the window. "Open up," he says.

I lift the window, letting all the good air out so he can shimmy his way in.

"You sweated less after one of your classes," he laughs.

"Shut up," I snap. "You didn't even try to hide yourself."

He rolls his eyes. "She was probably drunk anyway."

"No, she wasn't, and you know that. Why are you always trying to knock back her progress?"

He shrugs before sliding his bag over his shoulder. "Can I sit?" Now he takes off his sneakers, stepping on the back of each heel. "I'll be quiet. Just like old times. I promise."

I watch him try to butcher the promise swear me and Hannah made up before he just sits on the bed. Nothing is sacred with him. Not my life. Not my friendship with Hannah. And I want my bed to come to life and just toss him off. I want my room to feel weird and cold and spooky with him in it, but it feels, sadly, just like old times.

"Why are you here? What couldn't you text?" I turn off my main light with my reacher. Like its name, it's good for reaching things, but it also saves my shoulders, because the lights in here are all a stretch away. "Turn on the lamp, please."

Nolan does what he's told, even though we're both used to sitting in the dark with each other. "I want to do this right."

"What are you talking about?" I whisper. And not because I'm trying to keep my voice down. My volume won't work.

"I've been talking to my old swim coach. He thinks I'm too stuck on you. He's right. You know how I feel about us. It would be nice to have some reminders, but I got to let some of you go for now. For a do-over." His hands don't move, even though they're in position to unzip his bag.

"You want a redo even though your coach thinks you need to move on?"

His nose crinkles. "Why say it like that?"

Let's make it a true daily double, Alex. "Shit I'm Definitely Not Answering."

"Nolan, I'm confused. What do you want?"

"The way I left last time. That wasn't me."

"But it was. And you got what you wanted, so why are you here?"

He leans back on his elbows all Adonis and merman-like. "I was thinking that we both are having a hard time. So I was wondering what to text you to make you smile. But that didn't seem right. Then I got an idea. I had to show you something, not just text you memes and shit."

"The memes would be okay," I counter.

Finally, he unzips his bag and pulls out a doll. My doll that I remember throwing out because I got a stupid birthday card with two hundred dollars and Beats headphones from my father. It's one of those rag dolls with a bun on her head made of yarn. Dad gave it to me for my fifth birthday, and I cherished her until he left.

"You threw her out when we were cleaning out your room that day," Nolan says, inspecting her. "I couldn't figure out why you did it if she was on your bed. She clearly wasn't trash, so I saved her."

"You—" I stop myself from calling him an idiot. "I threw her out because she reminded me of my dad."

"Oh. I didn't know."

I can't tell if he's being sincere. Maybe I didn't tell him. Maybe he thought I would regret it. Because I did for a little bit. She looked like me, from her hairstyle to her jeans and red T-shirt. When I threw her away, I was tossing out my old life. I was seventeen and didn't need to hold on to her anymore. Because another birthday had passed and I got money and some hot new gadget when all I wanted was my dad to come and explain himself to me. That was the present I needed. I deserved it.

"Why didn't you give it back months ago?" Or mention it. I can't buy that he didn't know I threw her out for a reason.

He sits the doll on his lap like a real child, and I can't tell if he did that on purpose. "I mean, we wasn't exactly in a good place a couple months ago."

I snort. "And we are now?"

"No, but I thought maybe you'd like it for comfort or something? She lived on your bed, if I'm not mistaken. Like damn, I'm trying to be nice here, and open up a little after all this time of not having a decent conversation."

"What do you really want, Nolan? To sit and talk about what happened? I'm not doing that."

"But you will. We have to talk about it, because that night was crazy." He sighs. "I'm chill now, though. Even went by to see my dad tonight. You're not the only one I got to talk to. Can you believe he moved all the way out to Flushing? Bed-Stuy must've got too small for him."

I back up a bit. Nolan and his dad. He can get either really weepy or really shouty when it comes to this guy. "What happened?" Too fast, I get sucked into his drama. If I bring up my dad, we can talk about our respective deadbeats for hours and hours.

"I asked him how his girlfriend was doing, and he said, 'I cheated, she left, and I've got another.'" Disappointment swirls in his eyes. For some reason, he cares about his father's character. It's something I've never been able to understand, because some people simply suck and there's nothing you can do about it.

Nolan's dad is a serial cheater. I will give Nolan this, he's very much a one-girl-for-me kind of guy. His mother has been torn apart with the lies and the other women. Not only did his father cheat a lot, but he would stop taking care of his responsibilities to lavish the others with time and money.

"Some things never change. Did you leave him behind a dumpster or something?" I'm only half joking. Nolan has literally fought his father. It was that time that his dad finally left them alone for good, until now, apparently.

"I'm doing better, Genie. I didn't even yell at him." He gets animated. Proud, even.

"Good for you." Now's the time to break away from this. This has nothing to do with me. I want nothing to do with him. And even though I'm looking Nolan in his eyes, I'm not thinking about him. It's Kyle who's on my mind. What's he doing right now? Working out? Writing bakery reviews? If I used his number, I could simply ask, but I'm not sure I'm ready for all that.

A low growl comes from Nolan. "How have you not changed? Genie, I need you. I need someone to talk to about it. You do too."

"Pretty sure I'm the most changed out of this. I don't see you using a wheelchair be—"

"I didn't push you!"

"But you let me fall." I can't scream it. I need to scream it. Instead, it comes out airy like blown powder. My stomach has become a blender. The ingredients of bitterness, anger, spite, and betrayal swirl around and then drop before they splatter everywhere.

He knows all my secrets. I told him everything about my mom and dad. He knows I hate how Mom lived her life through my dancing, the drinking, and the pressure I felt from her to stay a prodigy. All of it I unloaded onto him. I owe him a lot for those nights he would sneak through the fire escape and just listen to me. Not telling me to work harder in class or to make sure people remembered me. He didn't care to tell people I was a dancer. To him I was just Genie. I fell for that.

My eyes stop on the picture of Hannah, Nolan, and me. A better time. How *haven't* I changed? I've changed a lot. I'm lying to Hannah. Been lying to Mom. The one place I want to be, I can't even think of myself there. It hurts too much. I'm too embarrassed by why I can't be there. Sometimes I think it'd be easier if I got hit by a car or injured myself dancing. That would be understandable. Forgivable.

"I remember when we took that picture," Nolan says, bending in front of me. When did he even get off the bed? "I'm right here, Genie."

Nolan's hand is warm. Too warm on mine. I flinch. "You need to go."

Our eyes meet but don't really say anything. Feels like all we can do is vent to each other. I don't want to vent and I don't want to fall back into our physical relationship. His hands roughly brush over my skin before he takes my hand and places it on his chest. Before any of this, he wouldn't have had to do that. I would've been on him already.

I wonder if Hannah is cozied up with Dez. She didn't even show me a picture, but I guess I didn't ask for one.

"Touch me. You'll see this isn't over." A trail of kisses burns my neck.

Right now, I don't want to think about Hannah, Mom, VAB, "Magic," or even this doll. I want to feel something other than unhappy. These kisses should make me feel something. There's nothing. I twist away from them, but he holds me steady.

"Let's. Move. To. The. Bed," he says between kisses, stopping right before my lips. "I'm giving you an outlet, Genie. You want me here, want to talk to me, look at me, love me, even. We both know you're hurting. I can see it."

Nolan's got my arms pinned to my sides. Licking his lips, he moves in for a bigger kiss. I can't push him away. "Nolan, don—"

My words are covered by his lips. Licking them didn't help. They're cracked against mine, digging into me so intensely, I expect to taste chlorine. I manage to wedge my arm from his grip to slap him, not caring if Mom can hear the ringing circling the room. Nolan stumbles back, falling on his butt.

"Fucking bitch."

I nurse my stinging hand. Why don't I feel even a smidge better? "This is over, Nolan. Don't come back here again."

Angrily he zips his bag. "That's it, your mother knows now."

"Tell her, Nolan. I don't care."

"All you ever do is care what she thinks." He puts his sneakers on and opens the window.

"What else do you want to take from me?" Why does he still even bother with me? Whatever he saw in me before my accident is gone. He can thank himself for that. "I'm hurting because I can't feel my legs. Because of you. Remember that before you waste our time."

Nolan squeezes out the window, not even looking back at me. He becomes a shadow again. I want to toss everything I own out the window, including my wheelchair, raining a hail of Genie down on him.

CHAPTER SEVEN

Accidents Happen

reate. Don't hesitate. Miss Kuznetsova used to tell everyone that if she felt we were holding back. *Don't think. Do. Don't stop. Go,* she writes in this morning's email. Normally I just look at it once, but she's hooked me today, and even now in the elevator at therapy I'm rereading it.

I hover above the reply button before the elevator opens up and I creep down the hall. *Create. Don't hesitate.* The choreography part of my head is broken. Has been since I came crashing down. Even if I wanted to make up a variation right now, my mind is blank. No way I could put together a barre exercise in this moment.

I can't tell Kuznetsova that I've completely stalled; that and disappoint her more. It probably doesn't help that I won't even look at a ballet, or listen to one. *Create. Create. Create.* With what? You have to have something. I always had something to spark me. Boredom, anger, even goofing around. If I told Mom, she'd tell me to see a shrink. But what can a shrink do? They can't put the steps back in my head. And Hannah thinks I can still be a choreographer if I help with "Magic." Magic isn't that type of magic. I don't even remember it. I just know how I felt doing it. That's not enough.

I can't even find the room I'm supposed to be going to until I see a sign for QUEST and an arrow pointing down the hall. I follow a few more of those to a yellow-painted door.

For some reason I thought group therapy would look like the inside of a waiting room. Everyone sitting in their spots, some magazines, a dreary wall color covered up by boring posters to spice it up, and maybe some light music in the background. And crying, can't forget the crying. I was wrong.

I roll into the room no trouble; they propped the door open for the kinetically challenged like me, who want to shit their pants just looking at a closed door. I can't escape the horror of those cheesy photos they like to plaster in every room, however. Light music is not how I would describe the sound bumping out of the iPod dock. I spot Kyle by a table full of refreshments, and from the size of the piece of chocolate cake on his plate, I'm going to guess they serve the good kind.

"Did you save me a seat?" I pull up beside him, eye level with a platter of Danishes, both apple and cheese. No stale box of peanut butter crackers and sugar-free cookies here.

I've startled him. He bumps into his walker, which knocks my knee. His mouth pops open and his eyes strain, searching for a word. "S-s-sorry!" he sputters.

"Relax, I can't feel it anyway."

"Still," he says.

I can see my joke didn't go over well. The fix-it light in my head goes off. "Can I at least carry your cake back to your seat?"

That puts a smile on his face as he nods His scars are covered by a new patch of curly brown hair overnight. I place his plate on my lap, and he trails me as I wedge myself between two chairs. A girl with a prosthetic leg waves at me, and the girl sitting next to her notices me and waves too. I give a small smile in response, even though I don't know them. They're friendly enough, but I'm glad I know Kyle.

He's wearing a red Stanford shirt today. At least he's still going, although he can't compete. I wonder how he told them. Short and sweet? Or did he just quit? If he quit, he doesn't need to tell them what happened.

I'll only be starting senior year of high school in the fall, but I have no idea what I'm going to do afterward. Apply to colleges? For safety I was going to apply to some dance programs. I'm more VAB than SAT, but it's all unclear now. Like learning choreography for the first time, trying to imagine what it's supposed to not only look like, but feel like. What's my future supposed to look like? How should I feel about it?

I shake my head and turn my attention back to Kyle. Nolan's behavior last night should have me off guys altogether. Kyle should look like a turd in my eyes. But he doesn't. There's this coolness about him, like he just lives and lets go. Somehow, he manages to make eating look adorable. He's one of those people that nibbles first before going for the wide bite.

"It was our last day of therapy today. Didn't see you down in the lion's den," I probe. If I had known you could skip the last day of therapy, I would've. I don't know which I hate more. The uncomfortable pain of therapy or the uncomfortable silence between Mom and me.

"Hooky." He smiles, a bit of chocolate on his upper lip.

Oh, I'm intrigued. This is the guy that says he can do "one more" after every rep, and actually does two more. Why would he skip a session?

"Stanford knows you don't play by the rules?"

"S-s-secret."

I know about those.

"I—I—I didn't think you would c-c-come," he says.

I feign shock. "I promised, didn't I?"

He had every reason to think I would flake out. I almost left right after today's session. But Hannah told me I sucked, and I didn't want Kyle to think I did too. I don't plan on participating. Just sitting here says I've participated in some way, and that's all he asked of me. Although this is feeling more like a glorified party than a support group. Everyone looks adjusted, happy, even. How? Seems like every psychologist who ever talked to me might have talked to them and actually gotten through. *You'll get used to it. You'll find new meaning. You'll be happy again.* How long did it take for them? How long for me?

He nods. "N-no text, though?"

Busted. I did think about it. But thoughts don't send texts. I didn't know what to say. I suppose I could've texted, *Good luck in California, sorry you had to meet bitter me, smiley face emoji thumbs-up.* I can send one now: *P.S. You have chocolate on your top lip. It's actually really cute.*

Before I can respond about the text, the music cuts off and everyone quiets down. All six of us. A woman with a cane who looks around Mom's age walks into the room. She's rushing but full of smiles as she waddles to an empty chair in the circle. Obviously, it's saved for her.

"Sorry, everyone! I apologize for my tardiness," she says, placing her cane on the floor, making eye contact with me. "I see a new face."

All eyes are on me. Even though I'm one of two people in a wheelchair here, I feel more aware of my chair than I've felt in a while. Everyone here knows I wasn't always like this. They're all probably wondering what my story is.

"Welcome to QUEST. Questioning, understanding, and expressing sudden tragedies. Care to introduce yourself? I'm Carrie."

Kyle gives me a supportive smile. I never would've thought there'd be a time where I'd constantly wish to be invisible. I tug on my pant leg like it matters, smoothing the top of my thighs. My seat belt suddenly feels too tight, and I unbuckle it.

"I'm Genie."

"Welcome, Genie," Carrie says. She scans the room, a smile still on her face. "Who wants to start this meeting today?"

I look over at Kyle with his chocolate-stained lip; he raises his hand.

"What's up, Kyle?" Carrie calls on him.

His mouth opens and closes, and everyone patiently waits for him to speak. "I want . . . t-to t-talk about . . . how . . ." He stops. His eyes sweep for the word. Carrie tells him to take his time. "How people see me now . . . not knowing . . . m-me before."

A collective sympathizing murmur floats around the room. I

lock my eyes on a photo of a girl jumping in joy. I used to be able to do that and more. Why would anyone care that he used to be a gymnast, though? To the people at Stanford, he'll be the guy with the speech impediment and slow walk. Even if he manages not to need his walker anymore, it's not like he can flip off a vault ever again. What does it matter to anyone that I attended the best ballet school in New York, let alone America? Standing on pointe means nothing if I can't stand at all. All everyone ever sees is this chair. It doesn't matter how I got into it.

Kyle taps me on my shoulder. "C-C-Carrie's talking to you."

"Do you have any worries about meeting people? People who weren't familiar with you prior to your incident?" Carrie's eyes are open and inviting. In a way they remind me of Mom's. She's still struggling to make sense of the fact that I'm not Genie her ballet prodigy anymore. She doesn't say it, but I'm not wrong to assume.

"Not really," I tell her. But I remember back at the park when that boy assumed I was shot or was born this way. People have no idea, and I hate that they make up their own stories. But that doesn't mean I have to go around with a mic into a bullhorn, shouting mine. Maybe it's no one's business.

She looks taken aback, and I keep my head trained forward so I don't look at Kyle. This is exactly why I avoided this place. Everyone wants to know something. Spill all the tea. I can't share what little of me I have left and let them know I'm afraid of being the girl who used to dance but got paralyzed. I want to be the Genie that oozed confidence and drew everyone's attention when attitude turns and Italian fouettés were just part of my drip.

Because she's polite, Carrie moves the conversation along, saying something about wanting people to know who we were before our injuries. I want to disappear.

"I can't help but feel like I'm . . ." Kyle pauses, but it seems voluntary this time. Like what he wants to say may just destroy him.

"Damaged," the girl with the prosthetic finishes.

"Yeah," Kyle whispers.

"Stupid," the boy in the wheelchair adds, his voice hoarse and labored.

Kyle clears his throat. "People get p-p-past the walker, but I open my mouth and th-th-they give up on me. I still go to speech and I remember not being able to t-t-talk at all, but I'm not where I want to be. People can see that and I'm pushed a-a-aside."

"These are all valid fears," Carries says. "Anything to add, Genie?"

I don't know why. Maybe because I feel like everyone just thinks if they tell people who they used to be, it would matter somehow. I feel differently, and I have to say it. "If it looks like a duck and quacks like a duck, must be a duck. I'm damaged. I won't walk again. I'll only ever be the girl in the wheelchair." The angry Black girl in a wheelchair, to be more specific.

Kyle looks like I spit in his Cheerios. If there was ever a time for me to jump into a magic lamp and disappear for centuries, it'd be now. Kyle and I don't know each other well, but what he gets of me outside of getting frustrated in therapy is that I'm an asshole. Logan is somewhere feeling secondhand embarrassment. I know it.

He's quiet the rest of the meeting. *See, this is why I didn't text,* I want to tell him. Giving me his number "for whenever" is cute, but there is no good time to deal with me. He's right: I have a lot going on without adding him to the mix. Maybe things would've been better if we'd just stuck to glances.

I expected to leave here happy, but now I'm confused. Instead, I feel like I've used a baby as a speed bump. That wasn't a good way to say goodbye to someone. Telling someone that if they sound stupid, they really are.

I rush to the elevator before Carrie officially ends the meeting, just so I don't have to deal with looking at everyone. I'm actually glad to be out in the sun and heat when I realize Mom wasn't sitting in the waiting area.

Searching for Mom, I look like a merry-go-round. She could be waiting in the car. I roll up the block. Maybe she couldn't get a spot close to the door and didn't want to double-park. More like she's still mad at me. Nevertheless, I text her and wait for her reply.

I open my phone to texts from Hannah. Her signature of "let's make up" emojis consists of watery-eye faces and hearts. That I can work with. Truth be told, I should've texted her first. However, I usually open it up with a *Hey, thinking about you. Made up a solo piece.* Of course, she manages to slip in that she has the cozy studio to work on "Magic" if I want to come by.

I know she's not being pushy, but oh, it pushes me. Didn't I say let me think about it? She just assumed I'd be able to drop everything I'm doing to help her with a dance she knows perfectly well without me. She knows my process. I can't just sit in the corner and yell out steps. I have to do them. Even at school I would take the hall pass just so I could work out bits here and there. Teachers called me hyper and unruly before I even realized what my body was doing. Right now, I can't respond. I pull on my braids as if they're some sort of stress string to yank on. I bet if I was entertaining the idea of going to VAB, Mom would appear out of the blue.

A text from Nolan pops up. He wants to know how I'm doing and what I did with the doll. She's on my bed, not that I'm going to tell him. For a rag doll, she's pretty plush and works great under my neck.

"W-w-waiting for your mom?"

Kyle.

"All the good daughters do," I tell him, tucking my phone back in my pants, as if he can or cares to read my text from Nolan. He steadies himself on his walker, and I wonder why he wouldn't just sit inside and wait for whatever or whoever he's standing for. Quickly I glance up at his face, and he's looking up to the sky. I look up too.

"Your ride coming by air?" I ask.

"Bit . . . out my . . . budget," he stammers, looking at his watch. It's a nice watch too, with a black face and steel band. One of those watches that look great but hard to tell time on. "G-g-going to be late." He taps his walker with impatience.

"For what?" I click my teeth in regret. It's not my business, especially after what happened inside.

Kyle sighs. "Mandated community service."

Mandated. As in he fucked up. Before my judginess can spread to my lymph nodes, I remember that I'm not exactly a saint either.

And the way he said it. After the sigh, it was said with dignity, as if he couldn't care less whatever I'm thinking now, and the way he's looking at me, I hope he doesn't take the look on my face wrong.

"Is it far from here?" I'm pulling at straws, and they're bendy.

"W-w-well, it's on the other side of Brooklyn. St. Nicholas, down by the Verrazzano."

"I know that church."

His posture straightens out. "R-r-really? How so?"

"My mom has . . . meetings there."

Really, I should say she has AA meetings. When I was little, I would go and play in the park next door. Afterward, sometimes we would go to the waterfront overlooking the Narrows and walk a bit before heading home. I think it was then that I decided I loved to choreograph, after I made up a dance on the spot for Mom to cheer her up.

Kyle's lips fold into each other. He knows exactly what kind of meetings I'm talking about. His eyes are relatable, though; soft, even. Makes me feel bad for judging him earlier.

"I hope your ride gets here soon, then."

"Me t-t-too. I really enjoy going." Before I can respond, there's a honk and our attention is diverted to a silver Honda. "That's me." He gives me a short smile before hobbling toward the car.

"Bye," I say as the car pulls off. This is it. No more Kyle. No more rehab. No more Logan, even though I know he and Mom are conspiring to keep me going with another six weeks of therapy. Logan thinks I haven't done enough. He'd be right. I did the bare minimum next to Kyle for four days a week. For the past three months, he worked like a horse. By the time I got in the headspace to try a bit more, using Kyle for some internal competition, it was just easier to stay mad.

Logan would tell me it's not enough to want to just walk again. It's not about walking for me, though. There's no point in wishing for the impossible. I just . . . I wish I were myself at therapy. I wish I could turn on what I see in Kyle: that drive. Regaining my strength and learning to live in this chair is hard work. Work I can't make look easy.

Kyle makes everything look easy. Even opening up in a roomful of strangers. Yes, I'm being a hater. How can I not? How can he just *do*? It's like he's getting Kuznetsova's emails too.

He wanted to talk about how people see him now, not having known him before. If he's this good now, I can only imagine the before. Then there's me before all of this. I don't think I want people to know who I was. Maybe still am. Because I do feel damaged. It has nothing to do with my legs. Ballet is gone, and I can see myself out in the open now. I don't think I ever worked like I should have.

What would Carrie say if I told her I'm the same person now as I was before? Scared and bigheaded. Hyping myself up to distract myself from the mess that is my life. So there's no point in knowing me before. *Questioning, understanding, and expressing sudden tragedies.* Maybe my fall wasn't the tragedy, just the mirror showing me I've always been the tragedy.

My eyes burn, and for a moment I think I've lost it and started crying, but it's only sweat. It's too hot out here. I could go back inside and wait, but I don't want to be here anymore and risk running into any more QUEST kids. Maybe Mom is at the store. She was here when she dropped me off, she wouldn't just leave me . . . right?

Starbucks it is.

As I roll up the hill, I think of all the things I've should've asked Carrie. How do I get rid of the air that feels trapped in all the wrong places? 'Cause drinking a Dr Pepper doesn't help. *Hey, Carrie, question: How can I not make guilt the first thing I feel when I wake up? Maybe it could be the second thing or the fifth. I won't be choosy. Another thing, Carrie. Why did my mom get the short end of the stick? Was it not enough for her to be an alcoholic and a teen mom? Now she has to put up with my injury, too.*

I push harder, seeing the countdown in the crosswalk. The combination of speed and blurry vision doesn't help me navigate around a crater in the pavement. My front casters hit the uneven cement, sending me flying out of my chair and onto the sidewalk. Everything from my waist up stings like I jumped into water from too high. The right side of my face burns, and I'm too hurt to look up to see if anyone saw.

"I'm calling for help," a woman's voice says to me. All I can see of her is green-and-blue running shoes; they move frantically, like her voice. "I need an ambulance. A girl just fell out of her wheel-chair."

Hey, Carrie. One more question; Why do accidents happen?

CHAPTER EIGHT

Stuck

onight on The Breaking Pointe, *we have a special episode about serving face with a bloody nose.*

What pisses me off about being dependent on a wheelchair: when my chair goes bye-bye, Genie's stuck. No one wants me to move. Even though they've checked my bones over and over, they're afraid I might break something or fall out of my chair again. Like that scares me. "I've dropped from bigger heights," I joke. When I say it, nobody laughs.

For twenty minutes I've been listening to some man in the emergency room argue with an orderly about why he refuses to be transported in a wheelchair. He keeps repeating that he "doesn't need it" and that it's a "waste of time."

"Just let me walk there. I can make it no problem," he says between coughs.

"Sir, for safety reasons you need to sit in the chair," the orderly tries to reason with him. This has to be the tenth time he's reworded that the chair is to make sure Mr. Hacker here doesn't fall when he coughs out that lung.

"I don't need it. It's a waste of time." I can't see him, but judging by his annoyed tone, he's got his hands folded across his chest, try-ing to be dignified in a paper dress.

"Sir, we just—"

"I'm not sitting in that damn chair!" An army of choking coughs come out of him. Serves him right for raising his voice. The nerve of some people. Hospitals are supposed to be quiet.

"Only for a few minutes," the orderly coaxes.

The orderly should just come to my cubicle area and ask me. I'd gladly sit in my chair right now.

"No, I refuse."

Too bad he can't see that the chair isn't the enemy here. It's just a minor blip in his day, but after lying on my back for weeks, finally being able to sit in a chair, back brace and all, was liberating. I could look out a window. I could make it to a vending machine, even if Mom didn't want me to ruin my appetite for that bland-ass hospital food. As weird as it felt to actually need that loaner chair, it helped me do things I couldn't when I was stuck on a bed, and, most importantly, I could do them myself. I wish he would shut up and get in the damn chair already.

I've folded this blanket ten times, tried developing telekinesis powers by tipping over my water cup, and tested my savant abilities guessing the number of tiles on my side of the room. Makes me happy that the last time I was in an ER, I was unconscious. I didn't have to stare at this puke-green divider.

Being stuck here has done one thing for me, though. I've thought of what to tell Mom when she comes. I settled on telling her I misjudged some crack and didn't listen to Logan when he said I really need to wear my seat belt.

"Genie, are you okay?" Mom rushes into the room, yanking back the thin divider, ignoring Mr. Hacker, her eyes overflowing with worry. They're the same eyes that followed me around parks. Telling kids to be gentle and for me to stop jumping from so high. Those eyes bulged at the sight of me running up or down stairs too fast. She would have kept me in bubble wrap and only let me out for dance class if she could have.

"You have to be careful," she says, checking me for herself, lifting my gown to inspect my legs. She has on a visitor's tag from another hospital. I ignore it. Just like Nolan.

"I may not feel you on my legs, but you're working my nerves, Mom." I throw my head back against the bed. I hate how she fusses over me. I'm not one of her AA buddies, always needing to be checked.

"I'm sorry." She composes herself and takes an apprehensive step back. "What happened?"

"I was waiting for you, figured I'd go to Starbucks, and misjudged if I could go over the crack. It was an accident."

She stares at me so hard I know she's going to call me out. I was distracted. Exhaling, she moves her twist behind her ears. "We'll make an appointment with the ortho to make sure you're okay."

"No more doctors." I mean it. She's just going to tell me what I know already about being careful to keep my bones healthy because of "osteowhatever."

"Keep your seat belt on. I know you weren't wearing it," she scolds me, sitting in the corner chair. Her pity eyes flash at me. "Your face." She touches her own face, as if to check to see if it's still there.

I don't need stitches, but my right cheek up to my eye is bruised. I caught a glimpse from a mirror in the hall as they wheeled me out of radiology. It looked like I let a toddler use an eggplant as eye shadow. There are a few scrapes and cuts, too. The doctor said, "They'll heal in no time," like it would cheer me up.

"I'll be fine," I tell her.

"Will you?"

Instead of answering, I close my eyes.

I hadn't realized I'd fallen asleep once I got home until Mom's yelling wakes me up. My hand smooshes a Twinkie as I sit up in bed. A few more empty wrappers crinkle as I roll on my side to alleviate some pressure. Swell, now I'm stress-eating. Forgetting about my bruise, I wince as I try to rub the sleep out of my eyes. When did I conk out? Who is she yelling at? I transfer into my chair, slower than I normally do. There's a party of pain on my shoulders, and it's lit.

Mom paces back and forth like a caged animal, her twisted hair hanging primal. I almost don't recognize her. She has always tried to hide any imperfection with cute outfits, tamed hair, and a smile on her face. Her youth helped. I didn't know Dad beat on her, until that one day. To see her like this scares me. I have to remind my hands to loosen up on my rims.

"Leave her alone!" she shouts into the receiver, losing her balance a little. "I won't let her see you, Bryan."

Maybe I should throw the doll out again. Clearly, it's haunted if he's calling.

"Mom?" I push forward. A big glass of ice water sweats on the table, but it doesn't seem to be chilling her out.

Her eyes shoot to me; they're red and tired. How long has this conversation been going on? It seems like her chest is going to explode by how high and fast it's rising. "Don't call here again!" She hangs up the phone and tosses it on the couch, plopping down next to it.

"What did Dad want?" It's a dumb question, but I ask anyway.

"Don't worry about it." She does her best attempt at fixing herself up, swatting at her twists like they're snakes hanging from a tree taunting her.

"How—"

"Genie, please, go back to your room." She waves me away, but there's an edge in her voice. "He made his choice at the café."

"No." I roll closer to her. For years I've been fine about not knowing why he disappeared. I won't just go to my room.

"Genie!" Her foot comes down so hard, the photos on the wall shake.

"Just tell me about the deal! You said something about a deal, and I know it's why he never came home. It's been ten years. Say something more than he's not coming back." The first month he left, I just kept waiting and asking for him. Every time she would give me those pity eyes, smile softly, and tell me he wasn't coming back. Then she'd ask me to perform for her. *Make Mommy smile, dance for me.*

I would give her something and get nothing back. Nothing more than her short-and-sweet answers. I'm tired of being her puppet.

"I'm not getting into this with you." Her voice is almost back to normal.

"No, that's not good enough. What's so important that all of a sudden you two are speaking and you're screaming about me?"

"You're important, Genie. He's—" She stops herself, rubbing her face.

"He's what?" I try to think of anything she might be hiding, but nothing comes to mind. This is the most emotion regarding Dad I've seen in a long time.

"I'm trying to protect you."

"Where were you today, then? If you'd been there, I wouldn't have fallen. But I guess someone else needed you more." It comes out of my mouth as easy as spit. I didn't plan to say it. I don't even know if it's how I really feel.

"If you hadn't fallen off that roof, you wouldn't be in that chair. You'd still be dancing! You'd be living your life instead of fighting it!" Her eyes are so wide, I think they'll never close again. The hands that used to give me massages after classes ball into tight fists, shaking at her sides.

Not sure if anyone gained a point here.

I recognize her face—cheated. It feels like the moment Miss Kuznetsova picked Hannah for the opening season "Kitri" variation. The one I worked so hard on, the one she knew I wanted. Rage and humiliation were—are—center stage. I stayed back after class to dance the variation, wanting to see where I'd messed up. Miss Kuznetsova sought me out. "You expect everything to go your way. I teach you humility," she told me. From then on, I stopped expecting parts. If I wanted a part, I had to fight for it. That much, I knew then. I'm struggling with this now.

Normally when Mom says something that might hurt my feelings, she backtracks and her eyes plead a thousand apologies. I'm looking into her eyes and they're not sorry. They're speaking the truth. She's been wanting to tell me this since she found out I would never dance again.

"Finally. You said it. I ruined my life. Can't dance. Can't take care of myself. I can't even keep myself in my own chair."

The pounding moves from my heart and settles into my temples, waiting for her to respond. All she does is look at me. More like glares. We stare at each other for I don't know how long before I get the sense to go back to my room.

That had to be a whole willow tree's worth of shade.

All I want to do is stomp and scream and throw something. I open my mouth to yell, but nothing comes out. No amount of force helps either. Pushing myself back here felt like rolling through quicksand.

I'm trapped.

There on my nightstand is the napkin. All balled up and wrinkled and begging for me to just put his number in my phone. I reach for it, stopping short of touching it. This is the whenever. Ugh, but I made an ass of myself today. What am I doing? I shouldn't bother him. He should forget about me. It's not like he can help me.

But he does understand me.

I called him damaged.

But he understands me.

The digits seem to dance around on the napkin, each number taking a turn doing a solo as if going down a chorus line. *Dial me.* I contemplate finding some Tylenol for my headache. Dancing numbers? You really need to see a doctor, Genie. While you're there, just check yourself into the psych ward. Hannah would miss you, but she'll be off to Paris in no time. And Kyle. He'll be at Stanford.

The numbers finish their movement, and I applaud by typing in his number, blinking away a few floaters clouding my vision. Pressing the message button, I write: I wish I could fly again.

Almost immediately I get a text back: Me too.

Thanks for understanding, I want to reply back, but my hands are stuck. All I can do is look at his reply. I thought I was the thirsty one. Was he really waiting for me to text him? How did he know that whenever it was, was right now? Does his mom hate him too because he isn't who he used to be? I want to ask him, but I don't want to pry. Just like I pried about community service. How'd that go for him? I hope his lateness didn't hurt him.

Slowly the pressure on my temples lessens. The cursor in the type box blinks at me. Like me, it's stuck, unmoving, waiting and wondering what to say next.

It's a sign. There's nothing else to say. I should leave him alone.

And I do leave him alone. But he doesn't leave me alone. He's all I can think about. Those arms, his thighs, and that smile. The curly hair that makes me want to run my hands through it. That face would most certainly keep me locked on him during a pas de deux. No acting required. Be in love. Easy, have you seen those eyes? Sensitive and brown like that chocolate Lab you wanted as a kid. When they look at me, they see me. The chair is invisible. And that chocolate-stained lip of his. I wanted to wipe the chocolate off for him. See up close if his lips are as soft as they look.

The last time a boy kept me up late was Nolan. I guess Davis women have a skill for keeping things behind closed doors. I quickly shake the thought of Kyle in my room, sporting those biceps around.

I do wonder how he knows it was me texting. My *Swan Lake* poster of the two swans Odette and Odile in mirror image doing an attitude derrière catches my eye. Long before Hannah was in the mix, they were my best friends. I talked to them about my dad issues and they replied, speaking the dialogue I made up for them. I've neglected them lately.

"Am I crazy to think that he cares, girls?"

"Guys like Kyle are special. He knows special when it texts him," Odette, the white swan, assures me.

"He's a player," Odile, the black swan, says nonchalantly. "He just took a guess."

"Don't listen to her, Genie. She's just trying to trick you."

"Odette has a point, Odile. You trick people. It's kind of what you do," I point out.

"I'm setting the record straight. Guys like him have a bunch of girls in their phones, texting them all day."

"None that fly like Genie."

"Thanks, Odette!" I say.

"Sweet, innocent Odette. He probably knows a bunch of gymnast girls." Odile pats Odette on the shoulder, comforting her optimistic attitude.

"But none are special like Genie," Odette adds with know-it-all flair.

"Genie, your number probably came up with no name on his phone. He filled in the blanks." Odile squashes the argument.

Good chance I'm tripping. Maybe he wants to say more but is stuck too.

CHAPTER NINE

More Than Dance

On this episode of The Breaking Pointe, *Genie is cranky because the house is no longer full of Twinkies. There must always be Twinkies.*

"I got you something." Nolan excitedly opens his bag. He's dropped by unexpectedly.

Sort of. I knew he would pop up eventually. I just didn't know when. I wish it weren't today of all days. All I can do is hope Nolan doesn't have a "hold my beer" moment and try to one-up the embarrassment of falling out of your chair the last day of physical therapy. Now he's here again and I don't want him to be, but I keep letting him in. It's just muscle memory. I see him, I pull up the window. He comes right on in, and for a moment I hold out hope he'll say something worth listening to. Something in the shape of an apology or that he's joined the military on a supersecret no-contact mission.

Another part of me wants to fight with him. But it never happens the way I want. I need him to apologize—to take responsibility for what happened—and then I realize I don't know how to get that from him. "Do you like seeing me upset?" I ask. "Or can you not recognize when I don't want you here?"

"Do you like ruining all things good? Or can you not recognize when I'm trying to spread positivity?" He squints at me before laughing. "You're not going to ruin what I have planned, so stop trying. If you didn't want me here, you could simply not have opened the window."

Nolan, one. Genie, zero.

"Would you even take me not opening the window as an answer?"

He ignores me. "I have something you might love more than dance."

"Another me is impossible."

He chuckles, and it's freaking cute. "Twinkies." Nolan pulls a box from his bag.

"Wow. That's actually really nice of you." In Nolan's universe, this is like a Nobel Prize contribution to the world.

Instead of smiling, he shrugs all bashful. "Peace offering? I hope you know I'm not going to tell anyone about . . . you know. Besides, I know you."

I'm surprised he doesn't fully name it. *Abortion.* I spoke it out loud just to normalize it. So it wouldn't sound so foreign to me. But he won't say it. I don't think he has a problem with them in general, but he didn't want me to have one. I know he thinks I skipped on my way to have it done and heel-clicked when it was over. That I probably didn't think too hard on it. And he'd be right about that part.

It didn't mean that I was any less upset about it. I couldn't even register the feeling as upset at first. Everything felt different. How could it be so simple a decision for me, and tear me apart, too? My life as I knew it wouldn't have to change. It was a simple backspace on what was written. A small edit.

I wish it didn't have to happen. That a decision didn't have to be made. Does Nolan know that?

"That's one thing I'll miss when I change schools. The treats you always slipped me," I tell him.

Nolan turns his head at the mention, unintentionally bringing attention to his earring. Different from last time. One I gave him. A baby gold stud left over from losing one when I was younger. "Sucks the school isn't accessible."

"You're telling me." Not only do I have to adjust to this chair, but a new school and all that comes with it, too.

"I have something else from your childhood, but I don't think your dad is responsible for them like the doll was. I figured you'd want them back." He goes into his bag and pulls out a small Tupperware of the other half of earrings. I must've lost a dozen earrings before I was ten years old. When Nolan pierced his ear, I got a kick out of making him wear my childhood earrings. I couldn't use them anymore, and hoops looked good on him. He touches his ear. "After all the pain I went through to pierce my ear I'm willing to let them go. Guess it's time to get big-boy diamonds."

"Son, the pain is like ten seconds."

"Says the girl who tells me afterward she was an infant when she got hers done."

"You look cute, so I say it was worth it."

Nolan was always fine, but jewelry really elevated his look.

When I brought up the piercing, I didn't expect for him to be down. I know he didn't do it just for me, but it was a nice thing for him to consider. I remember it being like one of the first couples things we did together (kind of; his mom had to give permission and she quickly bounced after doing so). Walking hand in hand in Kings Plaza to Piercing Pagoda. Afterward we bought like two pounds of oatmeal raisin and macadamia nut cookies to distract from his throbbing earlobe.

"Aight then, go get your nose pierced so we can compare."

"So you can take a picture of me crying?"

"You got one of me?"

"Of course."

"Can I see it?"

I answer by rolling to my bookcase. A box on the third shelf sits above me. There's a sharp pain in my shoulder as I stretch for it.

"Fuck," I hiss.

"What happened?"

"My shoulder just went ape on me." I should've used my reacher, but I'm stubborn about using it if I can stretch a bit to reach.

Nolan gets up and walks over to me. "Let me see." He touches my arm and brings it up. "I know some stretches to help. I've been having to do them lately."

Using my wall as a demo, Nolan models some stretches for me, and I humor him by following along. They're close to what Logan has me do. Before we lose any more time, I reach for the box and sift through some four-by-sixes. That one Halloween we dressed as Black Panthers. He actually grew out his 'fro for a whole year. The pic of him and me the day he and that boy had the fight at Broadway Junction like it wasn't barely thirty degrees outside. Unlike some of the other pics of us, there's some distance despite his arms around me. We both let out a sigh at the same time. I was done with him after that day. Until that March almost a month later that led to the makeup sex that led to the pregnancy. There's no denying that day at the train station changed both of us. I saved him from doing something he couldn't come back from. Then he chose not to save me.

The one I'm looking for is right behind that picture. I hold the crying pic up to him. He says nothing until I give it to him.

"Damn, you kept receipts on my emotions," he laughs. "I look vexed."

"Something like that."

It's one of those pics that I just got printed out and did nothing with. Not sure of its purpose, but just a moment in time. One not attached to a bad memory or feeling. Just a good old moment despite his tears.

He nods. "I can't stay because I'm going to get some conditioning in, but, um . . . thanks for turning me on to the earring thing, even if you did punk out about the nose piercing."

"I do what I can."

But he doesn't move.

"You, um . . . you going to be okay?" He motions to my face.

"It's a little cramped in this bottle, but Genies are always okay."

I'm being nice to him and I don't even know why.

No. I know why. I feel bad for him. Bad for me. For us. There is something I love more than dance. That's to be thought about. Cared for. Nolan's being a decent human. Why am I being nice to that? More so, why do I care? I don't want him back. Or need him, but when Nolan's not being a dick, he's cool to be around. And unlike being around Hannah, I don't feel as shitty. Like we're both in a cell together because we both fucked up. Right now, that's comforting.

CHAPTER TEN

Lucky Me

On this episode of The Breaking Pointe, Genie practices her "I got loosies."

I might as well be one of those guys that stand out in front of the corner stores all day. Finishing physical therapy is great, but what else do I have to do? The only thing I did outside of ballet was hang with Hannah, and she's in dance class. At least going to therapy filled up some time in my week. There might be an undiagnosed concussion, too, because I can smell the cookies from Kings Plaza. Now I'm craving them, and all I have is time.

It's one o'clock. Hannah's probably in advanced technique class, and I'm just wiping the cold from my eyes. Sleep didn't hit me until six this morning. Partly because I thought Nolan might come back after his swim, and the other half just not being able to fall asleep. I watched the sun set and rise. And you know what? It wasn't even that special.

I empty my bladder into the toilet through my catheter. People think being able to lift my leg over my head is unnatural. Try having to stick a tube through your privates just so you can drain your bladder completely. The consequence of sneezing or sleeping too hard is peeing on myself. My urologist said it should feel natural by now. Lies. There's nothing natural about not being able to pee on your own. I drop the used catheter in a baggie and toss it in the trash.

My left leg extends, locking in front of me, vibrating like I'm rolling over cobblestones. Almost sliding off, I grab the side of the toilet to catch myself, but my leg won't stop shaking. I'm accustomed to a knee sprain here and there, fatigued shoulders and general exhaustion, but these spasms win the Olympic gold for being a pain in the ass.

"Shit!" I shout accidentally. I bite down on my lip to silence myself. The last thing I need is Mom in here. Not that I matter to her anymore anyways.

I knead my thigh like dough, knuckling the spasm out of my leg, chopping at my calves like an amateur masseuse. These spasms make me crazy. I always end up talking to them. "Be quiet, left one. Don't wake up, right one." My left knee knocks into my right one like chattering teeth. Just as quickly as it started, it stops. "You're such a spaz, leg."

Baths help. I lean to my right, careful not to disturb my limp legs, which fire off with any wrong movement when I wake up. I pull the stopper to trap the water and watch it rise. I look toward the door; Mom usually comes to check on me when I'm in here. The bathroom is just as dangerous as the roof to her. I can fall easily or get trapped in the tub if it's too slippery to climb out.

She also hated how I had to balance on my wheel to lean over far enough to spit in the sink. Now I spit in the toilet. Even my spitting has become modified.

I pull down my shorts the rest of the way and toss them against the wall, doing the same to my shirt. I grab a towel and spread it over my seat to transfer into my chair.

If I don't align my chair just right, I can break my neck. One by one I place my legs over the side of the tub into the water. I check to make sure my locks are secure before leaning over to grab on to the support rail. Using my right hand, I push my body forward on the chair until I'm lowered enough to plunge my whole body in.

Since when did grabbing on to these cold metal bars become so familiar? I don't think I ever held on to the wall for support. Life before the accident is fading. I'm low-key afraid of hurting myself. There's always that fear in the back of my mind—slipping.

The thought of going out by myself challenges me like a set of Italian fouettés. I can't—won't—live with Mom forever. That I'm sure of. It shouldn't be too hard to bump down two steps. My will is there. I just need to find a way to never need to ask Mom for anything. She can live her life, and I'll work on my "nonexistent" one.

The bath did the trick for my muscles, but now I'm hungry. I know girls sometimes starve themselves, but I'm not one of them. I'll just go to the kitchen really quick and get something and bring it back to my room. The kitchen looks clean and unused. There's a whiff of cleaning products lingering in the air. Come to think of it, I didn't smell any cooking or coffee earlier. Where's Mom? She wasn't in the living room when I went by either. Why do I care? She's probably not thinking about me right now. Yogurt it is.

My phone rings as soon as I get back to my room. It's Hannah, and I happily answer.

"Genie-in-a-Bottle Services. Happy three wishes," I answer. I press the phone to the right side of my face, forgetting about my little bruise, and quickly switch it to my left.

"First wish: How's everything going?"

Technically it wasn't a lie that I couldn't make it to the studio because I fell out of my chair. She must be in the dressing room; I can hear the familiar chatter of girls in the background. The sound's so strong in my memory, I can almost put myself next to Hannah. We had the good corner, allowing for extra bench space under the air-conditioning vent. Often, we would just talk to each other, fix our buns, or sneak snacks Miss Kuznetsova would disapprove of. The smell of fruity lotion and perfume tickles my nose. I always sneezed first thing walking into it.

If she's talking to me in the dressing room, that means everyone can hear her. "Hannah, find some other place to talk. I don't want anyone to know you're talking to me."

"You should stop hiding," she whispers.

"Whispering doesn't count."

"Genie, relax. Answer my question."

I groan into the phone. "No, everything isn't okay. My life is . . . I'd rather not talk about it."

"What about Kylito? How's that going, then?" She says it like she's feeding me something to talk about.

I think back to QUEST. I wish I could go back to the meeting and keep my mouth shut. Then there's yesterday and how I texted him. Seems like he doesn't hate me, I assume. Yet we didn't say much, either.

"I know that silence. You're sprung like a mattress," Hannah hypothesizes.

Me too, he wrote. Just those two words got me weak.

"I'm too curvy to be a mattress," I say. But she's right. I've been thinking about him. A lot. He's got some secrets of his own, like whatever happened that led him to mandated community service. It totally could have something to do with his TBI. Knowing that about him twirls me for a chassé en tournant, but I don't care what he did, and I actually want to go to St. Nicholas to see him again. It's not like we'll meet at physical therapy or group for that matter anymore. I cover my face with my hands. I'm embarrassed just speaking of it over the phone. I can sense Hannah grinning on the other end. "Quit smiling!" I fight my own smirk forming.

"Somebody caught feelings."

"You'd enjoy that, wouldn't you?"

"I'm just saying."

There's a brief pause between us. I stick my finger into the peach yogurt and stir it around and lick my finger when I'm done.

"He's going to Stanford," I blurt. Why start something to have him leave? I'm beginning to understand how Nolan felt about me going to Europe. Kills me to even admit it to myself.

"I'm not saying you have to propose to the guy. If you're just helping Nolan move on, I say go as far as you want."

Maybe if I thought Nolan was actually moving on. Perhaps if I knew I could say more than five words to Kyle before ruining it.

I'm triggered by my ex checking up on me and returning my things. "I don't know what I want."

"You always know what you want. And you always go for it, too."

Then why can't I remember my dances? I want to yell at her. It's not enough just to want. Execution—that's necessary. So is the belief that you can. Confusion ain't it, and that's all I got. It's not fair to me or Kyle to bring him into the middle of that. Kyle is better off with someone who will help him get better. He already is. I left PT feeling less strong. When Kelly comes back for my OT she's just going to tell me I'm doing everything wrong.

"'Magic' is lacking its razzle-dazzle," Hannah says, switching topics. I'm actually happy she does, even if it is about "Magic."

"Maya lacks style. Tell her to get out of the steps and feel them," I say, stating the obvious.

"I've tried! She's too polished. Come by, she'll take your direction."

"That was an attempt." Unlike in Kuznetsova's email today, telling me I have unfinished business at VAB, going back there will need to take a number. There's a lot of things I need to do.

"Worth a shot. I don't know what to do with her. It looks good. Doesn't feel right." She's probably making that screw-face when nothing's going her way.

"Did you try the red pixie dust?" I tease. "I could grant some, but that'll be another wish."

"I'm being serious, Genie."

"Seriously, I don't know what to tell you. You know the dance, rehearse it with her."

"I wish you were here."

"I can't be." It's time for me to put "Magic" up for adoption. I want to love it and raise it, but I'm not the best parent anymore. It's a strong dance and if I'm feeling weak, how can I be useful? And why should I help?

I'm glad she doesn't tell me to stop frontin', because I could be there. It's not like I have anywhere else to be.

"Well, don't say I didn't warn you when you come to the gala and see it for yourself." She clears her throat. "Do you want your name attached to something that's just okay and not . . . magical?"

I want to tell her I didn't agree to go, but now isn't the time. I swallow a spoonful of yogurt. "Don't you have character class now?"

"For someone who acts allergic to the studio, you sure know the schedule."

"It's embedded in me."

"I should go. Hit me up later."

"Thank you for using Genie-in-a-Bottle Services."

She laughs before hanging up the phone. I notice a smile on my face myself. It quickly turns into a sigh. It's as if I can feel her feet dancing on my heart. I'm equal parts devastated and inspired.

Mom's ghosted me. I suspect she's either being sponsored because she wants to be at a bar thanks to me, or she's sponsoring somebody so she can be of some help to someone. I stare at my phone, waiting for a light to flash. Ten seconds is all I give before opening her room door. If she didn't want her privacy invaded, she should've been home by now. I just hope she's not alone.

I roll in farther. There's a lot I don't know about Mom. I know she teaches middle school math. With me getting hurt so close to summer, she was able to take her vacation early to look after me.

Her "friends" are mostly those at St. Nicholas. People with her struggles, her sponsor, and other volunteers. I've always suspected she didn't fit in with her teaching peers. The whole teenage-mom and ex-alternative-school history. When Dad was around, she was too busy dodging people's gazes. After he left, she kept to herself until she got help.

Mom's room is serial-killer neat. I imagine she keeps her class-room the same way. Everything must be under her control. Even the music she plays for her students. Only she would be peeved that a group of kids don't want to listen to *The Nutcracker* when it's not Christmas.

Her dresser is the perfect height for me to be face-to-face with the photos on top. The first one is a picture of me in a gold frame. I'm about two at the time, in a red tutu, a smile wider than my head. Mom is on her knees in the photo, looking at me, a smile to rival mine on her face. It never hit me before, but I'm practically her age in this photo. I could be mistaken for her.

The next picture is me and her at my first ballet when I was five, *The Nutcracker*. The first solo I ever got was Clara's dance with the doll nutcracker. That's when I knew I needed to continue dancing. I remember she asked someone to take a picture of us. The last one is of my first day at VAB. I'm standing in front of the school's logo on the front window, ballet bag in hand, wearing a confident smile. I didn't know then that not even twenty minutes after walking into the building I would meet Hannah, changing on the same bench spot she called me from.

Nosy much, Genie? I have no reason to be snooping around other than boredom.

I pull open her drawer. It's her underwear one, but inside is a small clay box. I open it to find her AA chips. She's actually pretty genius for keeping it in here. Every time you reach for a bra to hook on, you see seven years of these and know you got your shit together. I never gave her enough credit.

The doorbell rings. I push the drawer shut and close Mom's bedroom door behind me. It rings again.

"I'm coming!" I shout at the door. I can only go but so fast in this apartment. Of course, I can't see out the peephole once I get to the door. "Who is it?"

"It's me . . . your father." He must've come through the front door as someone was leaving or something.

Genie and the Cursed Doll, coming to theaters near you.

"I don't have one," I say, backing away from the door.

"Genie, open up."

"Mom's not here."

"I'm not here for her. Please."

Against my better judgment, I open the door slightly. "Say what you have to say. Quickly."

He looks around. "Not out here. Can I come in?"

What does he have to say that needs to be said inside? Judging by his jittery legs, I don't even think he's too sure about coming in. I peer up at him, giving no signs on my face of my decision. I'll let him wait it out like he made me after he left us. Every time I heard the front door open, I would run out to see, hoping it would be him coming back home. Or at the very least coming to pick me up for a few hours. It was never him. Now he'll get just a taste of the hurt and anxiousness I felt waiting for him.

"Genie?" he asks. "It'll only take a few minutes," he adds hopefully. "Please," he begs when I don't budge.

"The minute you piss me off, you're out." I open the door wider, and he pushes it open farther and walks in. "You remember where the living room is, right?"

I suppose I should warn him that if Mom comes home and sees him, he'll be murdered. I will do nothing to stop it.

He squeezes by me and heads right to the living room, standing in the middle of it, acting unsure if he should sit. I don't care either way, but I also don't tell him to have a seat, either. I give him the once-over; he looks the same, just prematurely gray.

"What happened to your face?" He finally looks at me good enough. "Who did that to you?"

"I guess bruises to the face weren't your thing." He always hit Mom where she could hide it.

He stares at me quizzically, crossing his arms.

"Why do you assume someone hurt me? Just because you did it doesn't mean someone else did," I say.

"I never hit you."

"Didn't say you did."

"Can I have a seat?" he asks, more annoyed than nervous.

"I already have mine, why not?"

Dad stares at me too long. Like he's just noticing I have a chair under me. It must be a shock. The girl he left was still able to be lifted on his shoulders. He doesn't know that if I could stand, I would be almost as tall as him.

He sits on the couch like this is his house again. Leg crossed and waiting like I'm supposed to ask if he wants a drink. The whole posture reeks of nothing good to come.

"Do you always glare at your guests like this?" he asks. His car keys swing around his finger. The emblem of a Jaguar.

"I think you should go."

"I'm not going anywhere, Orchid. Here's the deal. I've hit some streak of bad luck that my wife seems to think is because I have unfinished business with you and your mom."

"We're good. I never wanted to see you again, and I assumed the feeling was mutual."

Dad hisses like he just got burned. "That hurt my feelings, Genie."

"Good. Being your daughter hurts mine."

Even though he laughs, I can tell by his downcast eyes I got him good. Genie, one. Dad, zero.

"You got a smart mouth. Okay, fine, I deserve that or whatever, but I got a wife who won't stop nagging me about every little inconvenient thing, so we're going to talk some things out."

"So you think I cursed you or something?"

"Not me. Renee, my wife. Apparently, the last straw was Jade, your sister, getting sick."

"No, you too. You could've easily pretended you spoke to

me, but you obviously came here because you think it's true."

He runs his hands along the grayish waves on his head. "Do you have anything you want to say to me?"

"Leave."

"You're just like your mother. Always picking a fight. But fine. You have all the control here, if that's what you need to know."

The cockiness, the way he's trying to make this all my fault, is like I'm in my room having this conversation with Nolan. It's enough to choke me. I try to moisten my throat with my spit, but it's not working. I sure don't feel in control. Feels the exact opposite. It's not like I can go back to being eight and he doesn't just take off. I've learned to live without him and so has Mom.

"You do realize we're doing great without you, right?"

"When I found out about your accident, I assumed your mom's drinking had something to do with it." He looks up to the corner of the room. "I don't think I ever knew her sober."

I don't trust him. Mom's been a champ in her sobriety, even though he's a good chunk of the reason why she was off the deep end. He can't waltz in here and blame her. Whatever he's up to isn't working. Why does he want me now? He drove here in his Jaguar, has a family, a nice shirt and shoes on, and yet he's stuck on me. I can't do anything for him. I won't do anything for him. He doesn't deserve or need it. What little bit of sleep he loses over leaving me will just have to continue. I won't comfort him.

"I see you still looking at me like you want me dead, but I'll be honest. I wasn't ready back then, and me and your mom fought over that," he says as if he knows I'm close to throwing him out just like that doll. "They say if you love someone, you have to leave them or whatever."

Except it wasn't love that kept him away. There was a deal. Dad lost my trust when he laid his hands on Mom. When he stopped coming around, I stopped caring. He didn't come back because he missed me. Not even because he was curious about me. I'm a pawn to him too.

"You don't get it, do you?" I give him the same blank stare he's sporting. "God, no wonder Mom wants you far away from me. You're using me."

Dad stands up with a quickness that makes me roll back. If he comes any closer, I'll lock myself in the bathroom.

"I can't believe it. Not only do you look like Tasha, you act just like her. Why is everything always so difficult?" He goes back to the couch. "Relax, Orchid, I won't hit you. I don't do that anymore."

"I'm supposed to believe that?"

"I don't care what you believe. I see you think I'm the bad guy. Tasha made sure of that."

How is it that I can say one thing that gets Mom away from me, but when it comes to Dad and Nolan, nothing I say pushes them away? I fight with Mom because for years Dad wasn't here to fight with, and now he's here and my voice is dryer than my eczema in winter.

"I'm not using you," he loops back. "She had no problem using my checks to pay for your dance lessons, though. That school is expensive as hell. If not for me, you wouldn't have gone. Sure, I'll be the bad guy here, but I've done some good things."

"Oh gee, thanks. Thank you for wondering how your investment was doing. As you can see, it's turned out super well."

"That's not what I meant." He waves one hand like it will erase what he's just said. "I—"

"It doesn't matter. Thanks for the flowers, thanks for the lessons. We're even now." I back out into the hallway to make room for him to leave.

"Genie."

"You really need to go."

I hope he listens. If he decides to just sit here, I don't know what to do. But he rises off the couch and stops short of me before laughing the most insulting laugh. I follow behind him to the front door, hoping that at any moment Mom will burst through and Hulk-smash him.

He holds the door open with his large hand. "When you need my help, and you will, just know I don't have any hard feelings toward you, Genie. You're still my daughter."

"Lucky me."

He shakes his head, but he smirks. "It's a good thing you have your mother's looks. Use them, since you can't dance anymore. There's someone for everyone, right?"

He lets the door slam, and in the mix of feeling shaky and yucky, I feel lucky. Lucky that he left my life. Lucky that I won't ever see him again. Lucky that I will do everything and anything to never need him again.

CHAPTER ELEVEN

Daddy

Nolan hums as he lies across my bed. He's always had a decent voice, but he never did anything with it. In a way I missed hearing it, so I'm sitting in silence, the day turning burnt orange. The ice cream truck he's harmonizing with moves down the block, and now he sounds clearer, stronger, nicer than I've ever heard him before. Still no Mom, and after dealing with Dad earlier, I'm happy for his company, embarrassingly.

I almost wanted to hug him when he knocked on the window. *Hug* Nolan. That feeling was too close for comfort. I keep checking my phone for a message from Mom. Just because I'm not skipping into therapy doesn't mean I don't need her here. She's helping someone else when I need her help too, just not in the form of a psychologist.

"Mute tonight?" Nolan asks, picking at his fingernails. "Usually you're running that mouth."

I take a bite from my granola bar, ignoring him. Once I let him in, I decided pretty quickly that I don't want him here, but what if Dad comes back? Nolan feels like the lesser of two evils. Until he blows up, which seems likely. "Am I making you uncomfor—"

I can see it all over his face. He couldn't ask that question. I remember every time I look at him that he let me fall, so I know he does too.

"You don't gotta be across the room from me. I'm not going to grab or kiss you."

"I'm not lying on a bed with you again."

"There's only one person who has you like this," he sings. He takes the doll on my bed and shakes her.

"Nolan. I'm not fighting with you tonight."

"You say it like I'm starting it."

"You are—"

We both look away from each other. I shake my head in done-with-it fashion. How much longer can I deal with this? With Nolan? My stomach literally aches around him. I guess there's like some rotten butterflies still fluttering around.

I go through four more granola bars, my dinner, before I care to look back in his direction. Of course, he's staring at me. Not angry or menacing. More so curious.

"I'm not trying to start nothing, okay? What's wrong? I think I know when you're only moody or if something happened."

Nolan sniffed out my pregnancy like a hound dog. I can't lie. "I saw my father today. I don't want to talk about it."

"Why, what did he do to you?"

I hate how he's leaning forward like I'm telling some great story with twists and turns. I'm not entertaining him with a rant.

"Nothing you haven't already done," I tell him.

He doesn't blink. "What's that supposed to mean?"

"It means if I tell you, you'll only get mad," I sigh.

"Stop controlling everything and telling me what I'll do. You have no idea," he all but shouts.

"This is incredible. You've never even met the man and you act just like him."

"How? I'm still here for you. He's not," he says matter-of-factly. "Don't even get me started on your mom. You keep checking your phone, listening for the door, and it's not to warn me she coming, either." Nolan holds his finger up like he just had a eureka moment. "I bet she big mad you can't dance anymore. Tasha probably toasted right now."

"Keep her name out your mouth."

"Oh, come on, you're thinking it too. When she come home sloshed as fuck, you gonna want me here to tell you everything's all right, like I always tell you."

"No, you don't. You use me to make yourself feel better, and when I don't return your dumb affection, you gaslight me, like I'm the one with the problem."

Nolan shoots up, and I flinch so hard my feet slide off my foot-plate. Maybe this is it—the day he finally strikes me.

"Oh my God, I'm not going to hit you." He plops onto my bed with a thud.

I point at him. "That. He said that too. I can't always wonder if you'll hit me the next time."

"I've never hit you," he pleads like he's trying to get himself out of detention.

"Yet."

"Ever."

Before today I never saw Nolan and Dad in the same light. When I told Nolan about that night, how I tried to pull Dad off Mom and he tossed me into the wall, Nolan looked ready to find Dad himself. I had to tell him it wasn't even his memory to get so upset about. But he would just wrap his arms around me tighter like a snake would around prey. "Not us. I won't let that happen," he said. "We're better than them."

But now I can see it. We're no better than them. Worse because we're fooling ourselves.

I shake my head, finally putting my feet back neatly. As if it matters how well I'm aligned when I feel so misshapen inside.

"I would never. You know that. What your dad did to you when you were little was wrong, and he a bitch for that. I would never lay my hands on you. I love you."

Nolan's so full of shit. He wants to be here and pretend like he cares about me and what I'm feeling, so I can vent and so he can feel stronger. He's only tough when it comes to my weaknesses.

"That's not enough. It's not enough to love me or for me to be a daughter. I will not—" I was gonna say *not be helpless and broken like Mom*, but I am. I'm more broken than my shattered spine. Parts of me are still missing, and he can't even bother to step out the way so I can find them. Nolan claims to love me, but he doesn't respect me. Once upon a time Dad loved Mom, and ten years later, he can't even respect her sobriety.

My hands shake enough to move my chair back and forth, and I hope he doesn't notice.

"I scare you now? Your mom thinks I'm a monster—I can tell by how she looks at me—and now you believe her." His eyes narrow as he slides down the bed closer to me. No doubt he wants me to react, but I hold steady. "She can't see what true love is because it got beaten out of her. You can't believe her!"

"I didn't say all that." But he's not helping his case either. This is why I couldn't even entertain the thought of carrying his baby. The longer I stayed pregnant, the more chances he had to exploit me keeping it. And then what? I'd be standing there with a baby and a boyfriend capable of hurting me. I'd be my mother.

"You don't have to. I see it on your face. You're blaming me for everything, like you didn't want what I wanted."

"We never wanted the same things."

"We both wanted the makeup sex, even though we didn't have condoms. But it's all my fault you got pregnant?"

"That doesn't count, and you know it."

It wasn't like we planned not to use one. By the time we realized we skipped a whole step, sex was happening. I asked Nolan to stop so I could go in his drawer where he kept his condoms. It was empty. Had we really gone through them? "Go get some," I ordered. He laughed—said there was no way he was pulling out and running to the store in the random nor'easter we were having. I certainly wasn't. I still wasn't dry from making it to his house. "Relax," he told me. "You got most of it out of me already. Do you really want me to *stop* stop?"

I knew if we stopped, we'd likely end up fighting yet again.

"That doesn't count, and you know it," I repeat, trying to

convince myself. We made that decision together, yes, but it can't count, right?

"Maybe not, but the baby happened, and you acted like the world ended. That really hurt my feelings. But then I thought you were scared and just needed time because you were thinking about your dad. That I might leave you or something. Unlike him, I can handle my business."

"Can we please stop talking about my dad now?"

I think about how he sat on the couch like this apartment was his, like I was supposed to do him a favor because he pays child support. Him thinking he can still call me *his* daughter. I might've come from him, but he has no rights to me.

Nolan's eyes light up. "Yeah, fuck him. You don't need him. Let me guess: he's all guilty and wants back in?" Those same eyes look down so far, I tilt my head to see them. "Did he ask about your face? Want to know who hurt you?"

It's impressive that Nolan knows, but scary. Because now I'm starting to recognize what I suspect Nolan's known all along: he and my dad are so much alike.

"I'm sorry he still hurting you. My dad still hurting me. Still cheating. Why can't he be normal? He's such a piece of shit!" The thing is, Nolan is genuinely upset about it just that fast.

I saw where this was heading, and I let it go there. We cannot do this. Old times these are not and will never be. "Well, mine got a new wife and baby, so drop it." But I don't want to drop it. I want to be angry and talk shit and know that Nolan gets it. About Dad at least. And I want him to see that they're way more alike than not. But he won't.

"You have the right to be angry. We both do. They screwed us over."

Yes, Dad made my childhood a little less happy, but once I went to ballet it didn't matter. If Mom and I talked ballet, it didn't matter. It's the secrets and the mind games. I'm only important to him when it suits him, apparently.

"Wish we could get them in the same room and just . . . I don't even know," I say.

It's so odd to be having this conversation not wrapped in Nolan's arms. I'm clocking his movements to see if he'll try to creep for me, but he's firmly planted on my bed. Good.

"I never told you this, but I always wanted to show my dad that I'm better than him. I had one girl and she was all I needed. And when I became a daddy, he would see how much he sucked as one."

"How's that working out for you? 'Cause it's that thinking that has me in this chair."

"How?"

"You tried to force a family on me. and now you have this chance to move on and you're forcing a friendship on me. You got back into swimming. Focus on that and drop the revenge thing."

He pouts and hunches a bit. "You make me sound like a cartoon villain. Like I'm creeping around causing havoc. Should I leave and make some chaos?"

If I answer truthfully, he'll go off, no doubt about it. For sure since Mom isn't here. He knows it, and he's using it against me. It's working. I'm listening. I'm talking.

"It's so strange you got back into swimming when there's no chance of me putting on pointe shoes again." Coincidence? I don't know.

"Is it? I thought I lost you. I didn't hear from you and was freaking out. Mom told me I was driving her crazy, and then my old swim coach told me about the job at that Y. He has this friend there that's been getting me back into shape," he explains. "It's nothing serious."

The Nolan that won me over was the Nolan making and beating insane swimming records. It was amazing to witness, and instead of going to that pool and just doing what he did best, he came to me angry his dad wasn't there, upset at his mother for picking such a piece of shit as a father. I thought we were more alike, that we wanted to be the best at what we did. All he focused on was his father and hurting him.

Nolan never could push it aside like I did. Dad never came up when I danced. I danced and it wasn't about Mom's drinking or where he went. When I went on pointe and turned, it was all about magic.

"I'm just wondering how you went from being the best and only Black guy on the team, to literally drowning your swim career. What happened?" The first time I ever watched him at his swim meet, I swear Nolan turned into Aquaman. He glided through the water as easily as I could turn. Sure, he stood out being the only brown guy there, but it was his talent that did most of it.

"You happened," he says, low.

I check my phone again, then send Mom a text with three

question marks. *I happened, my ass.* That's not the first time he's strung those words together. I remember having to run down the escalator at Broadway Junction, pushing Nolan literally to keep going. If we had stayed a second longer, if I didn't tell Nolan the cops were coming, that boy wouldn't be alive, I'm sure of it. I was the only thing keeping Nolan from tossing that guy on the elevated tracks. And all because he smiled at me, and I returned the gesture. When we ran out the station and far enough to the next stop, I asked him what the hell happened. Could I not be friendly anymore? Nolan said simply, "You happened." He's not turning this on me. Not this time.

"So why do you want to chill with me, since I cause you so much pain? You could be rid of me and training to go D1. You're that good—were—before you got scared."

"I ain't scared of shit!" Nolan yells with a pound to his chest. "Don't you ever say that again."

I know I could find out the answer to the *or what?* I have on my tongue, but I have to think smart here. Use my words like the dances I draw out for a full company. Sometimes the corps has to stand there and pose while the soloist set up the scene.

"Since you like memory lane, remember when we had that free period and we got a copy of that college book from the counselor? We wrote dope or nope for potential schools. I noped everything not within a decent radius of a major ballet company, and you didn't even rank any swim programs."

Nolan shrugs. "I gave up swimming by then."

"Why give up a shot at D1?"

"It's not what I want. I wouldn't have time to be with you. And now you need my help. How can I focus on swimming when we have so much to do?"

It pisses me off that he walked away from that night with everything. He can still swim and still he won't. Still using me as an excuse for why he can't. Nolan set himself up so good for me. Ambitious, when really he was just lusting after me. Loyal at first glance, but actually obsessed. That persistence was manipulation. Chipping and chipping away at me.

"There is no 'we.'" And anything I have to do there's no way he can help.

I scratch my head and Nolan hums like he does when he's thinking.

He rests his chin on his pointer fingers. "I know what you trying to do. It's not working. Don't think I don't know you were humoring me while you booked that plane ticket for Germany. Semper Fidelis or something."

"Semper*oper.*"

"Right. That."

"Nolan—"

"No, you were going to leave me to be this big-time ballerina, right? Like that would make you forget your mom is a drunk, and your dad is a deadbeat. Maybe you would be all gucci. Right until nighttime and you needed me there. You always needed me when you were done dancing," he says, fist pounding my bedspread, digging in harder and harder, so much so that I feel it in my throat. "I'm tired of this shit. Let me be like your dad and disappear."

He barely looks at me before climbing out the window, but I feel like his eyes are on me. If I'm reading his shoulders right, he wants me to say something, maybe even pick a fight so he can stay. But I close the window and lock it for good measure and listen to the rattle of the fire escape, matching the one in my heart. I'll never be able to fix him. He'll do what he wants and I shouldn't care. Or waste my energy trying to remind him what he meant to me at some point, because the things I liked about him were all a lie. Nolan conjured up who he wanted me to see, but he's losing his power. He doesn't have the magic anymore. I see exactly who he is. And it scares me.

CHAPTER TWELVE

I Feel

I'm getting my Nancy Drew on, sleuthing through Mom's closet. Except this time, it's not for an outfit. Hannah always thought it was great that Mom and I could share a wardrobe. It's something I struggle with. On one hand it's one more way we're alike. The other hand says she spends money on cute clothes that I want a chance to wear. But I also checked her closet to look for alcohol once upon a time, early on in her recovery. Seeing as she's not acting like herself, I'm making sure she isn't slipping. I hate that Nolan might actually be right.

She's not home yet. Or answering my calls. I'm trying not to worry, but it's not going well. Mom's a grown woman, so I can't clock her, but it isn't normal for her to be out so late, especially since my accident. I know she thinks I'm angry with her, and I am, but not because I hate her. I wish things were different. Not just the fall, but everything with us. After all that happened today, I'd rather have her here telling me I need to work out my anger. I know she's just as frustrated with me, but she always comes back, or tells me she needs a break from me. But there's been nothing from her. I guess things really are that bad between us.

I lift a small box into my lap, shaking it to hear its contents. It sounds like a bunch of things, so I open it. A bundle of cards wrapped in a rubber band catches my eye. I slide one out. The cover has a big orange THANK YOU on the front. Inside is a handwritten note:

Dear Ms. Davis,
Bryce has always had a hard time with math. It was not until taking your class that he started to improve. He speaks of you daily, and he is finally grade level with his math, thanks to you. I cannot thank you enough, Ms. Davis.
Forever grateful,
Sandra

I read two other cards from happy parents before digging some more. Teacher pins and small items fill the box. She never talks much about her teaching, not even that she's good at it and parents let her know. Why hide it? I'm starting to think there're things I'll never know about her. Like why she never says a bad word about my father.

There's a second box just like the first one. This time I open it and come across my first pair of ballet slippers and a program nestled together, tied by the red ribbon I wore to my first dance recital. I squeeze my slippers like they'll regenerate life back into my legs. If only I'd known I would work so hard only to have it ripped away from me. I rub my hands over the white canvas. The shoe fits in my palm perfectly. I haven't seen these shoes in years, and never thought about them either. Makes sense Mom kept them as keep-sakes. They'd be even more precious once I became a professional.

Professional. I toss it all back. They're in the right place, just like my dance career. In a box left in the dark and hidden.

I remember the first time I ever told her I was committing to ballet for life.

"Mommy?" I asked as she cooked dinner.

I was doing my homework at the kitchen table and had class earlier that evening. My hair was still in its bun. I was eight, Dad was still around, and I was bored with homework, but Mom always said I had to do well in school before dancing. I was breezing through a page of math problems.

"Yes, Genie?" She was chopping cucumbers for a salad.

"I'm going to be a prima one day."

"Oh really?" She didn't look at me, but she smiled.

"Miss Gail says I have the attitude already."

"That you do. It takes more than attitude, though." She looked at me.

"Mommy, I'm going to be a prima. I'm really good." I stood up and demonstrated a plié. "I want to do it for work, like how you teach."

Her smile was huge. "If that's what you want, I want it too. But first finish your homework. Primas are good in all their studies."

She was so proud of me. So sure of me. Now she doesn't know how to feel around me, and I feel the same about her.

I came in here looking for alcohol, thinking Mom was keeping it a secret, only to find her hiding her praise from parents and great moments in my life. Am I the asshole? Yes.

Okay, so I didn't handle the whole *Relevé* thing well. Mom kept all this as a reminder of me, because she wanted what I wanted, and I haven't been fair to her. The massages after class, the late-night dinners, and she never once told me to stop dreaming so big. I said I wanted to be a professional, and she said go for it. Of course, she's just as hurt as me. She wanted it just as much. And now we're both trying to figure it out.

Curious, I go back to the cards. I pick one. It's a get-well-soon card. I try to think back to a time Mom was sick enough to warrant such a card. I open it to read another handwritten note:

> What's up Miz Davis,
> Sorry to hear your daughter is hurt.
> Wish you were teaching instead of the
> substitute, but we understand.
> Love,
> Ethan
> P.S. Tell your daughter she's awesome
> because you're awesome.

Mom hasn't mentioned any of this to me—not that I would've listened or appreciated it. I got tons of cards from people at the studio. Flowers came to the hospital, even. But I didn't care. All I did was throw them in the trash when I finally got home. I regret that now. People, kids who haven't even met me, wished me well. The front door slaps open and closed, followed by Mom's "sorry" because she didn't mean to slam the door. That was always my thing. I hear her shoes hit the wall with a thud as she kicks them off. I'm too slow to exit her room without her seeing me. She sighs as I roll toward her, but she ducks into the kitchen before I can say anything. By the time I get there, her leg is bouncing as she considers her beverage options before grabbing a Pellegrino.

"Is this what we're doing now?" I ask before she goes off on me.

The can harmonizes with her teeth sucking as it spritzes open. "I'm a grown woman, Genie."

"Says the lady that giggles like crazy when someone thinks we're sisters. You could've texted me and told me you were going to be gone all day." Even a note would've worked. I thought things were going back to those times when she drank enough to pass out on the floor, and magically got up in the morning like nothing happened.

"So now you need my help?" The can dents between her death grip.

Yes, I want to tell her. That all I ate today was granola bars and yogurt because I can't do anything. Couldn't remember anything I learned in OT to help me navigate this space. That I was scared because my father showed up and he wasn't the guy I remembered. He was intimidating and pushy and I see now why she kept him away and was trying to protect me. And my crazy ex she always knew was crazy was so close to hurting me again, but I swallow it all.

"You were teaching me a lesson?" Suddenly the fridge seems bigger, taller, heavier. If it for some reason decided to tip over, it'd squish me. I used to look over the top of it.

She sits down at the table. "No, I was with my sponsor."

My mind reacts like her words are a jump scare. I twitch and swallow a rock of saliva, but I know this isn't the real thing. "You were drinking again?"

Her head leans back as she gulps the sparkling beverage before setting it down. "I was thinking about it, so Flo, my sponsor, took me out. We had brunch and went to the movies, and I cleared my mind. Afterward I visited who I sponsor. You're not the only one not feeling like yourself these days, Genie."

And at no point did she think I would worry? But I'll take it. I deserved that.

"So what's this snooping-in-my-room stuff?"

"I was looking for alcohol." I come clean.

She chuckles smugly before her eyes go soft. "I went through your things when you were in the hospital. Your dance bag is as red as when I got it for you. I kept thinking if I opened it, the real you would appear."

"The real me?" Were my monitors and prognosis not real enough?

Her lips pull into a serious line. "Yeah, the Genie who *talked* to me. Who doesn't take a bite out of me every time I ask how she's doing."

Not only do my eyes roll but also my shoulders and head. She can't be serious. "Are you guilting me now?"

"See? This!" Her hands scan the length of my body as if presenting Exhibit A: My Disrespectful Daughter. "I'm just trying to talk and you're snapping. Believe me—I get it. There's so much hurt. I wish and hope one day we can be better." She takes a sip of her drink, her face sour like it's bitter. Or maybe it's my attitude. "Maybe I'm too close? I really believe you should be seeing someone. It doesn't have to be my therapist. There are others."

My neck tenses as I fight not to grunt and shout something I'll regret. We made it clear before I left the hospital that I was to be left alone. That if I wanted to see someone, I'd let her know, but for now all I wanted was to be.

"I don't need to speak to someone. I'm not like you. I'm not—"

"Not what? A drunk? No, you're not. Not yet, at least. You keep holding this in and you'll find the bottle or something else to be your therapist. I don't want that for you."

"Don't worry. I won't end up like you."

In my head it seemed more like an assurance, but spoken out loud it came out like I was judging her. My words roll off her like water off a duck's back. Or at least that's the face she's putting on as she finishes the remainder of her tiny can. She leans her head in the palm of her hand on the table as if she's wondering if she should get up for another one or leave the kitchen entirely. Both require me to roll backward completely out of here.

"I don't know," she finally says, adding that smug laugh. "You're behaving pretty reckless, like I did when I was sixteen, with you in my belly. Oh, I had a name to call anyone who I even thought looked at me funny. You couldn't tell me nothing back then. Thought I was so grown just because I had a chip on my shoulder, and a mother who wiped her hands of me. Then you were growing inside me and it hit me too late. My body was doing adult things, but I was cutting up like a child. The tantrums and fights just so I could have some attention, instead of telling someone I was in pain. It's not enough to just be cute." She sits up with a posture sharper than Kuznetsova. "Throwing out the magazine? You had no right to do that." Now her tone matches her posture.

"You can get another one if it matters that much to you." She can watch all the YouTube videos and recital DVDs she wants. Look through old programs, save my first costumes, and print all the articles she can. I don't care anymore.

"That's not the point. Are you really so angry that you can't see how you're treating me? What have I done to you? I've given you a lot of reasons to distrust me in the past, yes, that I will take responsibility for, but I will not let you keep lashing out at me. I didn't put you in that chair. I'm not even upset that you were doing God knows what on that roof. Genie, how can you not see that all I want is for you to be that happy girl I recovered for? I saw all that beauty you created with your body, and said I needed to be there for that. To be there for your wit and your dedication. When you love, Genie, you love so hard, but when you're angry it's even harder and it hits everyone." She exhales. "Your lack of respect these days is just uncalled for."

"Okay, I get it. It's all my fault." I grab my rims to roll back, but my hands are slick with sweat, confirming I need to get out of here. The kitchen feels like it's getting tighter, to the point I won't be able to move my wheels at all. I'll be trapped while Mom can simply turn sideways and slide out.

"No, Genie!" She sucks her teeth again. "I don't want you to blame yourself. This is worse than I thought. Why would you blame yourself? Am I missing something?" She cries spontaneous tears at her confusion. Tears that should've been seen on the forecast, like I can always predict Hannah's. "If only I let you see a therapist before you needed one. Would that have helped? Maybe I was too focused on my own recovery. Working on my profession and volunteering was so much easier than working on my relationship with you."

Instead of in my eyes, tears feel like they're forming in my throat. "No, Mom, there's nothing you could've done." She needs those meetings. Her students clearly need her too.

Her eyes look like those baby dolls with the flapping eyelids until she quits fighting it and closes them. Like some bullied girl hiding in the bathroom, she uses her shirt to catch her tears, because her eyelids aren't doing a good job at stopping them.

This time it's me giving her the pity eyes. I wear them all the way back to my room. The shaking in my arms is made clear when I rummage through the mess of papers on my desk. Where is that magazine? I go through all the drawers. I transfer to the floor so smooth, if Logan were here, he'd name the move after me. I always thought it'd be a school or an award for dance, but a transferring maneuver could be fun.

Think, Genie. I tossed the magazine out the window and—that's it. It's gone now.

On this episode of The Breaking Pointe, *Genie manages to fuck things up some more. Will the pixie dust fix things this time? Stay tuned.*

My posse of Black ballerinas stare down at me. I put them up there for inspiration and now they're just making me feel bad. Neck and eye rolls meant for me. *Not cool, girl. You oughta be ashamed, chile.* Finger snaps and stares in "disappointed Black Girl Magic" push me out of my room.

Soft cries come from Mom's room. I didn't even notice she came back here. Tears stream down her face. I bend over to touch her arm. She's hot to the touch.

"Mom?"

"I told myself that I would never leave you again, and I did it." She mumbles something. "Do you remember that night?"

I nod. Of course I do. I was maybe eight. Dad was gone. I was just as bad a sleeper as I am now, if not worse. So I woke up, crept to Mom's room. It was too quiet, so I turned on her light. She wasn't in bed. That wasn't strange. I figured she passed out in the living room and made my way there. Nothing was on. Not the TV. Not a light. That was strange. So I checked the bathroom. Sometimes she ended up in there, tucked between the toilet and the tub.

"Mommy?" I called.

My voice traveled down the dark hallway as I cut into the kitchen. My bare feet stepped right on broken glass. It was only then that I smelled the alcohol. "Mom!" I shouted as I hopped in pain, not able to stand on either foot. I fell onto the floor, my pajamas soaked in whatever rank drink had dropped on the tile.

In the dark I sat, trying to pull the shards from my feet, until my eyes adjusted to the blood on my fingertips. Suddenly there was a blast of light. The front door opened; Mom came in with two bags in her hand. The sharp clink of glass made me call out to her.

"Where were you?" My voice quivered, but I didn't cry. Crying never helped anything. It didn't help Dad stop beating Mom.

Mom flipped the light switch. The fluorescent bulbs hummed and made me cover my eyes.

"I didn't see you—oh my God. Genie—I—" She stumbled and slurred. Not really making much sense to me.

The rest that I remember was how red her eyes were as she bandaged my feet, promising we wouldn't talk about that night, promising she wouldn't leave me again.

But she has. And I was scared, just like back then, but somehow seeing her now, beating herself up for taking care of herself so she can deal with me, makes me feel like I left her. Mom's body is shaking like that night. I want to tell her that I'm going to be okay, that I handled being here alone perfectly fine, that I was sure I could handle myself, but I can't.

I couldn't stand up for myself with Dad or Nolan.

"M—"

She cuts me off with a sigh. "If you need something, Genie, please just give me a moment. Let me take a shower and then I'll be ready." She walks by me right into the bathroom. The door clicks, then locks, and on goes the shower.

Now's my chance.

I can do things myself. She shouldn't have to feel bad about leaving me alone anymore.

I need to get out of here. Far away from this constipated living. I'm tired of being stuck, so I roll away, closing the apartment door behind me. Except sitting in the hallway isn't enough. I need more than this door between us. I lock it. For the first time since my accident, I lock the door by myself. No Mom behind me. I can't reach anything but the bottom lock, but it'll do.

The air is muggy once I'm out front. It's a different kind of choking feeling. More natural. I check my phone for the weather. Satan's balls. I knew it. I'm in my best fruit-faced pajamas, so I need to commit to this nighttime stroll. There's still so much going on. My neighbors across the street sit on their stoop, puffs of smoke hanging above them like thought bubbles. Music plays from someplace to my right.

I exhale at the steps I'm supposed to get down. Of course those kids didn't put the ramp back where they found it. It's leaning against the gate that I need a ramp to get to. I could try to bump down the steps.

On this episode of The Breaking Pointe, *Genie might break her neck this go-around.*

Logan would disapprove, since I'm new to it. While he didn't teach me, he has said, *Some stuff you're going to have to figure out yourself. You can do anything with a little adaptability and patience.* But maybe he doesn't mean trying it out in the dark while I'm flustered.

If Brooklyn is good for one thing, it's people out on their stoops during summer. I'm about to do something I hate doing. I'm going to ask for help. I call over to the girl next door. Her headphones are on, so I have to wave to get her attention. She's a little older than me and wore a green plaid skirt to school until she packed up her dad's Mazda for college two summers ago, and while we never say more than hi, she's kind enough to set the ramp back up so I can come down.

"Thank you," I tell her.

She flicks her box braids over her shoulders. "Don't mention it."

I close the gate behind me. Tonight I feel like going left.

My stomach tickles as my phone vibrates in my pocket. There's no name on the caller ID, but I know who it is. I'm glad my finger worked ahead of my brain on this one.

"Hi, Kyle." There's cautious excitement rising in my voice and stomach. Something I've only ever felt when first dating Nolan. There's something different that I can't pinpoint. The indigo sky tells me most people are sleeping. Not calling girls they gave their numbers to in rehab.

"I need to see you again," he says in the smoothest way I've heard him speak.

"I'd like that," I confess.

There's nothing but his breathing coming through the phone. It's the most peaceful thing that happened tonight, reminding me to breathe. Slow and steady like *La Bayadere*'s "Entrance of the Shades," along with his breath, it's like an adagio. Kyle's Adagio. I can see it in my head. His breathing makes my dance come to life again. Tombé pas de bourrée, attitude derrière up into arabesque arms in high fourth.

I want him to stay on the line so I can dance to his breathing. I don't care how late it is.

CHAPTER THIRTEEN

Jesus, Genie

Mom packed some heavy baggage like we're going on a road trip. I know she remembers what she said to me early this morning, and that I was in her room. We should probably talk. Who starts, though? I can't exactly scold her for keeping in line with her program. And I don't want to tell her Dad came over, either.

Times like these I used to dance out my stress. Fouettés could literally turn my mood around. Afterward, I could think clearly and do what I needed to do. Maybe I need to make some donuts in my chair, leave behind a circle of worries, and push forward.

Three light knocks at my door, and Mom's head pushes through the tiny opening, her eyes slightly puffy. I guess she never really stopped crying. Just like I never stopped feeling shitty for starting our fight.

"May I come in?" she asks softly.

"Sure."

My eyes look at everything but hers as she leans against the door, hands folded diplomatically in front of her. No smug laugh in sight. Her exhaling reminds me of someone about to give a speech. All I can do is sit and wait for her next move.

"I realize"—she clears her throat—"I put you in a very uncomfortable situation leaving you alone without checking in. I want to apologize." Her voice gets stronger. "I feel terrible for unloading everything on you. That wasn't right of me. Sorry for anything I said and how you took it. You went to bed before I could tell you that."

"It happened. We just have to move forward, right?"

I don't know what else to say.

She moves closer. "You still are everything that is right. One look at you, and I feel guilty. I'm hurting with you." She glances from my chair to my *Swan Lake* poster. "Life is so unfair. . . ." Her voice trails off.

What is she thinking about? Me dancing? Does she remember holding me up when I first learned to go on pointe? *You're okay. I got you.* I wobbled learning how to stand again.

"Mom . . ." I keep my chin up to deter any tears that feel like swelling in my eyes. "I need to work this out myself. There's nothing you or anyone else can do about what happened."

I did a lot of thinking being out last night. Not that I went far. I made it back before she ever left the bathroom. Just around the block and then back up the ramp. It felt good to be out for more than just therapy or a doctor's appointment. I need to focus on something again. St. Nick's came to mind. It's perfect. Mom can work on herself and still feel like she has a hand in helping me. Plus, I get out of this rut and see Kyle.

She abandons her spot and moves toward me. Kneeling, she grabs my hands. Any other time I would have pulled them away, avoiding her, but not now. They're soft like I remember. "That's the thing—you don't have to do it alone."

"I don't have Dad to fall back on. You're all that I have. And if you just disappear on me—" She knows the rest. "And if every time we disagree you're going to bring up me needing a therapist, we'll never fix us, Mom. I'm learning to trust you again, so please trust me."

"I know, I know." She nods like I just gave her a second chance. "Favor? Come with me to the church? I promised I'd help out with the clothes drive, and we could use extra hands."

I would like to leave this room and apartment. "I was going to ask to come along today, but please, no therapy talks."

"Promise. Be ready in an hour, okay?" She turns to leave.

"Mom." I stop her. She looks scared I might say something hurtful. "I'm sorry about going through your stuff. Your students are nice . . . and I'm sorry about *Relevé*."

A small smile graces her lips. Mom gets to help, and I get to see Kyle again.

St. Nicholas seems stuck in some sort of time capsule. Nothing has changed, from the looks of things. The park on the corner still looks the same, and I find myself stopping to watch the kids playing. Wondering if any of them are like me, playing so their parents can get their life together.

"Genie?" Mom calls in front of the church. "Coming in?"

I speed up. "Yeah."

Mom takes the stairs, while I go up the ramp. Somehow, we both make it to the front door at the same time. Her face looks like she remembers every conversation and emotion she's ever felt in this place. She smiles down on me, and I feel like my heart is hiding under the bed. This place got her better. I was low-key expecting to feel better too just by being here.

Some guy exiting holds the door open for us. "Hey, Tasha!" He gives her a hearty hug. "Things are about to get done now that you're here. I'm doing a store run. Need anything?"

"No, no. Thanks, David. This is my daughter, Genie."

"No way, no way. Heard so much about you! The one day I leave my son at home, you bring your gorgeous daughter." He gives Mom a playful hug. "Nice meeting you, Genie."

I give him a nod before rolling through the open door. David has heard so much about me and he didn't say, *Sorry about your accident* or pout sadly at me. I'd call that a win.

Wooden beams tower above us as we avoid a line leading to the food pantry. I only know that because I rolled into the sandwich-board sign with the arrow pointing to the door.

It smells in here. Despite the modern upgrades, like the elevator down the hall, this place can't shake the fact that it's an old church. There's still the original stained-glass windows, not to mention the place is made of the wood Jesus probably cut himself.

"Good afternoon, Tasha," says a woman in a brown T-shirt and matching cap with the St. Nicholas logo. "The cavalry is here."

"Hey, Deborah. How's it going?" Mom asks in a chipper voice I've never heard.

"Girl, you know they got me doing ten million things. We need more people to volunteer. We are swamped."

"Uh . . . If I want to volunteer, where would I go to talk to someone about that?" I interject.

Mom doesn't move. She looks at me with shifty eyes. "Volunteer?"

"Yeah, I'll need to do something when you come here. Would you rather I stay in my room?"

"Of course not. I'm just surprised," she admits. "I think it's great."

"Talk to Gabrielle in room 105," Deborah informs me before looping her arms through Mom's and sweeping her away.

"I'll be around, Mom," I call out after her.

When did she become Miss Popular? I feel even more out of place seeing how everyone knows her. I decide to put some distance between us and push off toward room 105. The floors switch from wood to a heavy red carpet. I bet it just traps all the sins in this place. Jesus can walk on water, but Genies cannot wheel on carpets. When I get to room 105, I'm faced with kids my age. Boxes cover most of the red carpet, and they work together to put stuff in them.

"Gabrielle?" I scan their faces.

"Out." A girl with a stapler in her hand throws her obvious attitude at having to be here my way.

"I'm looking for a guy named Kyle too."

"Who?" the same girl asks.

"I only know his first name. Brown-skinned guy, big muscles." I even go as far as to flex my arm for them.

"Not sure."

"He's got curly hair." *Fine as hell, too.* I really don't want to say the boy with a stutter and walker, but they all just stare at me like I'm describing some alien. "He wore a Stanford shirt the other day." There isn't even a stare anymore—they look away from me. *Really?* I sigh. "He's got a walker."

"*Ohhhh.* Jimmy from *South Park.* He's down the hall."

"Guess that makes you Cartman. Jerk." He doesn't even use crutches. She just shrugs.

Will I go to hell for thinking about burning someone in a church? I sludge through the blood-of-Jesus-carpet and find Kyle at the end of the hall. He's by himself at a table, putting stuff in baggies. Yes, I'm being a creep looking at him, not saying anything, staring at the way he counts with his fingers before tying a baggie and tossing it into a box. He checks off something on a clipboard.

Pencil, pad, button, and close the bag.

"Mandated, huh?"

Jesus, Genie.

Why would I open my mouth to say *that?* I could've said *Guess who?* or even hi, but my dumb ass had to bring up why he's here.

Kyle's head shoots up. "W-w-what are you doing here?"

I rub my hand on the doorframe. "You said you wanted to see me again. We didn't exactly talk specifics, so . . . Anyway, my mom's doing the clothes drive."

Kyle only nods and goes back to packing the baggies. I move in closer. At least there's company and a chain-gang-like movement to get those boxes filled next door. They didn't even know who Kyle was without me mentioning his walker. Not thinking, I roll to the end of the table and begin to do what Kyle does, grabbing from a stack of clear baggies and reaching for the pen, then the pad.

"W-w-what . . . are you doing?"

"Helping." I nod slowly. The orange lighting makes his skin look like a sunset. "I watched you before I said that stupid thing," I explain, grabbing the button. He stares some more, and I look down at my lap. "I learn by watching, like I do dances."

He makes a *humph* sound and continues on. "T-t-technically my m-m-mandated hours ended . . . an hour ago." I think I saw a smile appear.

"And you're still here?" I stop throwing pens in the baggies.

He shrugs. "I'm n-n-not ready to go yet."

Damn, he just got cuter and my respect.

"And I just got here."

"Y-y-you got a free lap, t-t-too."

"Huh?"

"Can't exactly . . . carry this box . . . down the hall to room 105." He closes the box to the left of him and pushes it toward me.

For certain there's a smile now. And my God, is it gorgeous. I can see a small chocolate stain on the inside of his bottom lip. I won't say anything.

"I get it. I have to work for your company." I grab the box from him and pull it onto my lap. "Don't stare at my butt when I turn around, either."

To be funny he closes his eyes, the chocolate on his lip still showing, and this time I happily roll down the hall, stopping before I hit room 105. Can't have them thinking we're in the fun room. No one says anything as I drop the box by the door and back out.

There's still a smile on Kyle's face when I get back. I exhale loudly from the mini workout. Used to love carpet until I realized how hard it is to push on compared to everything else. "Why are you in here by yourself and not with the super-helpful ones down the hall?"

"No reason."

Either a demon has entered his body or he got really touchy. Whatever it is, I can take a hint and I move on, going back to filling the baggies. Kyle does the same, taking a deep breath like he dodged a bullet.

We fill up two more boxes before I open my mouth again. Which is great because while I love playing eye tag, I think we're a little too old to keep it going for so long. And if I clear my throat again, he'll think I'm harboring some sickness. That's not cute.

"I see why you stay. This is therapeutic. The repetition."

"Y-y-you must like m-m-math too." He makes a cute yucky face. "W-w-want to . . . do the count?"

"Don't insult me. I love math, and checking things is a specialty." I grab the clipboard from his hand, making sure our hands don't touch.

"What else . . . d-d-do you s-s-specialize in?"

Cute guys with muscles who do what they want.

"That's it. I'm normally fabulous." Counting fifty bags, I check it off on the clipboard. "I almost forgot why I'm here in the first place."

"Th-th-that's why I stay." Kyle looks up at me again. "Check this out." He gets up, grabs his walker, and hobbles toward a door that looks like it's a wrap if it closes behind us. It appears heavy and ancient.

"What's behind the door?" He doesn't respond, but I think it's because he's focused on walking. I follow behind him pulling the door back and moving a box in front of it to keep it open. "I swear, if we end up in Narnia, Kyle . . ."

"It's o-o-only a library or office."

The amount of dust in the air makes me choke. "It needs an exorcism."

"This isn't even a Catholic church," he says between laughter.

I like that he's laughing at me.

"Why'd you bring me here?" I can't move in any more thanks to the room being filled with old furniture and boxes. The book-shelves make the room feel tighter than it already is.

Kyle murmurs to himself, twisting left and right like he's trying to remember something. He makes an affirmative "ah" as he reaches for one of the shelves. "L-l-look what I found." He thrusts a dusty book at me.

I grab the book, brushing off the front cover. Most of the title is missing, but BALLET, though faded and scratched, I can make out. Opening it, I land on a page of old pencil-drawn figures of ballet positions and black-and-white photos of dancers.

"It's what . . . m-m-made me call you. F-f-found it and couldn't s-s-stop thinking about you."

His sweetness surprises me, and the way my pride is set up, I can only ignore him. "Balanchine," I say, pointing to his picture. He's so in control, holding Beryl Grey's leg in passé. I turn the brit-tle pages gently, dust rising like my heart, the pages bending like my will to keep from crying. He doesn't even know me and yet this is perfect. Nolan never so much as printed out a Google image of a ballerina for me. "So cool!"

"W-w-want it?" Kyle smiles like he's just remembered a private joke.

"It's not yours to give."

"I-I-I'm sure we can get it . . . out undetected. B-b-besides, it's sitting a-a-and rotting. You should have it."

"All right." I say it like it's nothing, but this is everything. It's like he offered me a board position at New York City Ballet.

"D-d-did you ever want to be in one of these books?"

"Of course. To be remembered forever. I made it on the cover of a dance magazine, though." It just rolls off my tongue like how I imagined saying it. *Genie Davis, cover of* Relevé *magazine. Yes, I was the first Black dancer to be on the cover, but who's keeping tabs?*

"You're famous."

"Hardly. I'm Genie Davis. Not *Geena* Davis. But I'm in a league of my own."

"That explains the bruise."

"Never caught a ball in my life." Now I'm the one sounding possessed. Why didn't I think to cover it? I check the time. "Been an hour already. I should go."

"I hope your mom feels better soon."

"Thanks for the book."

When I cross the red sea of carpet again, the kids in room 105 are gone, but a woman with an afro looks through the boxes and sucks her teeth. I knock on the door. "Gabrielle?"

She turns to me. "Yes."

"I'm Genie Davis, I'd like to volunteer here."

"You'd be working alongside people with mandated community service. Is that a problem?"

Not if I get to work with Kyle again. "Not at all."

Sifting through her pockets, she produces a business card. "Email me your details and we'll see what we can do." She goes back to rummaging through the boxes, and I see myself out.

Mom waits exactly where we parted an hour ago with a modest smile on her face. "Did you see about volunteering?"

"Yeah."

"That'll look great on your college apps." She looks relieved to talk about something else.

"Yeah, because that's the only reason why I did it." *Jesus, Genie.* "How'd the drive go?" I try to change my tune, but I've never been much of a singer.

"Just fine."

I used to end the day feeling like I did something right. Maybe I let go on a turn too much. Perhaps I didn't interpret the music correctly. But they were all things I could fix. Today I made a choice to volunteer and it feels right.

Sending myself to bed early, I get under the covers and direct myself to Hannah's socials . They're full of pics and vids of her and Maya at the studio today. I stare at them too hard, trying to picture where I'd fit if I were there. Standing. Posing. Living.

I posted a picture today, not of me, but the Verrazzano Bridge.

Hannah knows what the bridge means for me and Mom and she didn't like it or nothing. Yet she has time to upload four new photos? It's the first photo I've posted since my accident. But maybe she's busy, so I text her. With a smile on my face, I send: You'll never guess what I did today. I went to St. Nicholas and met up with Kyle. He's so cute. He got me a ballet book. It's old and falling apart, but it's the thought that counts. What's up with you?

It's me and the book alone in my room. I don't even have to open it to get happy. Hannah should be all over this. I send another text: Yo, let's talk Kyle.

Hannah: Hanging with Dez.

I wait for another reply, but that's it. Um ... did she just deflect talking to me for some summer intensive guy? It's not like he's permanent.

A text from Nolan comes in, and I'm about to chuck my phone before I stop myself.

Nolan: You weren't home today.

Me: You came by?

Nolan: Didn't have to. You posted a picture of the Verrazzano.

Me: That's not creepy at all.

Nolan: How'd your mom fuck up now?

Me: Who are you to judge her?

Nolan: She's an alcoholic.

Nolan: You're being dragged back into her problems.

Nolan: And I'm just trying to help.

Me: Don't help me. That's what I have friends for.

I slam the phone down on its face. The way Hannah just cut

me off, I'm feeling down a friend, if I can call Kyle one. It's a good thing Nolan isn't here currently, because he would be able to see clear through my bullshit. I'd love to talk right now and hear how Hannah is wrong. The crazy thing is, Nolan would absolutely take my side and say exactly that. That makes me dizzy with anger, and I don't get dizzy easily.

Same as Hannah, Nolan goes silent. I'm not worried about him coming over. If he wanted to be face-to-face, he would've been here already.

The book fits under my arm like a stuffed animal. It's the only reason I haven't lost my temper yet. I rub my hands over the rough spine, imagining it to be Kyle's arm. My room lights up in a blue haze from my phone ringing. *Kyle.* I bite on my lip before answering.

"Hey, Kyle."

His breathing makes me hold my breath. Sounds like he's changing positions. Is he in bed too?

"I want to see you again."

It's the same words as before, but I grin like I'm hearing it for the first time. And what he asks next makes me excited and nervous, just like learning a pirouette on pointe.

"I want to see you again too," I say.

Have it your way, Hannah. I just reached petty level one hundred. If she calls tomorrow, I guarantee it, I'll be with Kyle.

CHAPTER FOURTEEN

The Floor

I'm officially trippin' this morning. The music won't stop. Not unless I add movement to it. The music will just have to keep playing while I scavenge through dance notation books. I pull out several notebooks, some with lines, some without, all with circles and arrows representing travel across a stage and words in French: my life, before I lost sight of it.

Slowly, I flip through the pages as if they're artifacts, invaluable as the Declaration of Independence, or Van Gogh's paintings. These are all my creations, my visions put into 2D. I've guarded them with my life, locking them in a lockbox, as if a burglar would want to steal some girl's dance on pages.

I should email Miss Kuznetsova. Wait—no, not yet. Remembering choreo is one thing. It's another to go back to VAB. If the steps are coming back to me, though, maybe Hannah was right? Maybe I don't have to dance to be in ballet. But who will take me seriously? I mean yay, I made a magazine cover. That doesn't mean I have a following of people who want to see my dances or commission them. The CIA couldn't even find my choreography. All dancers put together little steps every now and again, and many go on to do it once they've made their way through the ranks. Still, I never put it out there. "Magic" was to be my debut.

There's not an empty page left in any of these books. When did I have the time to do all this? I have all the time in the world now, and I haven't gone back to choreography. Couldn't go back to my books. After I fell, the music stopped. Kyle breathed it back into me. A rescue breath of sorts.

I was chill with my confession on seeing him, but nothing happened until I heard his breath. I'm sure it was the breathing. Slow. Precise. Steady. I can feel a difference in me. Since the call, my arms are doing more than lifting me out of my chair or pushing me around. I caught myself practicing a port de bras in the mirror this morning, smacked my arm into my dresser, knocking me right out of my trance.

Kyle asked to see me again, but not at St. Nicholas, which makes me nervous. Not being at St. Nicholas makes it feel like a date. We haven't called it one either, so I shouldn't feel so antsy, and yet I am. Honestly, I won't be at VAB, and Hannah hasn't texted me back, so Kyle it is. It'll be a chance to get away from Mom, let her work things out without having to see me, or fix something for me just because I can't reach the stove safely. And I can tell Kyle about my dances, how for the first time in a long time I've done something that I could do before my accident. Remember my dances. Make new dances.

Of course, there's a good chance that I'm getting hyped over nothing. That's enough to get me to lock my books back up and come back to reality. No one wants to dance the work of a paraplegic teenager who hadn't even received a company offer. Maybe it's time I think about going to college, becoming a math teacher like Mom. I pretty much tutored everyone at VAB. Apparently, Mom did the same at her community college. That's how she made tuition credit and a little side cash.

The book Kyle smuggled me still rests on my bed. I don't open it, though, because I'll only stare at the pictures when I should be getting ready. I need to get dressed in actual clothes. No more Sweatpants Depression, aka Homeless Chic. The clothes in my closet hover above me. Jeans dark, light, and red line up neatly, ready to be worn. They're too difficult to put on, and I scan the corner of my closet. Several dresses sway back and forth as I run my hand over the floral and denim fabrics. A dress would show my legs. I don't want that.

Maybe Hannah could help? I quickly shut down that idea. I don't want Hannah finding out about this yet. She'll take it all wrong that I can be with Kyle but not at VAB. Pilates is on her mind right now. Dez too, probably. By the time she gets to her phone, Kyle might as well be on a plane to California. It'll take that long.

I've got it! I push everything to the left until I find the red culprit hiding all the way in the back. Bought just a few days before my accident. It literally screamed at me from the storefront window. *Are you really going to walk by?* it questioned—rather rudely, I might add.

The skirt is long and flowy from my chair's height, brushing the floor like a curtain would a stage. Easy to put on, with leg coverage.

Perfect. In this heat, a black crop top completes it. The only thing that would make it better would be if I could stand in it.

Mom has called me twice now as I dress.

"I'm coming!"

"Need help?" she shouts back.

"No!" I adjust my top. I look at Odette and Odile. "No need to respond. I look great."

A theater curtain opens from my room to the kitchen. Mid-bite, Mom gawks at me.

"Well, this is new."

I squeeze into my spot at the table and pick up my fork. The cinnamon is heavy on the French toast, just like I like them. Any other day, I would've told her I could bring my food to the table myself. Now, I try to come up with a nice way to tell her I'm going to meet Kyle.

"Actually, it's been in my closet for a while, but yes, it's newer." I swallow some hash browns.

Her eyebrows rise. "Is Nolan stopping by?"

"Nope."

"Still dating? He hasn't been by since your accident."

Why must she ask that? She has to know the answer.

If only she really knew the many times Nolan's been here without coming through the front door. How many times I've had to shush him, or Pinocchio an excuse to lock myself in my room. "Nope."

A small smile forms on her face. She merely tolerated Nolan. Thought he was straight unnecessary. Yet she figured she couldn't keep him out of my life. I wish she'd cracked down harder on the boyfriend thing.

"Something you want to tell me?" she demands more than questions.

"Remember that friend I told you about? From therapy? We're going to meet up at Brooklyn Bridge Park to look at all the able-bodied people."

"I'd like to meet this friend. Who is she? He?"

"He is Kyle and he's nice. Don't worry. He can barely stand without a walker, so he won't be kidnapping me." *Or getting me pregnant.*

She cuts into her sausage link. "Tell me about Kyle. How'd he end up at therapy?"

"TBI. Not sure how." No lie there. I don't know how he got his injury. It's something I've been curious about but never felt comfortable asking.

"How exactly are you two getting to the bridge?"

"Uber."

I notice she's cutting but not exactly eating. She doesn't approve, but she's holding back, not wanting to fight, either. "I guess it's good you're getting back to normal."

"Trying to," I say between bites of eggs. She still isn't eating, and I have to say something to ease her mind, gain her trust. Going through her things didn't help, and shitting on her attempts to tell me she's still proud wasn't good either.

"I don't want you to get hurt," she says.

Hurt how? Falling? Heartbreak? Making decisions on my

own? Kyle and I are just friends. At least that's how it needs to be.

She continues, reading my mind. "With the fall out of your chair, he's physically impaired too. I'll be up-front in saying this makes me uncomfortable. What if you get hurt? Can he help you using a walker? What if he gets hurt?"

I'd like to tell her that people fully capable of helping don't bother at all, e.g., Nolan. She'd never get the trust I have for Kyle. He's another distraction for me to her. And I planned on telling her that he does community service at St. Nicholas, but the way she's carrying on I'll keep it mum, just like the deal she made with Dad.

"Is it really smart to start something when you need to focus on school? It's in just a few more weeks, and things are different now. A new school and senior year. You need to be focused." The fork jabs the air like a sword. "Wouldn't you rather be at VAB? You're safe there. I'm not thrilled with the thought of you on some date out and about."

I blow out air. "Mom, he's a *friend*." I have to remind myself. If he comes to me looking half as good as I do, lines will blur. I accidentally touch the bruise on my face.

My face! How could I forget my bruised face? I press it softly, using a spoon as a makeshift mirror. It's still sore, but not as deep of a purple as the other day. "I need makeup! I have to hide this bruise." My juice rattles on the table as I push away from it. , My funny bone laughs as I round the corner.

"Genie?" Mom calls after me.

I scour my dresser for any sign of makeup. I only wear it for performances. The most I can do is put on mascara. I always relied on Mom and Hannah to work construction on my face. They enjoy the process more than I ever did.

"I can go to St. Nick's like this, but not *out!*" I call out to no one, correcting myself in case it sounds too suspicious to Mom, whose hands are on my shoulders.

"Okay, okay. You work yourself up. Let me get some things."

While she disappears, I stare at myself in the mirror. Lately my face has been the least of my worries. Looking good for Nolan has long worn off. If I didn't have to be in a leotard, most of the time I was wearing what Nolan wanted.

She returns. "Let's see what we can do."

Like I'm six again, Mom kneels in front of me, mimicking how I should hold my face for her. Back then, she only put a little blush on my cheeks, reminding me how beautiful I was without it. It was my first big recital and I needed to sparkle. I asked why I couldn't look like the other girls. They resembled stiff-faced showgirls with children's bodies. She told me they needed the makeup because they lacked the magic I had.

Her face is serious, as if she's working on the next masterpiece. Is my face really so bad it requires this much concentration? "Am I still going to look like me, or should my stripper name be Honey Bunz?" She presses too hard on my right side. "Mom, don't bruise me even more."

"Don't move your lips." There's a playful tone to her voice despite her demand.

I mumble my response about still having lips left. I'm holding the record for puckering my lips. If I duck-face any more, I'll turn into Daisy. I twist my head away for a time check: Kyle should be here in a few minutes. "I'm good."

Kyle's scars. My bruised face. Wouldn't be the worst thing he's seen, but I want to look put together. Like I tried today. "All right." A smile spreads across her face. "Been so long."

I turn back to the mirror. My skin is one smooth complexion again, and my lips are perfectly glossed.

"I know. I need to get outside, so he isn't waiting on me."

"I'll help you down the stairs."

"No need. The ramp is there." It's important I show her I can do some things on my own. And if it's not there, I'll be sure to ask for her help.

Just like the day before yesterday, I get down by myself. Somehow, I manage to keep Mom at the apartment door rather than the front door, leaving her with a face full of doubt. It's like doing center work. You have to find your balance, steady yourself. As Miss Kuznetsova would say, *Floor work is life, made to test your strength, flexibility, and balance.* I've come to think of Mom like the barre. Useful, very much needed. But no one comes to see dancers at the barre. Eventually we have to move away from it and take to the floor.

CHAPTER FIFTEEN

Banana Splits

The lines have been blurred.

Kyle looks amazing in a muscle-fitting V-neck shirt, with a gold chain on the outside. And that hair. When can I touch it? The sunlight adds a caramel haze to the frizz on top of his head. His curls are defined with the help of product. We're going to a park, and he's stunting to outdo Adonis himself. Hannah will swoon when I tell her. Of course I'm going to tell her. Eventually.

Our hands brush together on the seat of the car as I stabilize myself. I murmur a *sorry*, which he either doesn't hear or doesn't care about. My hand doesn't retract, though, and neither does his. The ride is silent for a few minutes. Are we both wondering if we jumped into this meeting too soon? Perhaps he's realized I've never apologized for the QUEST situation. I owe a lot of apologies.

"I didn't mean what I said . . . you know, at QUEST, about being dam—"

"Don't." His mouth makes shapes and forms like a dancer preparing to pirouette, judging their balance, correcting their arms and feet, before they let go and spin. "Y-y-you're right, in a w-w-way."

I'm right? He can't think he's damaged. The beat-up box doesn't always mean what's inside is broken. "No, I'm not. I was a bitch."

Kyle rubs his shoulder before pulling on his short sleeve. "Y-you're grieving."

He said the G-word. The psychologists who came by to make sure I wouldn't try head-diving out of the bed after the news was explained to me used that word. I closed my eyes, turned my head from them, and tried to remember the last time I danced, jumped, or ran down a hall. They told me I would most likely grieve the life that I used to know. Grieve? I thought grieving was the word used when your parents died, grieving meant crying and yelling to the skies to bring back your little brother who got hit by a car.

Maybe I don't grieve? The clinic psychologist where I got the abortion told me it was likely I would grieve the life of a child I wouldn't know. I told her there was not enough of a person to grieve. I was not grieving. I haven't cried yet. Not for the abortion or the fall.

"So, what's on the itinerary?" I ask instead of facing up to him.

"Ice cream. There's a really . . . n-n-nice ice cream shop down there." His face lets on a bit of disappointment contrary to his voice. He wanted to talk more about grieving. "Y-y-you know ice cream heals face bruises, right?"

"The doctors didn't mention that."

Kyle lifts up the shirtsleeve he was just adjusting. A bright bruise sits on his shoulder. "We both fall . . . you just have a shorter way down." He taps the side of his face. "You d-didn't have to cover the bruise f-f-for me today."

"It didn't match my outfit."

He smiles, and we talk of ice cream the rest of the way there. It's not until we get situated outside the car that I realize he's graduated to forearm crutches. Oh, that explains what that girl was talking about. He looks like he's just learning to stand on relevé without the barre. Now I see how he got the bruise.

"Look who's showing off," I tease. Secretly I'm proud of him.

"I—I—I can't l-l-laugh and use these things," he chuckles, stumbling through articulation. Without a walker to obstruct him, he looks younger, and a new confidence beams from his more upright posture. No more grandpa hunched shoulders. "Like w-w-what you see?"

I tilt my head back and forth, tapping my chin. "I don't know. I think I prefer the grandpa look."

"Th-thought Jimmy from . . . *South Park* look w-was in." He chokes in a laugh. "Shall we?"

Shall we? I said the same thing to Nolan on our first date. Going on three years now. I finally got Mom to let us leave the house after her millionth question. *Where exactly will you be? What rating is the movie? How are you getting there? Do I have your parents' number, Nolan? What is your mother's number? Genie, are you sure you want to go?* Once the door closed, knowing she was peeping through the hole, I gave him the biggest kiss I could. I placed his arms around my waist, wrapped my arms around his neck. I transferred my magic. The little speckle of glitter left on his lip told me so.

Mom opened the door and simply said, "Don't push it," and I rolled my eyes and pushed it out of her view the rest of the night. When I came home, I went to my room to find a box of condoms on my bed. Instead of taking it seriously, I called Nolan and we laughed about it. I mocked her. I was always pushing it.

Nothing good follows when I think about Nolan.

It takes us a while to cover some ground. Not because the ground is so hard to walk on. It's paved and smooth right up to the waterfront, there's just so many people. Everyone it seems is trying to get themselves photographed in front of the bridge. Kyle isn't quite as skilled with his new support assistance, so we move slowly, only talking when he needs a break. We get looks. A lot of them. Some man even looks behind us to see if someone follows. It seems that way to me.

If Kyle notices, he isn't letting on. I'm a little jealous he gets to concentrate on walking. I get to notice people parting to make life easier. I don't want ease. Only familiar.

We stop at a long line that curves out the door of the ice cream parlor. The bored looks and whining children say it isn't moving fast, either. I look up at Kyle, who has a sheet music of lines across his forehead. It's hot, he's sweating, and we walked a distance to get here. Standing isn't his strength. But he's glistening like a member of a boy band after their first set. All he's missing is some weird accessory, like goggles on his head.

"I. Have. A. Friend. Who. Works. Here," he says through breaths.

He walks ahead confidently. I follow. There's a ramp leading to a side door. Excitement powers my hands as I roll ahead of him, playfully blowing a raspberry as I head up the ramp. I figure I'll hold the door open for him. The door swings open as I reach for it. A group of boys with scooters barrel into me, shouting, "Oops" and

"Sorry," followed by a man shouting for them to slow down, sending me sliding back down the ramp. It happens so fast my reaction is to block my face from their elbows. By the time I grab my rims, my chair jerks to a stop. I feel for my seat belt. *Thank you, gods of humility, for I know better now.*

I look back to see a pained-face Kyle blocking me from moving even an inch more down the ramp. Did he catch me or did I run into him? "If I move, will you fall?" He lets out what I think is a yes. Panic sets in. "Grab hold of my handles, push, and I'll pull. Tell me when you're ready."

"Ready."

His breathing is labored behind me as I push forward, slowly pulling up the ramp with my right hand and pushing with my left. Best to keep a solid grip just in case we roll back more. I will not let my fingers give out on me again.

I lean my head back to look up at him when we reach the flat landing. "Sorry about that."

"It's f-f-fine. Let's get some ice cream." After catching his breath some more, he says more clearly, "I have to keep pushing you, since I dropped my crutches."

I look down the ramp, where his pair of crutches make an X. I'm no PT, but he can't walk down the ramp to get them. Not as tired as he is now. "I'll get them."

"N-n-no. We're getting ice cream."

"Kyle."

"I-I-I'll have s-s-someone will bring them to me. No one's going to steal crutches."

Pfft! What part of Brooklyn is he from? 'Cause my ramp gets stolen every other day.

"But—"

"O-o-open the door, please."

Someone pushing my chair is not something I've easily allowed. Mom has to help me up the steps, and the nurses did their job at the hospital. Being pushed makes me feel even less able. Any other time I would be peeved and tell him, *Hands off my ride.* I should've been able to stop myself, so I let him push me in.

He takes me to a table, using it for balance to lower himself into a chair. His face is beet red, and he rubs his non-bruised shoulder. Have I caused an old injury to flare up? This hopeful day is beginning to feel the opposite. The smell of homemade ice cream can't sugarcoat the disappointment of the last few minutes. If it didn't almost kill us getting up here, I'd ask to leave.

I do my best to smooth down my humidity 'fro. The top of my chest hurts—from some kid's elbow, I suspect. I press on the sore spot. Kyle's busy collecting as many breaths as he can. He's probably wishing he hadn't picked me up. The more I watch him struggle, the more I wish he hadn't given me his number. Maybe it isn't the meeting, but the chair. No chair. No ramp.

"I hate kids." I didn't mean to say it out loud.

"They're all right. They got . . . excited." Did he forget about his TBI? I could have caused a flare-up of the injury.

"Excited? I hurt you because of them. I hope one of them trips." I realize how crazy I sound, wishing harm on a group of ten-year-olds for behaving like ten-year-olds. Is the ice cream that amazing?

"They're . . . kids. You w-w-want any one day?"

The question catches me off guard. My paranoia over Nolan cools me like this place has air-conditioning. I have to remember Kyle knows nothing about me and I him. Back when I was being told of my paralysis and what I could and couldn't do, the doctor brought up pregnancy. Somehow I thought he knew, but he just explained that everything worked fine, and when I was ready, I could try for kids.

That moment was like being served school lunch. Everything I felt was separated into portions. One part relieved that yes, I could eventually have children. My abortion was a onetime thing. I had always planned on having them sometime later in my career. The other part held all my fears. I was constantly reminded how lucky I was that my fall wasn't worse. My fall could've easily crushed my ability to carry a pregnancy. Seeing my period for the first time again after it all was like an ending to a pas de deux. My body and I were in sync again.

"Only if they don't kill me over ice cream," I tell him with a forced smile. "How about that ice cream—I'll get some?" I lift the brakes up, ready to leave this conversation.

"W-w-wait." His smile brightens. "We've got . . . VIP treatment." He waves at someone behind me.

"Kyle!" A cheerful girl with a messy bun hugs him, squeezing so hard I want to whip her off him. "I couldn't believe it when you called."

She hasn't let up yet, and I may or may not be giving her the stink eye. Kyle certainly is happy to see her too.

"Ch-Ch-Chelsea, this is Genie."

I feel overdressed next to her work shirt. "Hi," I say, hopefully not too rudely.

"A-a-anything Genie wants, she can have." He smiles at me, and I think maybe I'm not being petty and annoying.

Chelsea teasingly gushes, "Breaking hearts before you go away to Cali?" She playfully runs her hand through his hair.

"Excuse me?" I shout it more than I mean to. Break my heart? Kyle and I are friends and nothing more. When the summer is over, that's it. Nice knowing him. I certainly haven't thought further than the summer with us.

Kyle has a sheepish grin on his face. Even he wasn't expecting that.

"Kyle made you sound super special, and he told me he wanted to reserve a table and we don't even do that here." She jokingly swats him. "You have to be really something to have this guy make sudden plans."

"Well . . . ," Kyle starts. I can't tell if he's embarrassed or searching for the words.

"Okay, I'll stop embarrassing you. What do you want?" Chelsea asks.

"Banana split," he says, eyes trained on me. They hold mine in place.

"Me too," I echo.

She's gone just as swiftly as she entered, and I must say I'm glad that he's looking at me instead of her. *Chelsea.* Doesn't she realize that I don't have much time left with him? God, I should've talked to him sooner. Hopped in on a conversation that Logan was trying to facilitate. We could've been coming here for weeks. I love ice cream! Now I have to remind myself that there's not much we can do because he's leaving soon. There're three tables in the small space. It hadn't occurred to me when we just pulled up to the table that it was reserved. The gesture is nice. More than nice. Kind and caring. I do my best to see what Chelsea's doing. A swarm of customers draped over the counter block her.

Even as a customer brings back the "lost crutches" that Kyle left behind, he barely lets his eyes off me. Not even to say thank you to the man.

"We trained at the same gym," he sputters, bringing conversation back into the equation.

"Is she headed to college too?"

He nods. "NYU."

"Gymnasts are really smart, I see." For some reason it comforts me knowing he'll be far away from Chelsea's friendly hands. *Am I jealous?*

"Not really," Kyle mumbles. His eyes disappear.

"What makes you say that?"

He looks at Chelsea, then back at me. Did I just Kool-Aid man it on something too personal? "D-D-Dylan was my best . . . friend. Gymnast too. W-w-we got drunk one night and . . ." He sighs heavily. I try to cut in, but he gives me the stop sign with his hand. "I crashed us." His eyes sink into his face.

I don't know what to say. I would never have guessed he was the cause of his accident. We both messed ourselves up pretty good. Mom wouldn't approve of Kyle's choices. But she's never seen him in physical therapy or at the church. He's working to fix his life. "What happened to Dylan?" I tread softly. It's his story to tell.

He shakes his head and buries his face in his hands. His body crumples like a dollar bill in a pocket. It would be easy to think he was reckless, but watching the remorse spill out of him, I can't think of anything other than understanding. Unlike earlier in the Uber, I want to touch his hands purposely. We all get into things we didn't intend to happen. Sometimes tragedy is the only consequence. I want to tell him he isn't bad, but you can't just tell someone not to feel guilty. I know myself.

I don't know what it feels like to be Kyle. To lose a friend. Yes, I ducked from Hannah, jealous, embarrassed, and conflicted by her presence. Now, as we're getting back into the swing of our relationship, I can't imagine picking up the phone to call her and her being gone forever. Hannah's one of the first people on my mind when I wake up. Maybe Dylan is the last thing on Kyle's mind when he goes to bed. Maybe that's why he called me.

"I—I—I get the urge to spill . . . my guts around you." His eyes dance around as he says it.

I feel like talking to him, too.

"Well, that says something. Most people just ask for wishes. Being a Genie and all." I try to lighten the mood.

He perks up a bit, and he's moved on to twisting his finger. "I—I—I wish for the . . . banana splits to be here."

"Doesn't work like that."

"H-h-how then?"

"*I'm a Genie in a wheelchair, baby, gotta push me the right way, honey,*" I sing. He laughs, bumping the table, which bumps my chair, reminding me that I took off my locks. I quickly lock them.

"Y-y-you're funny. I always thought ballerinas had l-l-little . . ."

"Personality?" I finish. He nods. "That's a myth. Dancers are full of personality. Many of us are just extremely focused, and it comes across as stoic."

"I—I—I went to a ballet once. It was . . . Christmas? The doll?"

"*The Nutcracker,*" I say matter-of-factly. "Everyone has seen *The Nutcracker.*"

"I c-couldn't do ballet."

"I couldn't hang from rings and flip over and over."

"Y-y-you're a great dancer, I bet." He says it like he's been dying to say it.

Chelsea sets down our splits just in time for me to ignore his compliment. I don't want to harp on what I used to be. But I'm stuck on his wording. Why must he say things like he knows? Like it's a possibility or still true? How would he know, anyway?

"You forgot the past tense."

"N-n-no, I didn't." He narrows his eyes at me, seeming a bit hurt that I would undermine his thoughts. "Y-y-you're s-s-still a dancer. E-e-even I can see that." He draws out a napkin from the dispenser to wipe spit from the corner of his mouth.

What does that even mean? I break the banana up with my fork. Nolan never wanted to talk ballet with me. He thought it took up enough of my physical time, and any time I spent with him, I shouldn't be thinking about it. In a way it helped. Thinking about something all the time can get tiring, but I didn't like how he wanted to rid it from me almost completely. Here's Kyle wanting to talk about it.

"I'll always love dancing. I just won't ever fly again."

"Not you . . . specifically, b-but what if you made someone fly? Like in a dance?"

"How'd you know I did choreography?" Suspicion creeps into my voice.

"D-d-didn't. That's really c-cool, though."

My choreography is sacred. I don't like talking about it. "Why the interest in ballet?"

"B-b-because it's like you." His face twists as he tries to start the next word. He takes a deep breath. "Beautiful, complex, and there's a lot I don't understand."

I need a map to retrace our conversational steps. My mind goes fuzzy on everything he's said before his previous statement. I've been called beautiful before. My lines, drive, and musicality. By Nolan when he buttered me up. Never have I've been called beautiful in comparison to ballet. It's the nicest thing someone has ever called me. Complex? I agree with him on that, yet he didn't mean it as a dig. It's as much a compliment as beautiful. He doesn't understand a lot about me, but Kyle understands a lot more than he thinks. I think that's why I'm scared to open up again. He's the fire to my dynamite, and if he gets close, I'll go off.

"Here's a joke: What happened to the pas de deux partners?" I ask.

He thinks about it, taking in a spoonful of ice cream—then shrugs.

"They split." His head rolls back in laughter. "If you can't come up with a better joke, you have to do one."

"I can't . . . compete with ballerina splits."

"But you can split."

"I'd s-s-split a lot better if . . . I went to ballet class with you."

I try to imagine Kyle in class. Is he a footed-tights or footless-tights guy? Is he one of the guys who would tickle us during partner-ing, occasionally sliding a hand down your leg when you held it over his shoulder? Would I kiss him during the bedroom pas de deux of *Manon*, like I did Chris, even when Miss Kuznetsova said to skip over it for the day? Did I do it to see if kissing somebody other than Nolan would make me feel different about him? Another reason to leave him. Another reason I ignored.

Chelsea walks by and playfully runs her hands on the back of Kyle's neck. Kyle blushes.

"I think she wants a piece of your banana split," I voice.

Kyle's eyes widen as he chokes on his split. "W-w-what?"

I rip the stem of the cherry off. "Ex? Friend with benefits?"

He smiles. "Neither."

I bite the cherry, giving him a suggestive smile. I'm just getting to know him too. This feeling is jealousy *and* inquiry. He hasn't offered any information up, besides them being friends, and who am I to read deeply into it? Especially when he's going away.

"You?" He raises an eyebrow.

I dissect my split while shaking my head. I feel labored, like I just finished the *Esmeralda* variation. "Ooh. I have caramel in mine," I say to distract him from his question. My vocal version of the high kicks required in the dance. I squeal in delight, adding the popular tambourine that makes the dance so exciting.

"The b-best thing about this split isn't . . . even on it." If my split hasn't melted from how warm his eyes are, I feel like I might.

The way Kyle looks at me. It's like I'm onstage again, being adored. He lays his eyes on me and I feel singled out from anything and everything around me. It brings me back to how Nolan looked at me. Except something is different. Nolan's look was possessive. Kyle's look is treasuring. And if he keeps looking, I'll feel like the title character in *Paquita* when she's allowed to marry the officer, like she was born to do. Nature must be healing, because I feel great right now. Looking cute, flirting like my old self. He's into me for however long he's in the city. Somehow chocolate ends up on his top lip again. I fill in the silence by dipping my remaining cherry like a tea bag into the whipped cream. Bad things happen when I feel, though. Nolan is my personal testimony. There should've been a warning label: *They tend to get possessive, lonely, and act like children when you don't want to be their baby mama.* Just thinking about Kyle romantically is dangerous. Besides, if he knew I had an abortion, what would he think of me?

"I-I-I'm too forward . . . aren't I?"

"It's not y—"

"Is that blood?" Chelsea interrupts, crouching down beside me.

I look down and find my right leg off my footplate and a small stain of blood next to my chair. There's a trail of it leading to the door we came in. Looks like someone squirted ketchup.

"I think it's you," Chelsea says, touching my leg.

I would yell at her, but as I lift up my skirt, I see a cut on my leg, oozing blood. "Dammit! I think I'm going to need stitches." Those damn Razor scooters live up to their name.

My leg's busted open and I didn't feel it. Couldn't feel it. Nothing I do stops me from looking into Kyle's worrying eyes. Sometimes I wish my emotions were paralyzed so I really couldn't feel anything.

CHAPTER SIXTEEN

As You Wish

O n this episode of The Breaking Pointe, *Genie does exactly what her mother was afraid of. Keep it locked for "I told you so."*

I'm googling whether I qualify for Access-A-Ride. This is what I'll need, since Mom will be against me traveling without her ever again. Now if I could figure out how to apologize to Kyle for wrecking his day, he can be my plus-one when I'm found eligible. There's no way he can say no to exclusive door-to-door service.

Kyle crinkles a pack of Skittles.

A nurse walks by my triage area without making eye contact. No doubt she's learned to ignore me by now. "Don't call my mom, please." She scurries away and another nurse walks by. "Can I please go before my mom gets here?" She slowly blinks at another failed attempt of mine. "I feel fine!"

My stitches were even done by an intern, so I know I wasn't a high-risk priority. And I thought arriving by ambulance was a bit much, even for me, who likes a good entrance, but Kyle insisted and so did the paramedics.

The head nurse marches into my section, wooden-faced and with pursed lips. "Genie, aren't you a little old to be carrying on like this?"

"If I'm so old, let me go," I counter. If I were a real concern, I'd be drinking slushies on the pediatric floor. I was getting my groove back, Nurse Ratched! Surely she has eyes that can see this. Now I'm sharing a partitioned cubicle with a kid who refuses to drink a sip of a child-sized juice cup so the doctors will discharge him.

"You're a minor. Mi. Nor," she breaks it into syllables like I have comprehension issues.

"Can I at least sit in my chair?"

"No, and don't you try it. If you so much as try to get into that chair, we'll restrain you." She gives Kyle a warning look, like a child who tried to steal from a cookie jar. "Don't help her either."

There goes that plan. . . .

I stare at my chair, parked directly in front of the nurses' station. Medical professionals are sadists. More so than I thought Mom was when she introduced the foot stretcher into my home dance regimen. It's meant to give more arch and flexibility. No pain, no gain. She was right, of course. The fiery eyes I gave her whenever she brought it out turned into just doing it on my own. I looked forward to her massages when I was done.

"Um . . . why do you want your chair so much?" Kyle asks.

"Because, whether I like it or not, it's my . . ."

"L-l-legs?"

"No!" I shout, forgetting where I am, rubbing my hand over my bandage. My outburst causes the head nurse to come back and give me a second warning glare. Kyle's obviously sorry and slumps over in his seat. Great job, Genie. You've managed to insult him, almost kill him, and yell at him. "Sorry, it's just . . . I don't see my chair as my legs. It's my only way to move around. I don't need to like it to accept it." My chair doesn't allow me to do splits, or a jeté, or even walk upstairs. Kyle might be bad at walking now, but he can still walk.

He looks at my chair. "I-i-is that w-w-why it's black?"

"It's black after Odile. *Swan Lake?* The ballet."

I think back to when I was given choices on the brands of chairs. Did I need it to fold? How well could I sit up? Measurements after measurements taken. A badly fitted chair equals a badly fitted costume. Dangerous. It's a costume fitting, I told myself. This is all part of the costume. When it came to choosing colors, I picked black. Logan was very new to me, and he spent most of the time telling me the best part came down to picking the color. Only I didn't pick a color. I chose black, after Odile from *Swan Lake.* Like Odile, this chair was evil, a trick to make me feel like I had "legs" again.

It's not something I want to get into with Kyle.

"That's i-i-interesting," Kyle says. "Ballet is still on your mind."

I nod slightly. I wouldn't expect him to get it. "I guess so. I never really paid much attention to it."

"I f-f-figured you'd have a red chair."

"Red?"

He nods like he just had a revelation. "Fiery, passionate, and sexy."

I can't help but smile. Secretly, I did want the red chair. I wanted to be bold. Red's been it for me as long as I can remember. And when my first recital called for a pink tutu and pink ribbons,

Mom placed her finger across her lips and gave me a red ribbon anyway. I know better now than to go against studio orders, but it made me happy that day.

"There'll be another one." I always thought I'd watch my legs grow old. I would retire, walk a little slower but still poised, leaving glitter trails in the form of a footprint. Like Kuznetsova. Now my chair will grow old, becoming a nuisance more than a help. I'll upgrade to something new. Maybe something red. It could take years before I'm able to stand decently if at all. I have to be realistic, right?

"Wh-wh-who's Nolan? You swiped his call away a bunch in the ambulance." Kyle turns the conversation around. And not for the better.

I try to keep my eyes from widening. Nolan doesn't deserve any emotion from me. Still, I ask, "How'd you see that?" If you can't feel your foot, can it still be in your mouth?

He scrunches his face. "I saw nothing else but his name."

"That was it?" I wrap the blanket around my bare stomach, suddenly colder. Good job picking out a crop top, Genie. I need to be more careful.

"C-c-crazy ex-boyfriend or something?"

"Basically."

His lips twist to one side of his face. "D-d-dancer too?"

"Nope," I tell him flat out. The questioning about Nolan has me wrapping the blanket around my hands as tight as possible.

The thought is laughable. Nolan in tights? He'd die first. I tried to give him a lesson once, but he was so adamant about it being so gay, so unmanly, that we ended up in a screaming match.

Kyle fidgets in his chair, eyes on the floor. I'm probably reading too much into his body language, but his puffed-out cheeks and tapping fingers tell me he's pissed with himself. Maybe he didn't mean anything by bringing up Nolan, but my answers say Nolan's name means everything to me.

"I-I-I'll be back," Kyle excuses himself.

I nod. Happy he doesn't have to see me look so tortured over Nolan. I'm ruining it. We should be having fun and talking. We shouldn't even be in a hospital, and to top it all off, I'm thinking about Nolan when I don't want to. Kyle asking if Nolan was a dancer brings back a memory I haven't thought about in a while.

Nolan met me at the studio. It was date night, and the studio was on the way to our favorite theater. It was a Friday and everyone rushed out, but I convinced Nolan to stay a few extra moments. It was rare that he watched me dance. He often got annoyed when I did anything ballet around him. I realize now the fire I had for dance was bigger than the fire I had for him. He could tell and didn't want to see it around me. His way of being more important when we were together.

"Curve your arms, and hold them down like this." I curved his hands and pushed in his stomach, forcing him to stand up straight. "Almost," I told him. "This is first position."

"Genie, I don't want to do this," he whined.

"How many days have I timed you in a pool?" I waited for his response. "I thought so."

"Ballet is for girls."

"Tell that to all the boys I've danced with. None of us girls complain about their biceps, either." He kept turning his head to follow me as I assessed his poor form.

"I don't like the way that boy touches you."

With my luck, he came in on Chris and me working through the choreography for the *Manon* final pas de deux. If he had paid attention to anyone else, he would've noticed that two other partners were learning it too. I don't know how he sneaked by the front desk and caught the beginning, where I lay on top of Chris as Manon is weak and fragile from fleeing through the swamp. If he focused a little more, he would have noticed that Chris and I were not on our A game, and Miss Kuznetsova had us starting from the top yet again. "Ugh, Chris, Genie, disappointment on my face. Do over. Do right," she lamented, hands waving in disgust. But I guess Nolan didn't hear that.

"Oh my God," I groaned. "Chris is my partner; he *has* to touch me." I turned his head back straight. "Besides, you're the only one to truly touch me." I pecked him on the cheek.

"Don't think because he's gay I won't kick his ass if he gets too touchy-feely. You're mine, Genie."

I didn't like how he talked about Chris. As far as I was concerned, I was the only one who could insult him. It was our little understanding, and I didn't mean any harm when I did.

"Really, Nolan? And he's not gay, so stop calling him that."

"Are we done here?"

"Not even close. I want to see you do a demi plié." I demonstrated a plié. "Go on. Try it."

Technically, students weren't allowed to have guests unless

approved by Miss Kuznetsova herself, and we certainly shouldn't be in any studios after hours without permission. Miss Kuznetsova disregarded Nolan's appearance, and I was cutting it close allowing his jeans-wearing body in her sanctuary. He reeked of hate for not only dance, but ballet. I'm sure everyone could tell. Nolan had better appreciate my effort.

We might as well have been on ice by how he wobbled. He was no Chris. Chris could make the elementary steps look beautiful. Even with me holding his waist, Nolan couldn't bend his knees to save his life. And I hadn't even asked for a grand plié, which would surely have had him licking the wooden floor.

"Well, you're no Chris," I said.

"I told you I'm not a fag."

"Don't call him that! I didn't expect for you to get it right away. I just wanted to share my world with you."

"I don't care about ballet. I don't care that you dance!"

"At least show some respect, then!"

"Show me some respect. I have to hear about you winding on some guy, his hands groping you. Now I've witnessed it. You spend more time here than you do with me." His stomping feet echoed around the empty studio, and I could feel the vibrations ripple through my feet. If he was behaving this way over a touch, he would lose it if he saw the kiss. His actions proved the kiss justifiable.

"Well, no wonder. Especially when you're behaving like an ass."

I stormed off and we didn't go out. I used the time alone to figure out why I stayed with Nolan. We had no common hobbies.

I wrestled with the idea that I loved his loyalty. He wouldn't just walk out like Dad did. But on the way home, I settled on the fact that he was good-looking and attentive. Mom was just happy to see me home early and alone.

Kyle knocks over his crutches as he sits back down. I turn to him.

"S-sorry. I didn't mean anything bringing him up." He sighs, offering me the pack of Skittles, which I decline. "W-w-was your mom a dancer?"

"In spirit." She's always been a fan of the art. Mom spoke of her own mother telling her she needed a practical job. Her mom put her in tutoring and math clubs instead of dance class like she wanted. I guess the *Fun Mom* subscription was lost in the mail.

"W-w-where'd you get your dancing genes from? Your dad?"

I shrug. "I don't know." Tired of talking about me, I push the questions on him. "When'd you realize you liked peeling skin the size of cookies off your hands?"

"My parents are doctors of sports a-a-and exercise medicine. A-a-a good family friend came to . . . know them after . . . a gymnastic injury. He's like an uncle . . . t-t-taught me everything."

"Were you always really good at it?"

"I was shit," he laughs. "I—I—I guess I'll always h-h-have to work really hard to g-g-get things right."

My phone vibrates on the bed. Mom's calling. I give Kyle the one-minute hand and take the call. "Mom, come and get me," I spurt out before she has a chance to go into her worried spiel.

"Are you okay? You work yourself up so." I know she's massaging the stress out of her face, rubbing her forehead or her jaw. "The car stalled on me and I had to get it towed. The mechanic can have it done soon. Sit tight, though."

"Mom, I need out of here."

"You need to relax, Genie. Twice in one week you're in the hospital."

"I'm fine." Really, I am. I don't even feel anything from being stitched up.

"You keep saying that—hold tight."

She hangs up and Kyle rubs his hands together like he's starting a fire. I swallow a few screams. They're my diet lately. The puzzle-pieces-print room dividers are driving me mad. Everything was going too well. "Y-y-you're sweating." Kyle points to my head.

I touch my forehead. "You can go home. It's going to be a while until she gets here."

"I'm staying."

"You don't have to."

"I—I—I want to."

"Your parents?"

"I'm eighteen. I c-c-can do what I want."

Just that quick I feel like a child. "Point taken."

There's silence, and whenever our eyes meet, he gives me a smile. I try to smile back, but sometimes I can't. Like our early days of rehab. "I d-d-don't like hospitals either," Kyle says.

"Your parents are doctors, though."

"A-a-after my injury, I've been n-n-nervous in them. Too many . . . bad memories."

"Same." I would hate hospitals too if my best friend died in one because of me. I came into the hospital alone and left that way. But we dislike them the same. "I'm sorry about Dylan." I start to say more, but I can't think of anything right to say.

"Thank you," Kyle says, looking at the floor. He gives a small laugh to himself before our eyes meet again. "M-m-may I have a wish?"

I stop shifting in the bed, truly focusing on him. What's he going to wish for? "What is it?"

He leans forward, licking his lips. Nolan has managed not to ruin lip licking for me. I'm reminded my lips probably could use some Vaseline. I run my finger over them. They're not dry at all. But my mouth is with anticipation.

"I—I—I wish to do this again. Not . . . this." He gestures to the hospital. "H-h-hanging out."

He's not going to kiss you, Genie. Why would you think that?

I didn't see the day going like this, but I guess I still got it.

"As you wish."

CHAPTER SEVENTEEN

Protecting

I'm in bed with Kyle, and we hardly had a first date. Since Mom still isn't here, Kyle and I have gotten comfy. Our arms touch as we watch videos of his gymnastic meets on his phone. Hours later and he still smells as good as when he first picked me up. He's a little sweaty, but after dancing with Chris for years, I'm used to sweat. Sweat meant effort. Kyle put a lot of effort into today.

I cringe as he spins himself on the pommel horse. I'm equally enthralled with his skill, too. Holding up his body weight, turning just his lower half. Kyle makes it look effortless. I use the blanket to cover my mouth as he dismounts. Gymnastics makes me nervous.

Not that I never got nervous for the ballet boys. One wrong landing out of a double cabriole and you could be out of commission for a while. Hannah and I would sneak a peek at the boys' classes, boxing ourselves into a corner. Mr. Balandin would spot us and stop the class until we got out. He usually only noticed when the boys would show off for us with who could jump the highest, attempting tricks Balandin didn't approve of. *You will kill boys here. Leave or I don't start class.* His hands would rest on his hips, and Hannah and I would blow kisses and wink as we strutted out.

Even though Kyle is smiling, I can see sadness in his eyes. I haven't been able to watch anything of me dancing for obvious reasons. How does he? I don't know. Maybe it's how he copes.

"You were good. No wonder Stanford wanted you."

He looks straight ahead. "Th-th-they almost revoked my admission."

Right, some actions require consequences. "Sometimes we get second chances." It feels like the right thing to say. It's what the psych told me. I've got another chance at life, and it's perfectly normal not to know what to do with it. He looks at his watch. "Sure you don't want to just call your dad?"

"No, no. If you're tired of waiting, it's okay to leave me." I hope he doesn't.

"No way." He looks at me again. "Th-th-thought you . . . wanted to get out of here?"

I do. If I had a dad in the sense Kyle is thinking, I would call him. "I'd rather wait for my mom." Anyway, I'm beginning to settle into Kyle's company again. There's silence again. Not awkward—needed.

"G-G-Genie, do you know her?" Kyle nods toward a woman with teal scrubs on. She's staring at me quizzically. I know those eyes. They're Nolan's eyes. It's his mom, Ms. Long.

I find myself holding my breath as she comes over to me. "I thought that was you, Genie."

The one and only.

"Hi, Ms. Long. . . . I thought you worked uptown."

"I transferred here a few weeks ago. You must think I'm

horrible." She hugs me. "I have to tell Nolan I finally saw you. Where have you been hiding?"

Let's try "People I Don't Want to Talk To" for one thousand, Alex.

"I've been home since the accident."

Ms. Long touches her heart as if it might drop. "Nolan's been so upset about the accident. Haven't seen that boy cry like that for years," she says loudly.

Why not say it a little louder, so the people in the back can hear?

Nolan crying over my fall? That's something I'd like to see. I don't look at Kyle, but I can feel his gaze on the side of my face. We never made it to how I became paralyzed. If she says anything before I can explain . . . I'll do nothing because I'm way punk right now. Still, it's not her story to tell.

"You have to come over for dinner sometime. Get your mom to set you free a bit. That way Nolan doesn't have to sneak over to you." She gives me another hug, but the squeeze says she knows about his visits. "I got to go, but please don't be such a stranger."

Of course he wouldn't tell his mother I broke up with him. I'm sure he also left out the part where he dictated what I wore, constantly texted to keep tabs on me, shoved me, and let me drop off a roof. How convenient, he failed to mention that he ignored my pleas as I looked him in the eyes. I feel my head pulse again and I try to ward it off, mashing my forehead into my palm. *Where are you, Mom?*

"Y-y-your mom will be here soon," Kyle says, like he's reading my mind.

I know he's figuring it out. I close my eyes, trying to block the noise from the machines and the crying kids. How am I supposed to take control of my life when everything comes back to Nolan? It doesn't matter if I tell myself he's irrelevant. Nolan is relevant. I'll never forget him. I won't forget how he made me feel when we first met, or how he comforted me when I was needy. Nolan was my first love, and although he loved me, he hurt me. Every time I think about my abortion, I think of him. Whenever I transfer into my chair, I think of him. If only he'd helped me, I'd still be dancing. Even if he'd hesitated, I would still be grateful.

We've reached the end of what we had and he's dragging it out. Kyle's fingers entwine with mine. I sharply suck in air. He doesn't say anything. I don't pull my hand away. I don't want to. Taking a chance, I lean my head against his shoulder, and as I suspected, he doesn't shake me off. I focus on his slow breathing, reminding myself to mimic it. If Nolan had helped, I wouldn't have met Kyle. And if there's one good thing coming from my accident, it's Kyle. I only hope Ms. Long manages to leave Kyle out when she tells Nolan she saw me here.

I close my eyes, trying to block out the chaos of the emergency room. I try to remember the calming circles Kyle performed on the pommel horse, the rhythmic primal music each time his legs rounded through the air. The beating of his hands as they slapped the bars. The rosin on his hands, like mine on my feet before taking the stage. We cast magic. Kyle and I are like the circles we turned. Going round and round. My fall. His crash.

"He let me fall," I murmur.

Kyle's thumb outlines smooth circles on my hand. I don't

think he knows how much it helps. My body tingles as he leans his head on mine. This is talking without words. Something Nolan and I never could do.

I've been protecting Nolan all this time. Leaving him out of it. Unintentionally allowing him to be made a hero. The one who called for help. Of course, he's sweating me. He knows he'll never get me back.

Mom's voice makes its way to me before she comes into view. Quickly, I slide my hand from Kyle's embrace and sit up. Worry blankets her face and she looks surprised to see Kyle, hesitating before she talks. "Genie, I'm so sorry. As soon as I speak to a doctor, we're gone."

I distance myself, moving over from Kyle. "Finally, let's get the doctor, then."

"Hold on. You must be Kyle," she says, not taking her eyes off him.

"Mom," I groan. "Bring me my chair."

"Hi, n-n-n-nice to meet you." Kyle leans forward, extending his hand. The one I was holding.

She shakes his hand. "Thanks for being Genie's company." She used the same tone when I first introduced her to Nolan. The voice of distrust. "I'm sure your parents want you home by now."

"They know ... w-w-where I am. It's ... n-n-n-no ... problem." His voice is markedly more distressed than usual. Nolan never got intimidated around her. He was confident, cool, even arrogant at times, like he had no need to worry about what she thought of us—him. He took pleasure in going against her wishes. *Imagine her face when we move in together,* he'd plot in the dark.

"The doctor, Mom. Find him so we can go." I try to take the attention off Kyle. Something kicks me to protect him. Veiling Nolan's part in my accident is me protecting myself. Making sure Mom was down for the night before allowing him to hop through my window was all me thinking about me. I didn't want to protect him. I flaunted Nolan in front of her every chance I got. But not Kyle. She can't look at him the same way she looks at Nolan.

Her eyes shift from me to Kyle to back at me. "Tone, Genie. I'll be back." She keeps looking back as she talks to a nurse at the nurses' station.

"She can be so rude," I tell him.

Kyle positions his crutches on his arms.

"I'm sorry," I apologize.

"She's o-o-only worried. She d-d-did almost lose you once."

Damn, Kyle's right. I look down, wringing the blanket as if it's wet. "Still rude."

"P-p-parents call it protecting you."

I cross my arms over my chest, not willing to look up at him. It'll be easier to let him go this way. The state of Mom's eyes when she walked in. She blames herself. Any chance of her lowering her guard again is slim to none. My breakup with Nolan makes her happy, but she can sense my connection with Kyle. The broken-not-broken club.

"You should go before she comes back." I don't budge. Being still means business. Piss off a dancer, and they'll stand still.

"I—I—I don't mind s-s-staying." His innocent tone tells me he doesn't get it. It's just making it harder for me.

"Thank you for keeping me company, Kyle." I keep my voice as flat as I can. "Mom's here now. No need for you to stay anymore."

"I—I—I c-c-can bring your chair and we'll . . . B-B-Bonnie and Clyde it out of here." He snorts a bit at his own joke. I would laugh too if it were the time.

He stops laughing when he realizes I haven't even cracked a smile or met his eyes. I want him gone by the time Mom comes back. I don't want her to look at him like that again. "Just go, Kyle." I surprise myself with how sharp my tone is, mimicking my mom when she told Dad not to call home again, to stop existing in my life. But that's not what I want.

"I—I—I—I—I—I . . . uh . . . I . . . o-k-k-kay." His speech sounds like it's been tossed down a garbage disposal.

He stumbles trying to move faster than he's capable of going. I cringe like I'm watching his dismount from the pommel horse. Even out of sight, I can hear his clunky movements. As Mom walks back in and notices Kyle isn't here, a small smile creeps onto her face.

I tell myself I was protecting him.

CHAPTER EIGHTEEN

The Other Genie

G enie, Genie! Over here! Who are you wearing?"

"*Shame & Regret. Shoes by Trying to Make Things Right. Thanks for nominating* The Breaking Pointe *this awards season.*"

Okay, so I'm a little in my feelings coming down the red carpet of St. Nicholas again. Two days ago, I told Gabrielle I was sick, which was why I couldn't make it in, but I can't keep the charade up with Mom anymore. I had to come clean on avoiding this place. I'm surprised Mom didn't follow me after I told her Kyle did his community service right here too. I guess she weighed having me here with Kyle versus not here at all. And as awkward as it'll be, it has to be done. I volunteer now, and deep down, Mom really wants this on my résumé for college season. And I enjoy it too. We have more than loving ballet in common.

Kyle stares at his phone screen as I creep on him again, same as the first time. Unlike that time, I'm not excited. He looks so absorbed with whatever he's watching, I think it might pull him in. The room is lonely, not like 105. Quiet, except the music coming out of his phone speaker . . . Something familiar. It's not until

I hear the pluck of the strings do I realize it's from *L'Histoire de Manon*. And then the announcer says my name, and I know what he's watching. Me dancing. And I don't know whether to be angry, shocked, or pleased by the look in his eyes. Like he just stumbled on something he never knew he needed to see.

I clear my throat and hope for the best.

Kyle doesn't look up. "Just taking a quick break. My head." He lamely rubs it. "R-really, I'm okay, Gabrielle," he says, flat.

"Just okay?" I ask. "Surely my dancing is more mesmerizing than that. I won first place with that variation."

Kyle's head springs up. "G-G-Genie!" He fumbles with his phone. Every press of his finger does the opposite of what he wants. The video starts and stops in tune with his fumbling voice.

"Wow, did you just play the disability card?"

For the first time, I watch him aggressively rub the nape of his neck. "I n-n-needed to not feel like . . ." A heavy sigh escapes him instead of the word. "F-f-feel like wanting to crash a car into . . . s-s-something."

"I should've handled it differently. Texted you or something. Please forgive me."

His neck snaps back. "F-f-forgive you?" The tone of his voice stops and starts my heart. He flings a chair to his left. His phone goes with it, and it becomes a game of pool as it hits two boxes, breaking the stack. His mouth works overtime but nothing is coming out of it.

If I were him, I would want me to keep my distance, so I stay back and peek out into the hall to see if anyone is curious about the commotion. No one's hearing any of this. The chair to his right slides across the room next, going farther than the other chair. Kyle holds his side, eyes watering with pain. Must be a bruise. Not sure if it's from before or now.

I roll forward with the same hesitation in my voice. "Kyle . . ."

Crunched over, only his eyes move up. "I—I—I watched you because"—he winces—"my competition v-v-videos just added to my anger. Not you. B-b-but me. I thought we were becoming friends, but maybe I don't deserve one after Dylan."

"I'm sorry he died."

"H-he's not dead . . . in a coma . . . because of me."

"Oh . . . Kyle. What happened?"

Kyle shakes his head.

"It's that messed up, huh?"

"D-D-Dylan was great, r-really good. Olympic material. He decided he was going . . . to train at this center in O-O-Oklahoma."

His mouth closes sharply, and all I can think is I've pushed him when he's not ready. But he rolls his neck and cracks his knuckles. "S-s-so before he left, we decided to have some drinks, get high. H-h-he was t-too s-s-stoned to take the train home . . . a-a-and, being stupid, I offered to d-drive instead of saying he could spend the night. I crashed us."

Kyle's hands are so big they cover his face, but they might as well be see-through because I can see the hurt all over him, as the tears rush to his chin.

"Here, let me—" I stop before saying *help*. He doesn't need it, but I would like to help. My bag has everything but what I need, as

I search for a tissue. "Can I?" I ask him once I find the tissue, holding it like some sort of white flag.

He nods and I wipe his eyes, dotting them gently down to his chin. His cheeks are warm and soft and that makes me self-conscious about how calloused my hands are these days. So I stop and back out of his face. I don't think I ever handed Nolan a napkin to wipe his mouth.

"Instead of actual punishment I get a slap . . . on the wrist and s-s-some community service," he continues.

"Well, that's not your fault."

"Y-y-yes it is, because my parents could afford . . . good lawyers for me and use my p-p-previous concussions to say I wasn't in my right mind." His face is red with anger or embarrassment. Either way, I understand where he's coming from.

"You do extra time because you feel guilty? You can't put that all on yourself, Kyle. Dylan made a choice too."

"B-b-but I was driving." His voice goes into a fragmented falsetto.

"And you're paying for it."

"It's not enough."

"When is it, though?" I'm asking not only him, but myself. I can't keep beating myself up for something I can't change. I made choices too. But it's easy to feel trapped. I look around the table, wondering what to do next, because we need a distraction. There's a pile of bookmarks printed with positive affirmations on them, along with the church's logo at the bottom. I can't think of anything uplifting to say. Kyle defeatedly puts his head down on the table.

"What's the point of all these bookmarks if they don't help in moments like this?" I ask him.

If Kyle were a dog, his ears would perk up. "'You only . . . lose the f-f-fight when you give up,'" he mocks, picking up one of them.

"Here's my favorite: 'Step into the new you.'" A woman poses outside the church, her arms open and inviting. I turn it over to read a list of things they offer here.

We give matching scoffs; our eyes meet. That's my cue to get closer. If there was an orchestra, the string section would finger-pluck the beats between us. I park in the space he created from sending the chairs to the corner of the room.

"I'm realizing I'm a stress-eater and would kill for a snack," I say.

"I got a blunt," Kyle suggests, putting the bookmarks in baggies with some stickers and pens, which is an upgrade from the pencils.

I think my lips just got caught in my casters. "You smoke still?" I fail at not sounding judgmental.

"P-p-promised my parents I'd quit after I s-s-split my head open." He gives me the silent finger. "But it relaxes me," he whispers.

"That explains the chill."

"Th-th-the TBI helped." A grimace takes over as he straightens himself up in the chair.

"Aren't you full of surprises?"

"You too."

"I'm a fuckup."

"W-w-we all are. At l-l-least you didn't take someone's life. He may never wake up."

"Debatable," I mumble.

He doesn't say anything. The silence between us gets louder. I consider leaving, the opposite of what I want. We're both angry and frustrated. If he were Nolan, the anger would turn to lust, and I wouldn't have to confront whatever the problem was. Sex would be so easy to fall into right now. Watch his face change from hurt to pleasure. But Kyle isn't Nolan. I have to use my words to make this right.

"So . . . you were doing your research on me?" I nod to the phone on the floor. The video of me as Manon, frozen mid-pirouette.

He picks it up. "T-t-trying to understand you."

Kyle looks farther than at me—in me. Like he can see right into my foolishness with Nolan. I think if he stares any longer or harder, he'll see what I'm afraid of.

"Before . . . how did watching yourself not anger you? When we watched your videos?" I ask.

This brings him back to looking at me.

"Sometimes it did. B-b-but I like to remember. E-e-even if it's just walking to the vault."

I try to put myself in his shoes. Must be hard knowing that if he bumped his head harder, he'd be sitting for the rest of his life. Or like Dylan. Not waking.

For me, it's not being able to feel weightless, or not feeling what it's like to look as if I'm walking on air, to spin on my toes, the sensation of doing something as simple as a plié or testing my balance doing an attitude on pointe. All forgotten by my legs, but vivid in my memories. I have to be okay with that.

"That's not the same for me," I tell him. "I wasn't going to change the world by walking. Dancing was my revolution."

Kyle moves his chair so close his knee touches mine. I wish I could feel it. His head tilts as he listens in, and I can see an eyelash on his nose.

"Do you know how hard it is to become a professional ballet dancer? Even harder to become principal, and even harder when you're not white."

Kyle sports the *go on* look.

"A lot of the ballets weren't made for people like me. Many of the best schools don't accept people who look like I do. Even if we have the talent, bodies like mine aren't classic enough. They can easily pass us over, color aside." I think about when I auditioned for VAB. At twelve, I was reminded that I was busty. I put on two bras just to make sure I had enough support. "Ballet was getting a new face. A new body. A Genie. I was making dances with girls like me in mind. We're going to stand out anyway, so might as well stand out in a piece that's made just for me. Now, I feel like I've . . . let other Genies down."

"I d-didn't know . . . it was so . . . hard."

"It's not exclusively ballet. How many gymnasts at your level are brown like you?" I ask.

He thinks. "Not many." The revelation sparks on his face. "My p-parents are white. My l-life would've been different if my b-birth mom k-kept me." He sighs. "I'm g-good because of my training, and I have good . . . training because my parents could pay for it." He frowns.

"I didn't know you were adopted."

He nods. "L-l-lucky to have them."

As much as I find it hard to admit, I'm lucky Dad paid for the best five years of my life. "VAB has scholarships, but they're based on need and not so much on merit, because everyone is great there. Mom makes a decent living, but quality training is expensive. She never spoke to me about the financials, and I never questioned how I was able to just show up the first day of class. Now I know Dad came in. I know it couldn't have been easy for her to accept his help."

I rub my forehead. "I've said too much," I add.

"Am I g-g-getting closer?" he asks.

I look down at his knee on mine. Then up at him. "To what?"

"The end of your . . . story."

"There's still quite a few pages left to turn."

His phone chirps and he looks down at it. "Chelsea."

"Late for a date?" It slides out, and I immediately hear the jealousy in my voice. I've got to stop doing that. Part of me wants to pry the phone from his hands and tell Chelsea, *I'm with him. He's great. No need to text back.*

That playboy smile—he's enjoying my jealousy. He smushes his lips together, suppressing a laugh. "I-I-I'll tell her I'm all better now that m-m-my Genie is here."

I pretend to flick my hair in true diva fashion. "You seemed to be doing okay watching my videos."

His cheeks go rosy. "I w-w-won't live that down, will I?" His finger pops up like he has an idea. "I'll let you touch my hair . . . if y-y-you let me finish watching this Manon that won first place."

"You say it like it's simple."

"It is. I s-see the way you look at my hair." He grins. "Might help." His face gets serious again.

He's attempting to actually help. . . .

I try to think of a way to shut his proposal down, but I can't. He didn't tell me it *would* help, he said *might* help. As weird as it sounds, his uncertainty is comforting. He isn't telling me how it'll be. No, Kyle is saying there's only one way to find out. Maybe I just have to think of grieving as steps in ballet. We only get to the full combination by putting what we learn all together. Kyle's way ahead of me in this grieving thing.

"Deal," I tell him.

"I'm h-here if you need a hand."

He gives me one long look before pressing play. I come to life like the toys from *The Nutcracker*. My chest rises as I take a deep breath. I still remember how hot my feet got before going on. Manon was a dream role for me. I especially loved this variation because of how the movements were suggestive and sultry, yet picked up on a dime into something more powerful. With this piece I could add my personality. Like Manon, I was torn between two loves. Hers were Monsieur GM with his wealth, and Des Grieux, her love for whom involved a lot of questionable choices for them to be together. Me, I was stuck between Nolan and ballet.

I watch myself reach for my invisible lover, and a gasp escapes me. I was so happy at that moment. Even now I remember how the lights warmed my skin. The way my maroon dress brushed my thighs as I covered every inch of the stage.

The curtsy when my performance ended was like a kiss at the

end of a letter. I wrote a love letter to the judges about my passion for ballet, for the stage, the lights, the audience, the story—all in under three minutes. In under three minutes again, my life has changed. The ache I feel from missing ballet has intensified just from watching this short clip. I won't be able to do that again, but maybe if I can create a ballet for someone to feel the way I felt—even just for three minutes—that would make things better.

"H-h-how'd that feel?" Kyle asks, leaning forward to see my eyes that are staring straight ahead.

"I feel . . . I don't have a word for it." How can I describe pain, joy, disappointment, and gratitude? Watching isn't the same as being able to step foot, or a wheel, in my case, in a studio. Will my face still catch the natural sunlight from my height now? Will the barre block my face in the mirrors? I still don't know if I can brave it.

"Y-y-you don't have to have one." He grabs my hand. "Y-you'll get through it."

I'll get through it. Dance is hard. We have good days. We have bad days. You all learn from me. You will get through it. If you don't, well, you get through to something else, Miss Kuznetsova said. I was twelve when she said it. I thought I was invincible. It became truer when I got to high school: harder academic classes and even harder dance classes threatened to kill my sanity. But I could solve any problem and finish any lab easier than I could please Miss Kuznetsova.

I squeeze Kyle's hand back. "Thanks." I give him a smile. "Now I want to touch your hair!"

"Hold on." Getting up, he grabs his forearm crutches and

hobbles to the door with the library. He opens it and looks back at me. "N-Narnia awaits."

There's so much space in this room now. Kyle has cleaned out a good portion of it, moving most of the things to the right side of the room. Using his crutches, he drags a rug front and center. It's definitely not from this room. The gold trim is way too bright, and there's no trace of dust. This was brought in by him.

"Magic carpet? Did you bring this in here?" I ask.

Out of breath, he just nods and begins his slow descent to the floor. While I'd rather do anything but transfer to the floor, I do it for Kyle. Now on his back, he looks like he's at the beach, tanning. His shirt crumples, showing me his side.

With patience, I bend my legs to cross. Kyle puts his head on my lap. At first my fingers only graze. Puppy soft. My fingertips tingle as they nestle deeper. His curls wrap around me as if they're responding to my touch.

"F-f-feels better than it looks, right?" Kyle says.

While some parts of his head are smooth and silky to the touch, I can feel the coarseness of his injury. Before I understood his hurt. Now I can feel it. *Gayane's* "Lullaby" plays in my head. My fingers dance on his scar, small, gentle circles. Too far. I stop. "It really does."

"D-d-don't stop. . . . Y-y-you're good with your hands," he mumbles. "S-s-sorry! That sounded d-d-dirty."

I laugh. Probably too loud. "Dancing doesn't just stop at your wrists or ankles. I follow through to my fingers and toes."

"I s-s-still s-see it—happiness . . . you have for . . ." He stumbles out of rhythm, but he doesn't need to finish it.

We stay quiet as Kyle settles on my lap. The girl with the attitude problem bumbles in, box in her arms. "Y'all just relax while some of us do everything," she says. She rolls her eyes at us before she steps out the room. We could be in so much trouble, but I don't care. It feels like the moment when I'm so focused that nothing else matters. This is why people dance. To inspire, to talk in a language everyone understands, even just a little bit. I know I can't be that Genie again. But this Genie can make another dancer feel like that Genie.

I still wished night after night, even hours after my accident, that I could be onstage again. I wished so much that these prestigious awards and competitions had a choreographer award for youth. There would be no contest. I'm that good. Like Balanchine, Petipa, or MacMillan good. I love the idea of other girls performing a variation I've made from a ballet. Even better, awarding someone with the "Genie Davis Choreography Award."

I didn't believe until now that I don't have to be the one onstage. How many productions keep the original choreography? Great choreography lasts longer than a dancer's life. It's timeless.

I need to help Hannah with "Magic."

If she ever speaks to me again.

CHAPTER NINETEEN

Tricks

On this episode of The Breaking Pointe, *Genie sustains an "um" for record time.*

Hannah and I have made it to Shake Shack, and it was no easy feat. I called her after I came home from St. Nick's, and she wouldn't even talk to me. Then, in true Hannah fashion, she just exploded. Told me she never knows what she's going to get with me. That she needed to protect her sanity. Of course, I agreed and offered to buy us lunch. Said I'd wait for her and secure a table. That she could show up or not.

Now her Chick'n Shack crumbles in her fist. I remove her Shack from her hands and set it down, pushing her cheese fries in front of her. "Here. Be mad at the crinkle fries. Don't take it out on the Chick'n Shack. It's way too expensive."

"I don't get why you're still entertaining him."

"He won't leave me alone. I don't know what to do."

When I called to patch things up with Hannah, I knew I'd have to answer for something. She asked if I was done being salty, and I told her about Kyle and the hospital. I wish she'd let it go about Nolan, though.

Hannah waterboards her fry, dunking it aggressively into the cheese, looking at me as she does it. "Genie . . . he's using you."

"I know." Now I'm doing the same with my fries. "We're fighting like my parents."

"He's a stupid ass," she says, moving on from her fries to her shake with her straw between her teeth.

"Not arguing there. I also don't want to fight with you anymore."

Her eyes get misty. "Me neither. What were we fighting about again?" We do our special promise swear. Kissing our hand, then heart, our hair and feet. "But I do want to talk about Kylito and what's going on there."

I fill her in more on Brooklyn Bridge Park, not glossing over my stitches either. "We do some work at St. Nicholas together. It's nice having someone who understands . . . what's happening with a new body."

"That explains the Verrazzano. Does Nolan know?"

"No, he doesn't, and I'd like to keep it that way. Ms. Long must've pitied me somehow. The only place I can be sure he won't bother me is at the studio. And you deserve to dance the best piece ever. I deserve to see it happen. I can't have you looking busted. So I'm going to come to VAB and show you how to work real magic."

"For real?" Hannah bangs her cup on the table. She takes in some air. "No way! Yes! I've been—wait—what made you change your mind? I thought stepping into the studio would make you melt."

"Well, bring a mop. Everything's been so . . . hard and unfair.

I'm so proud of you, Hannah." My voice flies away from me. "It—I—it doesn't seem real—not dancing together. You're practically eating croissants already."

"I wish . . . ," she groans, picking at her sandwich and then putting it on the table. "It's not going to be the same without you. We made plans to do it together." Hannah sighs. "But we still are going to do it together. Just differently than we planned."

I know all too well how plans can be changed or ruined. If I'd picked the movies that night, I wouldn't wake up sweating and screaming. Focusing on that is counterproductive, so I lift my strawberry shake and clink it with Hannah's. "I can't control what might happen when I get there. How bad is Maya? Wait—no—don't tell me. I need to go in with an open mind." I wipe the air in front of me like a clean slate.

"Oh please, Genie. You know you already have a list of insults waiting."

"Critiques, not insults. She's going to murder my genius work if I can't whip her into shape. Then you can kiss Paris goodbye, and I'll never work as a choreographer."

We both laugh. I miss the high-pitched laugh Hannah has. It's like listening to a child being licked by a puppy.

"Maya's coming to my par—get-together. Are you bringing Kyle?"

I actually think about it. Not much for wanting to share Kyle right now. He's been super supportive and we're connecting in this way that I can't name, but it's like finding the perfect combination to the music you have. Or the right music to the combination. Something is working between us.

"No, not this one." I text Kyle a quick Hey. "It'll be nice to be somewhere else for a change. Nolan won't just pop up."

Hannah gives me the sucks-to-be-you smoosh lips. "He's too intense for me to jump in there."

"He'll just have to deal with me having something better to do. Duh."

Kyle texts back a smiley face. I'm glad he's feeling much better. After "Magic" I definitely have to see him, show him some of my other magic tricks.

CHAPTER TWENTY

Back to the Barre

I watch as a few VAB students file out of the high-rise. Mondays are meh, but Mondays after VAB were always great. A new week to improve. A new week to remember why I danced. That used to be me. Dance bag slung across my shoulder and all. I can tell just by looking at them what year they're in or if they're just here for the summer intensive. Whether they're visiting or local, they all share something in common—pride with a pinch of ego. There's a certain aura that beams from ballet dancers. Something that says, *I can do something extraordinary*. Half of them probably think they're so special that nothing will end their dance career. The other half won't even make it professionally. And I'm sitting in the car just staring at them. I haven't even popped off my seat belt.

There isn't anyone from my class leaving. It makes me suspicious. I bet the minute I go in they'll all come prancing out like "Waltz of the Snowflakes." Then there's the chance Kuznetsova will be making her rounds. She'll be the hardest to face.

"Hey, you aren't still upset about wetting the bed this morning, are you?" Mom asks, finally turning the car off.

Don't remind me. "Yes. I mean no. I . . ." I wish that were it. This is like being away from home for so long, you wonder if you should use your key or knock out of respect.

"If you want me to turn back around, I will." Mom shifts in her seat to look at me. "You have to want it yourself."

I keep my eyes on the front door. "No. I'm getting out. Waiting for it to die down a little."

I don't know what's going to happen once I pass through that door. Everyone knows who I am here, regardless of the wheelchair spoilers.

Sorry-not-sorry, I was a big deal here. People that used to look up to me will literally look down. Still, I make a mental note of who I would be okay seeing. The way my insecurity is set up, Chris would be nice, but I'm not counting on it.

Mom gives me a slightly worried look before she turns to biting her nails. "Let me know when you're ready."

"Feels like cars will be flying by then," I stall, hoping she'll talk and give me more time.

"I felt the same the first time I stopped drinking. That things would be so changed before I actually had the guts to quit."

"That's just it. Things changed the minute I hit the ground, Mom. I'm so . . ."

Mom looks directly at me.

"Embarrassed."

She nods. "Genie, it's scary, taking the time to heal. No one hates you for it. If anything, they'll be happy for you. Your chair doesn't limit you. That's why you're even here." Her door flies open and she quickly gets out.

With my eyes I follow her as she walks around the front of the car. Then my door opens and she's crouched beside me. "I've been coddling you. But not anymore," she says matter-of-factly. "I will not be Giselle's mother," she adds, holding my hands and kissing each one. Even quicker, she sets my chair up for me.

I transfer into my chair, mouth hanging open. "*Giselle* reference. Mom, two, Genie, one," I tease.

Pointing myself toward the front door, I look back at Mom and shake my head, but a smile works its way out of me too. "Thanks, Mom."

She gives me a small wave before getting back into the car. "Call me when you're close to leaving." She restarts the car, pulling off a little faster than I would expect her to leave, but if she's feeling like me, it's to save face, because my "allergies" are acting up.

The door is heavy, but I manage to get it open enough to push myself through. The clerk is out on a break, so there's nothing in the entry but a small photo gallery of the school. Most of the pictures here are of Kuznetsova, back when the school was growing from a hole-in-the-wall. One room. Barely enough windows. It might as well have been a basement. Now Kuznetsova has this beautiful multi-floor space, with many more than the five students she started out with. But there are other photos. Kuznetsova back in Russia. Dressed in luxurious costumes of the Bolshoi, her posture tall and confident. She stands the same now. Even at her mature age.

I have to lean my head back to glance at them now. I need to put as much distance between me and the front door as possible; otherwise I'll be tempted to leave, so I head for the elevator, but I can't bring myself to press the button. Feels like I'm phoning home, the way my finger is out, wobbling as if pressing the button might collapse the whole building. The front door opens and two girls no older than twelve walk through, giddy with laughter. I press the button quick so I don't have to listen to them laugh like Hannah and I did every day after we first met. Luckily, the elevator is at the lobby. The door opens and without a thought I hurry in. Just like old times, Ellie the elevator makes a *klip, klip, klip* noise as it rises. "How's it been, Ellie? Probably don't recognize me coming in here alone, or . . . sitting. You sound the sa—" I'm on the third floor now.

I roll out onto the eggshell-painted floor. It's eerily quiet. No piano or music coming from any of the rooms. *Slackers.* I look down the hallway and expect one of the lights to flicker, signaling that a murder is about to happen. Hannah's probably in studio four—the cozy room. The room I turned a million pirouettes in, working over my technique, my presence, everything I learned. It's where anyone knew to find me in this place. It's perfect for just three people. I turn my chair in the right direction, but I can't move. *Who is that?* A tall broad-shouldered figure backs out of the boys' changing room.

Chris? Who else walks like a prince even out of tights? Open chested, extended neck, and feet in first position. *Has to be him.* I've only had his hands on my hips for practically five years straight.

"I know I'm a bit shorter now, but someone had a growth spurt."

Chris stops in place. His head tilts, but he doesn't turn around. "No way. Can't be."

"Drop me and die," I laugh.

"Definitely Genie!" He turns around and walks to me, slightly faster but still regal. I want to extend my hand out to him for old times' sake. Have him finger-turn me or control my pirouettes again. "I'm going to hug you," he warns me.

I'm so grateful for the warning. I get lost between his expansive shoulders and feel his arms tighten around me. If I weren't buckled in, he'd lift me out of my chair. "Okay, okay. Let me breathe." I pull away from his arms. Logan's arms still have nothing on Chris's.

"I've missed you so much. I sent you cards and flowers. You went pretty dark. So happy to see you. Class just isn't the same anymore." His eyes light up. "I think Hannah's still here somewhere."

The sides of Chris's hair are shaved into an undercut. Just the top of his head houses his legendary shag. "You cut *the* shag?"

"New partner, new look." He rubs his hands over the top of his head.

So much time has passed. It's more than changing hair. He looks more company than schoolboy now. "Who's this new partner?"

"Maya." He shrugs slightly. "I'm still getting used to her. She's good. I'm back to the whole starting-over thing. I'm in need of Genie therapy again, that's for sure."

Figures it'd be Maya. Can't do anything about that, though. But I will have to chat with her about how to work with Chris. He just needs to be given tough love. You can be a perfectionist without second-guessing every step, especially when you're learning to lift a girl over your head.

"You're a great dancer, Chris. Believe in yourself. Just remember: you drop her, you die."

He laughs, but his face changes to sour. "How can I forget?" Chris walks backward and sits on one of the benches that everyone crowds around before and after class. I follow him down the hall. "I can't believe the last partnering we ever did was *Manon*." The way he says it makes me feel like a child that grew up while he was away.

"Forever ago, right?" Shortly after *Manon*, I realized I was pregnant. Spring seems so long ago now. I'm so glad I got to dance it with Chris without the weight (ha!) of knowing I was pregnant. It explained so much of my nausea after dancing and how much faster I got winded. "I'm glad you were my last partner. Thanks for dealing with me."

"Dealing with you?" He shakes his head dramatically. "You're a legend, Genie Davis. More than you know." His eyebrows wiggle suggestively.

I peer at the spot where the cast list goes up. I always had a reason to be happy there. "Is Kuznetsova around?"

"Probably in her office. Why?"

"My business."

He sticks his tongue out at me. "What brings you here, anyway?"

"You'll learn at the end of summer."

"Anything to do with those books you kept around and guarded like a Rottweiler?" I'm sure I look surprised. "I've known you since before you started on pointe. You can't hide from me." He playfully pokes me, sending me into laughter.

"Jeez, you ballet boys have no shame using any medium to feel a girl up."

"It's an occupational hazard." Chris checks his watch, scrunching his face. "Sorry to cut out, but I have to go." He stands up and gives me another hug. "Don't stay away so long. We miss you, Miss *Relevé*."

He waves before stepping into the elevator. I wave back, wanting him to stay so I can remember for a little while longer. Chris's voice sounds through the door. "Remember. More than you think," he shouts over the *klip, klip, klip*.

I push toward the last studio on the left. Additional photos cover the walls. These are recent, though. From the past ten years to now. I recognize people that were in their last year when I first started here, standing idly at barres, some smiling at the camera, others caught mid-stretch or in flight, and even a few of Miss Kuznetsova modeling arm placements.

Is that me?

I'm no longer looking at the photos on the wall, but of one on top of the door. There's my headshot and a gold plaque above studio four. *Genie Davis Studio*. That's what the plaque says. I look behind me. Chris is gone. Can't ask him what sorcery this is. I would shout at him to come out and stop playing games, but Miss Kuznetsova hates yelling in the halls. I won't disrespect her rules. I wasn't gone for that long.

I turn around to check the adjacent studio number. That one is three, so this has to be four. Maybe I'm seeing things? No. I know this place too well. My vantage point is different now, but mothers don't forget what their children look like.

"Leave now," Hannah's voice floats from behind the door. A curtain blocks the glass, so I can't see in. "I don't know if she's coming." There's some acid in her voice. "And no one can see this dance until it happens—if it happens."

She? As in me? The door opens and Hannah's head cocks to the side when she sees me. She shoots a death glare at Ashley, Noelle, and Vittoria next. They're the pas de trois to the pas de deux Hannah and I always got cast in. The odalisques from *Le Corsaire*, Hannah termed them.

"Genie!" Noelle shouts. She wears her signature headband to hold back her short hair.

"Genie, you're here?" Maya asks, shoving back Noelle.

I don't have time to answer before Ashley and Vittoria knock me into studio three's door, smothering me with questions and shrieks of surprise and happiness. It's all too much love for this hallway. I can't get my head around them to see Hannah's face. Unlike when Chris hugged me, my body tenses up.

No one was supposed to be here. I wasn't supposed to be seen by anyone. Let alone hugged. I struggle against the girls like they're boulders and not well-trained, serious ballet dancers. My mouth opens to tell them to get off, but I can't say anything. I'm stunned.

"I can't believe you're back!" Ashley's raspy voice scrapes my nerves.

"And in your studio!" Vittoria adds, her Italian accent even fainter since living here for two years.

"Get off her." Hannah raises her voice. "We have work to do, so if you please . . ."

"We just wanted to see Genie. It's been like forever," Ashley says.

"Sorry, Genie," Noelle adds.

"Me too," Vittoria throws in her apology.

"*Out*, girls. See you tomorrow," Hannah says more sternly.

Ashley's doing a bad job at whispering, because I can hear her wishing she had a copy of *Relevé* with her for me to sign. I take in deep breaths, my eyes stinging with water. Maya looks on in awkward silence at me, clutching imaginary pearls.

"Why would you let them be here, Hannah?" I stun myself with how calm I sound.

I want to break on her. Scream at her. Tell her how horrible it is for me to see them all, standing tall, confident, straight out of *Relevé* magazine. There's a storm in me wanting to destroy all their existences.

Hannah has one hand on her hip and the other smoothing the back of her bun. "I didn't say 'Hey, wait around for Genie.' Give me some credit."

"Did you tell them I was coming, Maya? How'd they know?"

Maya's hands quickly unclutch her pearls. "It's news to me. And I would never do that to you, Genie." Her watery blue eyes bounce from me to Hannah.

"Nobody else is here, Genie. I swear," Hannah says.

Smoke is coming out of my nose. At least it feels that way. I look at Hannah again. "No one was supposed to see me. . . ." I can't even raise my voice. I just leave.

I back out the door and roll to the only other place I know. The changing room. I push through the swinging door and glide over the tile floor. The lockers feel like they're closing in on me. What was I thinking coming here? I'm so stupid for thinking I could do this. That I could be of any help. This isn't my world anymore.

My hands clench around my rims. I want to go home but feel trapped there. I want to see Kyle, feel my hands melt into his, and listen to whatever he's always right about. And the studio named after me—what's that about? Isn't that what they only do for dead people? Name places and rooms after them in their honor? I'm dead in the ballet world.

The door swings open behind me. I can hear the scuffle of pointe shoes. "Genie, I'm sorry. I really didn't know they knew. They've been trying to peep at what Maya and I've been doing for a while now."

"I don't care anymore. I'm leaving." Mom can't be too far.

"Don't—please, Genie. We need you. I need you."

"No, you don't."

I'm seriously questioning why she wanted me here so badly. Why'd I agree? Maybe Hannah isn't as nice as I remember, and all she wants is to watch my downward spiral up close and personal. She's finally tired of being my understudy and wants to use my choreography for her company auditions, now that her biggest competition is eliminated.

There I go sounding clinically certifiable again. Hannah's my best friend. But I didn't think I had to send an I'm-trying-to-be-ghost memo.

I hear her take steps forward before she slides down the bench toward me. "Hey, look at me, Genie."

My knuckles have turned into Casper. I don't look at her. I give her the same treatment I gave her when she came to see me in the hospital. The same jealous, hurtful feelings flood my insides. It's like I'm choking. I can see her pointe shoes plain as day. They're stained to match her mahogany hue. Mine are still in my dance bag, never to be worn again. Never to feel the smoothness of a polished studio floor.

Hannah leans forward, craning her neck to meet my eyes. "This must be so hard. I can never repay you for being here for me." There's a strain in her voice. "I'm sorry you're so upset."

My hands visibly shake now. I inhale deeply. *Don't cry, don't cry.* I'm hoping the suffocating feeling passes.

"It's okay to cry, Genie," Hannah says softly. "We're alone. Maya's in the studio."

My head involuntarily shakes *no*. My breathing becomes gulps—short and fast like I'm drowning, gasping for oxygen. Panting noises escape from me as I wheeze, sucking in air. I look at my stomach, how fast it's expanding and contracting against my T-shirt. I didn't even feel like this after my fall. Everything is rushing up. First my stomach gets warm, then my hands, and now my face.

"Stop fighting it, Genie." Hannah's crying herself.

I fix my mouth to tell her to stop telling me to cry and a screeching noise comes out instead. Tears follow. Too heavy to stop with a flick of my fingers. They throw me forward, shaking my whole body. My right foot falls off my footplate, and I don't even care if I wake up with a muscle spasm. My stomach spasms enough as it is.

I can't believe it. I'm crying. At VAB of all places! I don't even have time to catch my breath. Everything's coming out. *My wheels are going to rust.*

Hannah rubs both my shoulders. "It's going to be okay, Genie." She sniffs back tears. "I'm going to light into them tomorrow. Don't worry about those three."

Like they haven't already informed all the class by now. Someone's probably texting *pics or it didn't happen*. That just breaks another levee in me, and it shows no signs of being repaired anytime soon.

Hannah's stretched out across the bench by the time my body stops jerking and rocking, and the only sound left is a dry snivel, periodically, from me. She holds my hand in hers. I look up at the air vent as it kicks into overdrive, letting out a burst of cold air. Definitely what I need to help cool my face down.

"I don't know what came over me," I say.

"You can't hold in emotion. Eventually, it works its way out of you."

I use my free hand to swipe the moisture under my eyes away. "I haven't cried for my accident or the . . ."

"I know. I could tell. I thought I might have to go get Kuznetsova." She pulls at her pink tights.

VAB has always given me time. Time to work on me. Time away from home when it was too hard there. And now time to cry. I've always been my most vulnerable here. I thought it was because I needed to be open and dramatic to tell a story, but really, I've never been comfortable enough anywhere else.

"Sorry, I'm not a crybaby like you." I bring up the first day she cried in this exact spot. Our first day ever at VAB.

"That's low, Genie. That wasn't a dig at you."

"Sorry."

"Forgiven." Hannah gets up and opens her locker, bare because we aren't allowed to personalize anything on it. She pulls out a washcloth, wets it, and hands it to me. "Here, wipe your face. You look horrible."

"So is your turnout," I retort. It's not true and Hannah knows it. She ignores me, continuing to tug on her tights. I accept the washcloth and rub it against my face, allowing the coolness to rejuvenate me. "How long have we been in here? Think Maya left?"

"Don't worry about it, and who knows about Maya?" she says. "Let's find out."

Hannah stands up and I make a Y-turn, pushing through the door. Hannah makes her way to my side once we're both through, and we head down the hall together. Side by side like we used to. "I ran into Chris." I look up at her.

"Like his haircut?"

"It works for him. Dare I say he's cute?" I give myself short pushes as if Kyle's walking alongside me. I don't want to forget this feeling. Safety. I'm safe at VAB.

"He has a girlfriend now. One of the summer intensive girls."

"Good for him." I stop. "Why didn't you tell me Maya was his new partner?"

Hannah's shoulders drop. "The same reason I didn't tell you about the Genie Davis Studio. I wanted you to come back and see for yourself. Stupid now . . . I should've told you, but I didn't think you'd come if I did. You'd see how much things have changed, and you'd cut me off again." She clicks her tongue.

"You had doubts, didn't you?"

The look on Hannah's face says it all. I push forward and Hannah skips ahead of me, opening the door to studio four. I stare at the wooden floor. So, this is it? Finally, back into a studio. I push gently and let the floor take me in farther. I don't know what I expected. A flash of lightning? Birds to fly into the window? Insidious whispering? God Herself to be all *Where ya been, Genie?*

Nothing?

That's it. Nothing happens. I expected all the emotions to flood in the studio and not the changing room.

Maya is laid out on the floor, belly down, arms outstretched, and her legs bent like a frog, with headphones in her ear. Through the mirror she catches my eyes.

"Everything okay?" she asks, taking her headphones out.

I look at Hannah. "We're good."

"What she said," Hannah adds.

"Great," starts Maya. "I'm warmed up again." Her chocolate-brown hair is neatly tucked into a bun. "This is going to be amazing!" She tosses her music into her nearby bag and takes to the center of the floor.

Hannah takes a spot at the barre and looks like she's trying not to laugh, but her mouth isn't obeying because she's snickering rather loudly.

"What's so funny?" Maya looks back at Hannah.

If Maya thinks we're starting with the dance, she's mistaken. Back to the basics. Back to the barre.

CHAPTER TWENTY-ONE

Everyone's Magic

Although we don't have live accompaniment, I still close my eyes and listen to the speakers push out the sound of a piano. Hannah's and Maya's shoes softly scrape the floors in sync to the keys. So far, so good. For now. I'm not getting ahead of myself. I know they can handle the basics. I open my eyes to see Hannah focusing at a spot on the wall, a well-worn look of wanting to get to the good stuff on her face. Maya's been sporting the same quasi-polite smile since I told her we were starting with the barre.

"Keep these up, ladies, and you might be primas," I tell them.

"Not trying to rush your creative process, Genie, but I get it— the basics. Can we move on?" Maya asks, breaking correct head placement to look at me.

I should make her start over for that, but I don't. "Of course. By all means, be mediocre."

Hannah shoots me the same glare she gave to the three odalisques. "Come on, Genie. We've been at the barre for twenty minutes now."

"You of all people should know how I operate, Hannah." I stop the music. "I thought you wanted my help."

I'm stalling, really. I can't mess this up.

"You know I do," Hannah shoots back quickly.

"Then stop breathing down my neck." Maya whistles nervously as she looks on. "Now that the party's really started, let's see some 'Magic' then." I roll backward and wait for them to take position.

Hannah walks to the corner of the room, readying herself, while Maya gives me a doe-eyed look before taking the center. She nods to tell me to start the music. At the first string of the violin, she assumes my pose of my first day at VAB, on pointe, left hand on her hip, right hand outstretched to hold an invisible dance bag. A smile.

Right away I see the problem. Although Maya's piqué tours en manège are technically flawless right out of the gate for the first big combination, she looks like she's thinking about it. Those turns are the whirlwind of emotions I felt. They can't be technical. Not fully. I need to see the passion. I look at Hannah, who patiently waits for her entrance. The music slows down so we can see the theatrics of our introduction. Hannah and Maya sync into a small flight together with some *assemblés*. I notice, of course, that it's not as perfect as Hannah and I were, but no one would bat an eye. Well, Kuznetsova would.

When they close out the music, face-to-face as mirror images, I shut my eyes again. Out of breath, Hannah speaks up. "See what I mean about the failli bit?" She holds her hips as if she'll fly away if she lets go. That's what Hannah does after she dances. My eyes don't need to be open to see it.

I don't respond. Ruminating exactly over the failli assemblés. Maya's was too sweet while Hannah was giving sass in hers.

Hannah and I give lip in a minute, and we can channel it into the air. Docile Maya, however, doesn't have the attitude I worked up for it. This dance is about Hannah's and my friendship through the years. Not just the cute first day.

"I know my chaînés aren't as good as yours," Maya says.

When I don't respond again, Hannah gets annoyed. "You're supposed to help us, Genie. This is your dance. Tell us what we need to fix."

"I know I need a lot of fixing," Maya chirps. "I can handle whatever you have to say."

"Can you guess why my eyes were closed, Maya?" I ask, opening my eyes.

She shakes her head. "No."

I hear Hannah huff.

"My eyes were closed because I'm imagining that Arthur Mitchell is my father, and that Raven Wilkinson is my mother and Alvin Ailey is my cool uncle that everybody loves." It helps to imagine my family as famous dancers and brilliant choreographers. I sigh. "I'm trying to make myself happy before I come out my face and regret something I say."

My attitude isn't because of them. It's because "Magic" isn't magical anymore.

"Thanks for the insult anyway," Hannah sasses me.

"You're welcome. I can play the cripple card and say my feeling of lacking control is manifesting in the need to make your life hell until we fix every step, every turn, and every jump in this dance until I'm happy." I alternate my hands like a scale. "*Or* you can chill out."

Maya takes a seat on the floor and picks her fingernails while Hannah leans on the barre. I rest my face in my hands. Where to start? Dance for sale: everything must go. I know it's harsh to make Maya dance it exactly like me. Hannah and Maya aren't matching because Hannah can't match me anymore. They aren't complementing each other. With Hannah trying to make Maya dance like me, she's not changing how she dances, and it looks a mess.

The way I see it, Maya doesn't know magic, therefore she can't comprehend "Magic." She's great in other roles, like the Sugar Plum Fairy and even Clara, but this is much more real.

"Do you know what magic feels like?" I ask no one in particular. I get no replies. "Magic feels different for everyone. It feels like heat, a tickle, deep pressure, soothing sounds, the perfect taste, or a great smell."

"For me it's staying strong when everything shatters around you. My magic is heavy. I feel grounded with it," Hannah adds.

"I'm not following," Maya says uncertainly. "I can do it over."

"Nope. Don't move unless I tell you to." Maya goes back to picking her nails. I go back to thinking. "I think I'm forcing my magic on you. You need to find your own."

"I thought that was just a Hannah-and-you thing." She looks at me and Hannah, completely lost.

"We're all magic," Hannah adds, and we do our promise swear.

"Thank you, Hannah. So I think we need to come at this dance differently now. Maya, you aren't me. Your magic is different from mine and therefore works different with Hannah's. I can't expect you to tell my story. It has to be your story. Get it?"

"So now it's a story?"

"Now you can get up. Let's try this. How about you're discovering your magic for the first time? Let it be your story. What's magical about you? When do you feel the most powerful?"

"Honest?" Her hands pat her sides. If she had pockets on her leotard, I'm sure her hands would be in them. "I hate wearing buns. My mom . . . she's pretty sick these days and would always braid my hair. But her hands are weak. My brothers aren't very helpful, so I'm the one she relies on. I don't mind it. That's my magic." She stands a little taller.

"Perfect, Maya. The audience needs to see your reliability," I tell her.

Maya hops up and down. "What about four détournés?" She goes on pointe, pivoting in each direction. "Since I'm looking for my magic—if you don't mind!"

I tap my chin. "That would work great if instead of the piqués earlier, you switch into a bourrée en couru, because you're really good at those, and when you sync up with Hannah, I'll see if that fixes the rest of it." I clear the floor. "Good?"

"There's boss Genie." Hannah smiles.

"Let's get to work, then."

"I'm ready," Maya adds, taking the center.

"Magic" got a nip/tuck. It has a new magic to it. Maya's dancing like herself, therefore feeling more like herself. We still have a lot of work to do and I can't promise it'll look the same next time, because I'm about as constant as the A train on a Sunday, but I think Hannah and Maya are done. I keep forgetting that they've been here all day, unlike me.

"I think we can call it for now," I announce as Maya gets up to practice her fouettés.

"Oh, thank God," Maya plops back down and begins taking off her shoes.

Hannah follows suit, unveiling her blistering feet. She makes a pained face, but no noise comes out. Maya lets out a little hiss as she bends her toes.

"I can't remember what that feels like anymore," I say. Hannah and Maya look at each other. Then at me.

"I think you can. It just won't feel the same way. If that makes sense." Maya unravels her bun. "Look at Geoffrey Holder. He was making dances on his deathbed."

Hannah doesn't say anything. She just gives me a comforting smile.

"I'm going to go see Kuznetsova. I'll see you later," I tell them before leaving the Genie Davis Studio. It still doesn't feel real.

I take the elevator down one floor. No one seems to be here either, and I can see Miss Kuznetsova's door open. *Breathe, Genie. It's Miss Kuznetsova. Not a dragon lady.* As I get closer, I can hear her singing in Russian. When I reach the door, Miss Kuznetsova is singing to her plants as she waters them. She tips the water can so gently, but her wrinkled hands are the only things giving away her age.

"Miss Kuznetsova? It's me, Genie," I say to her back.

"Dorogaya moya! My dear, Genie! Of course I know you back!"

She puts down the water can and shuffles over to me, planting two big kisses on my cheeks, saying words I don't understand in Russian.

It's really good to hear her voice. I thought I remembered it well, but hearing her soft, low voice in person is the difference between recorded and live symphonies. There's no comparison.

"It's good to see you, too. If I'd known you'd greet me like this, I would've come up here first."

This is a side to Kuznetsova I'm not used to seeing. If she's tough on you—good. If she's soft—not good. She's mostly tough in class. I know she cares a lot about her students. When it came to me, there was a balancing act. Tough yet kind.

After pushing the chairs in front of the desk to the side, Miss Kuznetsova directs me into their spot. "I knew you come back home." She takes a seat behind her desk.

"Everyone knew but me, it seems." I notice the light gray hair peeking from the corner of her temples. It blends in from a distance with her blond hair. I wonder if I always had my chin up so much, I never noticed.

"Blinded by your own light, Genie. Though you disappoint me too. Don't confuse my excitement. I very mad at you. I tried every day to reach you. Not one reply?"

I have a hard time looking into her blue eyes. "I know. I was afraid everyone would look at me differently."

"Everyone always look at you different, Genie. Not news. Your hair, your skin, your beauty, and talent. You were always different. Now you worry what people think?" She looks at me over the top of her glasses.

The truth is real. I was going to stand out anyway. I couldn't control the fact that my dance friends in elementary school lost interest in ballet, thought it wasn't cool, or were lured away for various reasons by bigger schools. So my bun took longer to do—I have 4C curls, dammit. Besides physical looks, I stood out because I was good and I just happened to be Black. All out of my control.

There is no diversity card in ballet. It took years to get to where I was. That's why coming back here hurts so much. Why did I work so hard to have it snatched from me? Would my injury sting as much if I weren't so good? If I hadn't put in the time?

I scratch my head. "I can't walk anymore. I can't even point my toes, Miss Kuznetsova. That's something to worry about." I do my best to hold a steady look, but I end up staring at a ballerina figurine on her desk. "If it wasn't such a big deal, then why'd you name the studio after me?" I hope my attitude doesn't come off as me trying to be rude. I'm not. I don't think people realize how hard it is being here. Even if everyone is so accepting and happy to see me.

Miss Kuznetsova leans forward, folding her hands on her desk. I prepare myself to be cursed out or banished, but she smiles. "My school. I do what I want." She leans back and studies me. "I know what happened to you is tragic. Do you know why I started to teach?"

I think back. Not sure I ever knew. I shake my head.

"Back in Moscow, I got a phone call that my father die. I was so upset; I didn't look both ways across the street. A car hit me." There's a down curve of her lips, and she rubs her hands together.

I've seen old footage of Kuznetsova in her heyday. Her talent, combined with the best training in the world: she was a force to be reckoned with. Struck down by a moment of grief, a distraction. I would never have guessed anything got her down. And yet somehow, she's sitting in front of me, one of my biggest inspirations.

"I'm sorry. That's horrible." I suck in my lip. Why did I not know that? I should have.

She swats the air. "I am recovered, as you can see. I tried to go back, but my spot was taken. Even though I had to reaudition with other girls who did not have a serious injury like me, I tried anyway. They say my injury shows. Of course, that was not really true. No one wanted to take me on. I was a liability. Not physically, but my mind. It was like my fire died with my father. I lost what they trained me to be." Her lips curve down again.

"Then you decided to teach."

"No. I left Moscow to be with my mother. I was angry at everyone. Then a teacher I love from school, Raisa Vasilieva, she told me I had talent for working with other girls. She said she wanted me to help with her school she started in her hometown. That is how I start to teach."

But I'm not her. I didn't even get a chance to have my spot back at the barre.

"I can't teach. Those programs require that I be able to dance." No one will certify me if I can't dance.

"Nyet, Genie. Listen. So stubborn." She shakes her head but gives me a motherly grin. "I think you are a choreographer. You create things. Like your audition piece for here. I asked you who made the variation, you said proudly, 'I did.' I watched you in studio for five years. You tell, Genie. Not just with your mouth, but with your body. Your spirit. The stories that come out of your head. I need your help."

"My help? With what?"

"I want to start a program here. A class for kids with disabilities. I want you to help me with it. They should tell stories too, no?"

"No way. I can't do that. You just said I was a choreographer." I'm not a teacher. I definitely can't teach kids that aren't typical. Not even sure if I'm helping Hannah and Maya.

"You are, but you have a new way of seeing life . . . and now, of seeing dance. And I know you will be applying to university. This will help with that, make your mom proud. Yes?" She talks quick and fast because she knows she's losing me. She's got a big point about Mom, though.

The only thing making noise is my phone vibrating against me. I don't bother to look at it.

"I don't know, Miss Kuznetsova. Can I think about it?" If this conversation happened even a few days ago, I would've bounced. Now, it can't hurt to think about it. Miss Kuznetsova deserves that much from me.

"Of course. Let's say at the end-of-summer gala, you give me an answer." She sighs. "Just think about this: all kids deserve to show their magic. Even if they can't stand on their toes."

"Are you really using my magic against me? That's not fair." *Can she do that?*

"We both know fair is not a part of life." She stands up and comes around the desk. "Don't ever stay away again, Genie." If life wasn't fair to Miss Kuznetsova, would I have known her and not just admired her?

I get two pinches and two more kisses before she sends me on my way.

I don't get far. My hands are too sweaty to push. This is all too much for one day. VAB used to be the place I went to, and I didn't have to think or question anything. Ballet was what I did best. Made me feel my best. To leave and feel . . . what do I feel? There's so much to be excited about, to feel relieved about and worried about.

I didn't even run my hand across the barre. Next time. That doesn't sound too scary.

Mom could only get a spot around the corner, and when I roll up to the car, she's on her Switch with that gamer's focus. She doesn't even see me until I knock on the window for her to unlock the door. We do the transferring and chair dance, but when it's over, she doesn't start the car.

"You're going to make me ask, aren't you?" She's twisted in her seat, her right knee digging into the green seat cover. "Please, please tell me everything."

Her excitement is like a bass rattling in my bones. Or maybe it's my happiness too. I didn't think it'd feel like this. I guess I am excited about it.

"I can't lie. 'Magic' is probably my best work ever."

"Cold Stone Creamery it. Would I like it, love it, or gotta have this ballet in my life?" she asks with that mother's these-are-your-only-options tone.

"Gotta have it!"

"I can't wait to see it under all those lights. You've always been good about where things go. That's from me."

"You think everything good I do is from you."

Only when it comes out do I realize she could take it the wrong way.

"Of course I do. But if it helps to know, I would love your choreography even if I weren't your mother."

"I'm listening."

"That right there. The endless need for compliments you do not get from me," she laughs. "More seriously, though, you aren't afraid to push what your body can do. It's the technique of Vaganova with the storytelling of Ailey. And you love to turn."

"No, not love," I correct. "I gotta have turns."

"And what does Hannah gotta have?"

This is something we've never talked about. She's picked me and Hannah up from class on several occasions, but it wasn't like Hannah was spilling her deep love for the art to Mom.

"That girl could jump over the Atlantic."

"She must love your *Relevé* cover."

"Yeah," I sigh.

Mom sighs too. "All that talk about gotta have it makes me want some ice cream. Cold Stone? My treat."

I click on my seat belt in response.

CHAPTER TWENTY-TWO

Gentle Genie

I'm freaking out. All the way out. Everything I did Monday seems stupid. "Magic" feels stupid. Guilt swarms me, on Hannah's birthday of all days. Normally I can push it back. Not today. Now it's too much.

I pick up the phone. "Hannah, I can't make it tonight," I push out as soon as I hear her breath.

"Real funny, Genie. What time are you making your entrance?"

"Seriously, there's something sitting on my chest, it feels like. You don't want me there," I say, tracing the *B* on the ballet book with my finger. "I don't want to ruin a perfectly good Saturday."

"Is this because you're not entertaining Nolan's bull tonight?"

Oh, snap. Maybe that's it. That is it. I'm afraid Nolan will tell the story before I tell it. And Mom and I just got back to a good place. We talked about ballet again after VAB, even days later. And she didn't mention college once or therapy. It was almost like it was before. She was so happy to see me doing something for me. There was excitement about something in the future to look forward to.

"He'll tell her about the abortion, Hannah. She can't know about it. We just got back to good." I don't tell her how Nolan's been acting weird. Like he can tell there's a change in me. A good one that doesn't have anything to do with him. Now he's being super supportive like I care that he's been googling the different prognoses on my injury.

It's quiet on Hannah's end for a little while. "You need to tell her. Talk to someone about it. Don't wait for Nolan to get lonely and angry with you and spill everything."

"I don't want to talk about it to anyone." I put the ballet book down so I don't rip the weak pages out.

"You're impossible."

"I'm fine with it. It's just telling someone about it that makes me . . . So I had an abortion. Why do I need to shout it from the rooftops?"

"Maybe if you had, you wouldn't have fallen from one."

"Woooooow. I don't like this Hannah. Does it turn Dez on or something? Because this isn't you."

"I don't like this Genie."

"I'm angry I had to have one and pissed that I'm not heart-broken over it. At the time it was easy. Abort to dance. Now I can't dance. I'm in a wheelchair, showing you a dance I should be doing."

There's more silence on Hannah's end. She sighs after a while. And I smash a mosquito on my big toe.

"Genie."

"No. Listen. I don't want to tell Mom, because I'm a failure. My decision was a joke in the long run. Ha ha, Genie, go through this procedure to increase your chance for a future. Then—BAM!"

"You're not a failure, and I won't let you think that. Whatever is going on with you and Nolan is you and Nolan. I'll respect that, but Genie, come on. 'Magic' has felt better than it ever has with you this week. That's why you feel like this." She sighs. "You got a taste of you again, and you're back to punishing yourself for feeling happy with what you did in your chair."

There's a mistiness in her voice and I feel even guiltier. I run my hands over my braids. Combing my hair will not be gentle today, but I have to do it. "Fuck, Hannah, I'm sorry to dump this on your birthday. I'm the worst. I'll be there. Let me go make this call to Nolan."

We hang up and I almost feel better. That damn "almost".

Here goes. I press Nolan's number, which is sadly in my most frequent contacts. Nolan answers his phone way too quickly. "Genie, what's up?"

"If you were planning on coming over tonight—don't."

"Why not?" He sounds more confused than angry.

"I have something better to do."

"So, let me tag along. I can help you or something."

"I don't need your stupid help."

"All right. Chill. Fine, go do something else." He hangs up without even a threat, and I don't know what to do with that.

I find pants to put on. Not easy when all my pants besides sweats are skinny jeans. I have two choices of shoes to wear. My beat-up sneakers that'll look ridiculous with what I have on. They're neon orange and pink, and I'm wearing a combination of moss green and shit brown, because it's how I'm feeling. Then there's my shoes

I wore to go see Kyle at the park. A patent-leather Moroccan flat. Fine but a little too formal for this event. Or—and I might be crazy—but I can wear the sandals Hannah and I have.

It has to be the sandals.

As I hold them in my hands, I wonder if I should just call off everything. Wait, that'd make me a bitch after telling Hannah I was still coming. Her present sits on my bed, and I kind of want to ask Mom to take me so I can drop it off and go.

"Those are perfect, Genie." Mom's voice taps me on the shoulder. I turn to see her standing in my door. "You were so excited to get them," she says, stepping in.

"Yeah, well, I can't put them on myself."

"Would you like me to help? I will if you want."

Raising them to her, I say, "Please."

Mom lets out a sigh, as if she was expecting a verbal kick. I watch her lift my foot gently, like she used to when I finished class. It's so different from how she's been touching me lately. As if I'll break and crumble in her hand.

"You don't have to be so nice to my feet. I can't feel it." I'm careful to not sound like I'm bitching at her. She really doesn't have to be.

She stops, still holding my left foot. "Genie, just because you can't feel doesn't mean you can't be gentle with yourself."

There's a brief moment that fills the space between us. I could tell her now about the abortion. She'd die of secondhand embarrassment and feel like she didn't do enough, then blame working on her sobriety when she should've gone over my birth control options. I didn't even tell her I was sexually active. I figured she assumed. How can I jump into "I was pregnant and now I'm not"? I open my mouth as she looks down to fix my sandal, but even telling her gently won't help, so I close my mouth and smile when she looks back at me. No, I can't be gentle with myself. Not on this. If I do, she'll take it hard on herself, and that isn't fair.

CHAPTER TWENTY-THREE

Selfish

O
n this episode of *The Breaking Pointe, Genie feels like the night isn't going to go well, because why would it?*

Before I knock on the door, I take a deep breath and reposition Hannah's gift on my lap. Suddenly the wrapping paper isn't right. It's gold, sparkly, and textured in my hand. Hannah's turning eighteen; maybe a gift bag would've been more appropriate. I just want to go in and forget about the conversation we had earlier, and enjoy whatever snacks I know she has in there.

Hannah lives at the cusp of Fort Greene and Downtown Brooklyn. Her family has lived in this garden apartment for as long as I've known her, but it's gotten a face-lift. The facade is made to look more upscale, with its silver door instead of the comparable wooden ones lining the block. What else has changed? I knock on the door.

He opens it. Dez. It has to be him. I didn't expect him to look so old, though. He has a full beard. An actual beard. "You must be Genie," he says, standing there.

"Yeah. Watch your feet," I tell him, pushing forward so he has to scramble to get out of my way. I just know whenever I see a door to push a little harder to bump over the hump. Everything but the way the couch is set up is the same. Hannah probably did that so I could maneuver easily. She's so thoughtful. "Where's Hannah?"

"Her room. Getting dressed. Maya's here too." He plops down on the couch with a cup that seems to appear from out of thin air.

Maya's here already? I thought maybe Hannah and I could have a moment before everyone arrived. I don't have time to pout, because Hannah and Maya come from around the hallway, giggling. They both smile upon seeing me, and I do my best to return one. Now I wish I'd taken Hannah's offer to invite Kyle over.

"Happy birthday, Hannah."

"Genie, you're here!" Maya gallops over to me. Her hair is in two French braids too, and she notices. "Twinning!"

"Lazy." I point to my head. "Where's the food?" I ask no one in particular.

"Kitchen. I have to take the pigs in a blanket out the oven," Hannah says.

"Did your mom not make empanadas?"

I follow Hannah into the kitchen, glad Maya doesn't feel the need to tag along. Hannah's kitchen is even more boxed in than mine. Hers is short and square and we barely fit in it together. She turns off the oven and takes out the breaded dogs.

"You met Dez." Her tongue sticks out in that silly-emoji way.

"Yes, I've seen him."

She leans on the fridge and makes a motor sound with her blue-painted lips. I actually like the color. It's navy. Haven't seen her wear it yet, but it goes great with her blue floral top and navy skirt. "Cute, right?"

"I mean if you like the Paul Bunyan look, yeah, he's cute."

Hannah smirks at me, rolls her eyes, and puts the pigs in a blanket on a serving tray all at once. Opening the microwave, she hands me a plate with empanadas. "Just for you, mami said."

I sniff the plate. Thank you, Mrs. Hernandez. "I told you I was your mother's favorite."

"You might be right," Hannah says, going back out to where everyone is.

It's dim in here. The only glow comes from some white Christmas lights hanging around the living room. Perfect.

Dez is running his mouth a mile a minute to Maya. I pull up next to the side table with a picture of Hannah's little sister, Leah, back when she was so chubby you could hide coins in her arm rolls.

"Maya, why did I have to hear from Chris that you're his partner now?" I would've asked earlier in the week, but I didn't want to ruin the vibes before we rehearsed.

Maya's eyes get wide and she holds her cheek like I slapped her. "I should've told you. I didn't know how, though. It's for summer only. Until Matt comes back."

"I'm not mad, but I could've told you how to get him not to start over a million times."

"He's so weird with that," Dez butts in.

"It's not weird, and you don't know him like that," I tell him. Not that it's Dez's business, but Chris has told me he struggles with mild OCD, and that's why he got into ballet. The order and control.

Dez looks over at Hannah, who looks at me, and I'm locked and loaded, but Hannah gives me the "chill" eyes and it's her birthday, so it's the only reason I do back off. There's a knock on the door, and Dez saves himself by getting up to get the door he's way too comfortable opening.

"Babe, are you expecting some guy here?"

Hannah, Maya, and I all turn toward the door. "Some guy?" we all ask together.

"Hannah, it's me."

Oh fuck.

Hannah gets up and goes to the door. "What are you doing here?"

"Happy birthday." I hear Nolan say. "I got you a gift." Something crinkles. "May I come in? I saw you were having a party on Instagram."

That explains it.

Hannah looks over at me, and I give her a look to say it's her decision. She used to kick it with Nolan sometimes too. I'm hopeful she'll kick him to the curb until she says, "Ay Dios mío. Don't start anything, okay?"

She and Dez make space to let Nolan in, and I want to scream. Instead of screaming, I twist my hands around my rims hard enough to generate smoke. It's a good thing Chris spends the weekends in Westchester with his grandparents, because I have a feeling Nolan would start some shit with him.

"Hey, Genie."

"Nolan."

I let Hannah do the introductions for Maya and Dez, and we all sit in the living room with the radio playing reggaeton. It's Maya who breaks the silence.

"Let's play truth or dare," she suggests.

"I'm in if Genie is," Nolan adds.

I ignore Nolan and talk to Maya instead. "You're up first, then, Maya. Truth or dare?"

"Truth," Maya chooses.

"Have you ever crushed on anyone from VAB?" Hannah asks.

"Yes . . . Mr. Balandin."

Hannah, Dez, and I erupt in laughter. Maya shrugs coolly, but her face is a fire hydrant. Nolan's eyes glaze over. Good. Maybe he'll leave early.

Dez goes next and chooses a dare to drink hot sauce for ten seconds. Hannah goes after and also chooses dare. To impress Dez, most likely. Her dare is to prank call her dad, which fails miserably, because Hannah is the worst at lying and changing her voice. We can hear him chastising her for making him leave the movie he's in to take the call. He says something about her mom and sister too. It's all good fun as she apologizes through her laughter.

"Truth or dare?" Dez asks Nolan.

"Truth," Nolan picks. His earring glistens against a white light.

"How many people have you screwed?"

I hate how Dez is the only one smiling. Even Maya gives him a funny look. Hannah conveniently turns on hostess mode and grabs the empty plates up.

"Dez, this was a PG game," Maya reminds him.

He sounds as goofy as he looks. "I'm spicing it up."

Nolan looks at me, and I try to keep a straight face but end up chewing on my lip.

"Just one," Nolan answers.

"Got that off your chest, Dez?" I ask.

"Genie, it's just a game." Hannah comes to his rescue.

"Is it?"

"Truth or dare, Genie?" Dez asks confidently and wrongly. I think it's Maya's turn to ask.

"Dare," I say anyway.

"Kiss me."

Nolan pops like a starter gun. "What the fuck you dare that for? And why are you smiling at her like that?"

Oh great, it's Broadway Junction all over again.

"Why would I kiss you, Dez? You're with my best friend."

"Hannah, can't your friends take a joke?" He makes a face that makes me want to shave his beard . . . with tweezers.

"It's not a joke, though, Dez, and you know it," I counter.

"Cheek?"

"Switch kiss with slap and sure."

"Bitch," he says under his breath.

That's all Nolan needs to hear before he lunges for Dez. Used to pissing people off, Dez moves out of the way too swiftly.

"Nolan, stop it," I say.

To my surprise, he stops. Dez struts around Nolan and marches into the kitchen.

"Genie, come here," Hannah calls.

Maya nods at me as if she knew I was silently asking her to babysit Nolan to make sure he doesn't go ape on Dez. I follow Hannah into her room. Her four-poster bed suddenly seems huge to me now.

"Why are you freaking out on Dez?"

"Because he deserves it?"

"It's a game. You're telling me that you, of all people, are pretending to be modest?"

"Because I almost had a baby, I should be okay with kissing guys I never met before in front of my jealous ex?"

"No, I'm saying this wouldn't have bothered you before. What's changed? Even at VAB you've been different—"

"Of course I am. I'm not the same person anymore. I mean, I fucking cried, Hannah. I sat and watched you dance a piece I'll never be able to do. This is exactly why I didn't want to go to VAB or here tonight. Everything's changed."

"I know that, but that's not it. I'm worried about you. And Nolan showed up. What the hell?"

"I didn't let him in. That's on you." I throw my hands up. "We rushed things. Maybe I'm doing too much too soon, with VAB, hanging out with everyone, and I got this thing going on with Kyle and volunteering. . . ." So much has happened in a couple of weeks.

"Genie, if you quit—I can't do this with you anymore. I've been patient enough and so has Maya. I can't sit and wait for you to stop with this punishing thing. I have to move on and so do you."

"So what? You don't want to be my friend if I don't come and watch you dance?"

"That's exactly it."

"That's not an overreaction or anything."

"Is it? If Nolan asked you to be there, you'd make time." With each word her hands clap.

"This has nothing to do with Nolan."

"This is all Nolan, chica. You only move mountains for him, apparently."

"Shut up, Hannah. You don't know what you're talking about." But she's right. I don't blow Nolan off like I do her.

"You okay, Han?" Dez steps his stupid bearded face into the room.

Han?

She walks into his arms. "I'm fine."

"Maybe you should go, Genie," Dez tells me. He's petting her hair like she's, well, a pet. Hannah would never let anyone, especially a guy, touch her curls. I get popped when I try.

"This isn't your house, Dez, and you don't know her like I do."

"You're upsetting her."

"Oh, then stop everything. This is Hannah, Dez. She gets emotional. Hannah, are you really letting this guy step between us?"

"You let Nolan do it."

"Again, with Nolan! You're so jealous of what we had. I bet you're happy I'm in this chair. Guys look at you first now. That's fine. Have Dez, flirt, dance, be happy. Just remember I'll always have the talent!"

"That's fucked up," Dez says.

He's right. Now that it's out, I know I didn't have to take it that far. I didn't have to say anything. I didn't mean it and she wasn't wrong. But I am. "Get out and take Nolan with you," Hannah cries, so deep I know she won't stop for hours.

I push around them. Nolan stands by the door like he knew what was going to happen. Funny he didn't see himself out. Maya stands and looks toward Hannah's room, then at me.

"Genie?"

I ignore her, looking at the present I got for Hannah on the side table. It's a vintage gold lipstick holder. I've had it since the start of the year, and I know she'll love it.

Nolan opens the door for me and of course I haven't called Mom because, well, I was supposed to be here for a while. So I push as hard and as far as I can, only to find myself on the corner. A dollar van pulls up so close to me, I realize how dangerously close I am to the edge. Nolan grabs me back. He wraps his arms around me.

"Genie, are you trying to kill yourself? This is Atlantic Avenue!"

I push him off me so hard, he bumps into a woman walking by. "What did I tell you about helping me?" It comes out like a hiss. "You didn't do it that night. Don't start now."

"I'm comforting, not helping."

"Semantics. Why couldn't you have fallen in love with the girl next to you in English?"

He's not even screaming right now. Who is he? The Nolan I know would've flattened Dez like roadkill. This looks like the same Nolan that got us running out of a train station for blocks over a smile, but he's not acting like him. Dez crossed a line and he stopped like a well-trained dog when I asked him to?

"Genie, no one gets you like me. We're different from everyone. We get angry and no one understands it. We used to be able to comfort each other."

"We used to have sex."

"It was more than that." He whispers it, like he's afraid someone will take it.

"Not to me. If we weren't having sex, you were nothing but a boy too afraid to be great, so he hid behind me, instead of swimming to the top. The only thing I feel around you is regret. I'm happy I had an abortion, and no one is going to make me feel bad for being the best that I could be. No one. Not even you."

He bucks at me so hard, it scares me, but only his words move forward. "I oughta knock you flat on your selfish ass."

"Do it. I fucking dare you, Nolan. You can't push me or help me up." I have to lean my head back to see him in focus. He's so close.

He grabs his head. "I'm so sorry! I'm so sorry. I love you so much it hurts, Genie. I'm just trying to be friends and I'm messing it up."

"We can't be friends. Or anything. Besides, there's someone else."

"Who?"

"Doesn't matter."

Nolan looks at me as if I didn't help him up. Like he's the one sitting in a wheelchair trying to figure everything out. Yes, I'm selfish, but so is he.

"You're selfish. More than selfish, you unhinged piece of shit. Stop coming over, stop texting me. Don't call my house. Get me out of your head. Leave me alone for good. Having you around makes everything worse. I wish we never met."

The only way I can describe the sound that comes out of him is a cross between a roar and a cry. It makes me jealous that he can scream and let it all out like that. There's no point in looking around, because I can feel the passing glances. Nolan does too, and he takes off running just as fast as he swims.

I pull out my phone to text Kyle. He's the only person who gets it.

Me: Accepting new friend applications.

Kyle: I kind of thought I was already.

Me: You are.

Kyle: Everything okay?

Me: I'm just like Nolan. Selfish.

Kyle: You're talking about Nolan.

Me: I don't want to talk about him.

Kyle: We won't.

CHAPTER TWENTY-FOUR

Magic Wanted

There's traffic on the Belt Parkway. I wish there weren't, because Mom has been looking at me like she wants to say something since she picked me up at Hannah's yesterday. If traffic weren't creeping, I think she'd drop it, but there's no moving, so she might as well talk. And once we get to the church I know she'll be swept away.

We're stopped at the exit for the movie theaters. I wish I could go and get lost in the darkness. Still haven't decided if I'm going to meet up at VAB today. My problems are with Hannah, not Maya, and she doesn't deserve to suffer because Hannah and me can't figure our shit out. "Genie, I do wish you'd talk to someone. A good therapist will change your life. I went through three before I found Anne." The concern in her voice makes me wonder if she thinks I'm going to find the nearest roof and roll off. "Or go back to VAB today. What's this about not going back because Hannah doesn't need you? What happened at her party?" Mom asked earlier about the plan for today, and I only mentioned volunteering and home because Hannah doesn't need me. She's been itching to talk about that since breakfast, but I've been shutting it down.

"I can't go back or face Hannah. I mess everything up." I'm surprisingly honest with her.

A car sustains a honk behind us and Mom throws her hands up in frustration. "Because that helps," she mumbles.

Maybe it does, and they know it'll piss people off. Might make them feel a little better, too. Who are we to judge?

"I was able to get some referrals from Anne. They specialize in trauma," Mom continues. "The mood swings and fights with Hannah are all because you won't address your anger and resentment. Don't let it spread until you can't have any good relationships."

"Addressing My Anger for two hundred. 'She is now paralyzed.' . . . What is 'I fell off a roof'? That is correct."

"Genie . . ."

"Resentment for eight hundred. 'You hit the daily double.' I'll make it a true daily double. 'This dance was supposed to change her life.' . . . What is 'Magic'? 'You won the daily double.' Everyone claps."

"Enough, Genie."

"We can't skip Final Jeopardy. 'This person promised to stop bringing up therapy, but continues to push.' Doo-doo-doo-doo, doo-doo-doo, doo-doo-doo-doo . . . 'You wrote: Who is Mom? That would be correct. But did you wager enough? And you did. Congrats, Genie! We'll see you tomorrow to see if you'll keep your title.'"

"Okay, Genie. You made your point. You don't have to be so rude about it."

"Sorry, I'm not trying to be rude. You're just making me so angry."

JOY L. SMITH

"Okay, why am I making you angry? Is it because I care?" She looks right at me. "What is it?"

Everything. Mostly it's knowing she was right. Nolan and I were screaming at each other in public. Nolan and I are completely entangled, and she said it would happen. Why'd she have to predict this? Why couldn't I balance Nolan and ballet? I told her Nolan and I were just having fun. Well, this is not fun. This is the time the city shut down because of Hurricane Sandy and I couldn't go to ballet.

"Don't make me ask again, Genie."

"You were right, okay? That's my answer."

"Right about?"

I open my phone to text Kyle and tell him I'll be late, fighting the urge to turn up the radio. He sends me a selfie of a sad face, looking like a freshly baked snack in the light of that room.

Mom peeks over into my phone and I jerk it out of her view. "Can I have some privacy? Damn."

"Really, Genie? I'm trying to talk to you about your mental health and you're sexting some boy."

"I'm not *sexting*. I'm talking to Kyle to tell him I'll be late. We partner at St. Nick's. Can I live?"

"Don't be disrespectful. You're being ridiculous about talking to a professional." She taps the steering wheel.

"I talk to Kyle. He gets it."

"Why'd you volunteer, Genie?" I can tell she wants to turn to me fully but can't.

"Because I felt like it." I don't owe her an explanation.

"Maybe you shouldn't make decisions based on boys."

My neck hurts with how fast I snap it. "What does that mean?"

"I mean you made such a fuss about Nolan, and where is he now?"

"We don't all marry our high school boyfriends." *Or have their babies*, I want to say, but don't. "Kyle's different."

"I don't get you anymore, Genie. I'm disappointed in you. Do something. Want it for yourself."

"Well, maybe I want to not want to do anything."

That isn't true. But I don't bother clarifying.

Finally, at St. Nicholas, I storm into the room. I'm wearing my mood on my wheels today.

"H-h-hey, you okay?" Kyle asks, putting down his baggie.

"No. I'm a disappointment." I start throwing things into a baggie. "I knew that, but I've been reminded."

"No—"

"From the minute I showed promise, I couldn't disappoint. My mom was so excited by me—what I could do. She just wanted me to be different. Then it became I couldn't disappoint my teachers and the dancers that looked up to me. When you're singled out in class it's an honor, but also a responsibility."

I hear a rip and realize I've shoved a pen too hard, putting a hole in a baggie. *Great.* I slow myself down.

"I'm a disappointment because I wanted a boyfriend. It just so happened that we both have daddy issues, and he sat next to me in class."

"M-m-makes you n-n-normal." Kyle scoots his chair closer to mine.

"Makes me stupid."

Kyle touches my shoulder. It helps a bit. Swayed by touch right now is not what I want, though. I want to be in a studio with the sun on my face, as the people across the street watch me tell a story with my body. I need to feel the wind of a triple pirouette.

Mom's words about doing something nag at me. Kyle shouldn't be hiding here. He should be by Dylan's side.

"Kyle, do you go see Dylan?"

"I-I-I've done . . . enough d-d-damage. I don't need reminding."

"That's an excuse."

"W-w-what do you know? You didn't . . . take away a life. Someone's son. I—I—I did that." There's a viciousness I've never heard come out of him.

"Okay, but how is sitting here shoving pens in a bag helping? Seems like you're hiding."

He shakes his head fast. "Y-y-you're hiding. W-w-what's this hanging out with me . . . because you can't be the perfect Genie with your friends or mother? I-i-is this how you want to spend your summer?"

I snap my head away from him. It wasn't my intention to start a fight, and yet here we are. Everything is already sucky from Hannah and me getting into it at her party. Now Kyle too. Mom just keeps being right. My anger is just like shit and I'm the fan. It's flinging at anything and everyone who doesn't deserve it.

"I don't even know what to say to that, Kyle." Unlike what

Mom thinks, I'm not following a boy. "You think I'm here because I have fragile feelings?" I wish that were it. I'm here because I like his company. I found some meaning in the work. There's more to me than turning pirouettes.

"Y-y-you say you like b-being here, but you rather be s-s-somewhere else. A s-studio."

I still don't look at him, focusing instead on my dirt-stained palms from my tires. I don't have to explain myself to him either. "That doesn't change the fact that you're backing down from this. From Dylan. Show up, say you fucked up, demand to see your friend. Apologize to him personally, even if he isn't awake."

"N-n-not that simple."

"Why not? You had the balls to get high and drunk and drive a car. Walking into a hospital should be simple enough. Don't punk out now."

I face him. He looks at me as if I've told his secret to everyone at the Barclays Center. *Take it back.* I shouldn't have thrown it in his face like that. There's no backtracking from me. My jaws clench instead.

"D-d-don't you have to . . . go dance?"

"Fine. I'm out."

I swing my chair to the left and don't look back. Checking the time, I can make it while Hannah has the cozy studio today. So I wait for Mom, and while she seems surprised to know that I want a lift to VAB, she's still peeved. All that matters is I at least try to fix things with Hannah.

CHAPTER TWENTY-FIVE

Cygnets

Thinking I'd come in on Hannah and Maya, I've instead crashed Chris and Maya's *Sleeping Beauty* Act III "Wedding" pas de deux rehearsal. I watch silently as they end in a one-handed fish dive. Balandin should probably be overseeing their lifts, but I won't tell.

"That was beautiful, but you're letting go of Maya's back leg too early," I say as I inch in. "She needs to be in a perfect arabesque, Chris."

"Hey? What're you doing here?" Chris says with a slight confused smile.

Hannah pretends not to see me from her spot in the corner. It stings.

"I thought—you're busy. I'll go."

"Why? Stay. Me and Maya could use a break, right?" He looks at Maya, who has already grabbed her water bottle and nods.

Now we're in an oblong circle, like some mandatory awkward camp icebreaker.

"Do you have the Black Swan edition?" Chris asks, pointing to my chair. He's sweating more than Kyle at rehab, wiping his neck with a rag.

"Hell yeah. But I think I want the Genie edition now. Might make it red soon."

"I'm good with a spray can and can paint a black swan on it somewhere."

"No thanks, I've seen your graffiti skills. Besides, this chair cost too much to experiment on. I'm thinking tape and stickers?"

I look at Hannah, who's on her phone. I'm actually surprised she hasn't run out of here. She and Maya should be rehearsing "Magic," but asking why they aren't would kill the vibe Chris is trying hard to keep civil. No doubt he knows Hannah and I came to blows.

"I have a question to ask. Do you think I'd be a good teacher?" I say.

"You could be. Whenever you explain moves, you make it relatable," Maya says.

"Why?" Hannah finally speaks, but she doesn't look at me. Still, I can see the lines of questioning on her forehead.

"Just thinking."

Thinking about my place in the ballet universe and if it'll slow its turning so I can stop watching from space and enter it. And I think about life outside of ballet—Mom and why we keep missing each other. And Kyle. How he's still hurting and how I want so much to help, too, because he's been helping me.

"Have you asked Kuznetsova?" Chris asks. "I'm sure she'd have something to say about it."

"She's the one who brought it up," I confess.

"Maybe she'll give you a job here!" Maya taps the floor. "That way we could still see you and you could still be in class. That would be awesome. Right, Hannah?"

Chris gives me his nervous-emoji face.

"Mhm," Hannah says, her thumb heavily swiping her screen.

I turn to her, but I look to Chris and Maya too. "Let me say some things." I exhale and use my hand to block the sun beaming through the window. "I want to be here. I don't just mean helping with 'Magic.' I want to be at VAB. I need to be here. I deserve to be here."

"Then start acting like it!" Hannah shouts loudly.

"Maybe we should go," Maya says to Chris.

"No. Stay," Hannah says, eyeing me. "We all should hear this."

"I'm sorry for everything I said. I don't mean any of it. Dez deserved to get his ass kicked, though, so I won't apologize for that."

Hannah crosses her arms. "I don't like being mad at you, but you make it so hard to root for you. I'm constantly worried about you. You're all over the place with what you want. How can I believe you?"

"She's here, Hannah," Maya says. "I think that's a good start."

Hannah stands up, not looking totally convinced.

"Look, I can't dance 'Magic' anymore, but I can do 'Magic.' Let me help you. Let me make it the best thing you ever danced. I thought I didn't want it anymore if I couldn't do it. But that's not true. It has to be us. You, me, and Maya. Please, Hannah."

"Genie . . ."

"I almost died because I love this place so much. I promise I will tell you more—I really will, but all I want is to be here with

that." He pulled me back into his arms. "I love you, Genie."

That was the first time he ever said it, and the first time I realized Black girls blushed, but it also came with a warning. At the time I thought I loved him, too. I tried to play it cool, like it was nothing.

"She told me to watch out for you saying that."

He played with my hair, wrapping his fingers to make quick curls. "Because it's true?"

"Because I want—need to be a professional dancer. I have to stay focused."

"I know what you need." His arms snaked around my stomach tighter. He kissed me deeply, his fingers aimlessly roaming my stomach and up near my breasts. I had to suck in air when he pulled away. "Focus on that." He kissed me again, guiding me until I was on my back and he was on top of me.

"Nolan . . ."

I knew what he was suggesting. We talked about sex a lot. A lot of what we did prior to that night might constitute sex to somebody. I was no prude, and we got intimate early on. I hadn't thought that full-blown sex would come out the blue, especially when I was so down.

"I'm just trying to make you feel better." I was used to his weight on top of me. He wasn't heavy, but I was still locked under him. Only his eyes were in the light, and I could hear the zipper of his pants come down. I looked to the unlocked door. "Don't let her get to you." I felt his fingers on the top of my pants.

"She's not." I let him slide my pants off.

I'm not saying I liked it the first time when it was all over. It took me the rest of the night to come to terms with what happened, but it got better the next time and the time after that. After a handful of times, I felt like I was getting something out of it. I started to initiate it.

It became a cycle. I complained about Mom. We had sex. Real talk, and for a while I thought sex could fix it all. Then Nolan became different. We couldn't talk anymore. He wasn't attentive, he was smothering. After every class, he was right at the door, leaving his classes early to meet me after mine, eventually making himself late so he could walk me to my next subject. During class my phone would rattle my thigh to the bone because he couldn't just wait until lunch to talk. We were fine when we were having sex, so I used him as a distraction. Luckily, Hannah keeps me grounded now.

"Hello?" Hannah shouts into the phone. "Earth to Genie. You're still ignoring his calls?" Her voice is weak from a stomach bug. It's why she's not at VAB right now.

"What else am I supposed to do?" Kyle hasn't stopped texting or calling me since after the cygnets thing three days ago. I can't bring myself to block his calls, but he's making me wonder if I made the right choice to cut off communication. I don't want this to become a Nolan 2.0 situation.

I moonwalked around telling her why Kyle and I aren't talking. I was downright mean to him. Told him he was making excuses and hiding, while disappearing myself. My hopes of Kyle coming through this okay are thinning more than my edges, but Hannah won't drop Kyle, and with me avoiding him, I'm needy right now, so I indulge her.

"Talk to him. Normal people do it." I hear the hiss of soda opening. Probably a ginger ale, the only soda she drinks even when not sick.

"Odile said the same thing this morning when I asked her what to do."

"Odile, the swan? What? Never mind. Simply explain to him how your mom is one of those super-protective parents. I'm sure he'd understand. Maybe he doesn't mind sneaking to see you? This is about your mom, right? Why do I feel like you're not telling me everything?"

Yeah, sure, I'll ask him to climb the fire escape. What is Hannah getting at? Of course Kyle understands. He told me himself Mom was just protecting me. And I can't exactly waltz back into St. Nicholas after I quit volunteering. And yes, it's about Mom too, but I lashed out at him and for no good reason other than I was upset with Mom and Hannah.

"I don't want to do that!" I take a deep breath. Not interested in repeating history with Kyle. "Sorry. No sneaking." How can I look at him again? It would've been easier to punch him.

"What's she so afraid of, anyway? It can't be that he's distracting you from a dance career."

"She sees every boy as my dad reincarnated." Instead of throwing my phone, I rub the frustration out of my eyes. I really just want to spoon with the book.

"You're not her."

But I could have been. And my accident only happened because I was fighting against the very thing she wanted to protect me from: being stuck with a boy who is no good for me, but staying because of a baby. "Time won't make a difference."

"Honesty will."

"You're gonna just fix my life like Iyanla?" I actually laugh a little. "I'm such a hypocrite. I fought with Kyle because he was making excuses, and here I am making them. Hannah, I was uncalled-for rude to him."

"We all make mistakes. I let Dez get to third base before the party started. That's my excuse on why I let him act like a dick."

"We can do better."

"You are with Kyle. Answer his calls, Genie. I've been on the other side of you thinking you're helping someone. It doesn't feel good." She moans softly either from her stomachache or dragging out how she felt about me "helping" her, before I hear the ginger ale opening again. "If it matters from this girl, I don't think you should push your mom out either. She made her decision regarding you, and you made yours."

I chew on my fingernails. My biggest fear after my abortion was Hannah agreeing with Mom about me not being focused enough. I couldn't even tell Hannah beforehand about it. After I told her, she gave me the biggest hug and asked me how I was doing. She didn't even bring up the amount of time I spent with Nolan. His name never came out her mouth. I thought the abortion would change the way she looked at me. Like a dancer coming back from surgery.

It happened to one girl at the studio who broke her ankle in addition to her Achilles tendonitis. She recovered, but we all knew. We all watched how she would look on from the corner after warm-ups, her hands memorizing the dance for her until she was able to fully join back in. Miss Kuznetsova would single her out because she wasn't where she needed to be. We all gave her the same thank-God-it's-not-me look. Time off is good for the person—not the dancer.

"Call me later. I got to sleep this sickness off."

"Yeah, yeah. Thanks, Hannah."

"Besos."

Now what?

My phone buzzes the same time the intercom goes off. I try to ignore them both by straightening the contents on my desk. Somehow it reflects my life. A mess. Papers switch around like a game of shells. I do my best to put everything in a spot, but I can't focus. Not with the intercom buzzing. Must be the crazy UPS guy again!

I turn my phone off as Kyle calls again. When Hannah feels better, we'll have to go old-school and use the landline.

Did he tape his finger to the damn intercom? I stop what I'm doing and clip my elbow on the corner of the desk, giving it a quick inspection as I head to the intercom. Mom sits on the couch, Switch in hand, as if there's no noise.

"Mom, who is it?"

"No one."

"Can't tell 'no one' to go?"

She doesn't look up. I wait for a response. Nothing. I turn back into the hallway and stretch to press the talk button.

"Whoever it is, go away," I shout so they can hear me.

I press the listen button to see if they say anything. Maybe it's a delivery guy with the wrong address, or someone hoping to get let in.

"Genie?"

Kyle.

"Genie!" Mom yells. Before I know it, she blocks the intercom. "Why didn't you say it was Kyle?"

"Ignore him." I can't tell if it's a threat, an order, or an appeal of sorts.

The same choking feeling of her sabotaging my plans with Nolan comes back. I know the amount of energy it takes for Kyle to move around. The fact that he came here tells me I wasn't right, cutting him off without an explanation. I'm afraid of treating him like Nolan—someone to keep on the hush. Kyle deserves a ride or die. Not someone who has to fight just to talk to him without Mom breathing down my neck, controlling every relationship I have that isn't with her.

"He came all the way here to talk to me and you were going to ignore him?"

"Genie, try to understand."

"Move. Let me talk to him."

She steadies herself. Makes me wonder if she's had a few drinks. "No, you have to focus on you. We have to come up with plans. I know how easily you become distracted."

Like she's one to talk. She's the one volunteering and always at her meetings so she doesn't have to be alone, because she's afraid she'll walk into a bar.

"Here's a plan: leave me again so I can talk to him. You have no right to bring 'focusing on me' into this. We can barely get two words in without fighting." The buzzer keeps going off.

"Listen to me! You'd listen if I were Kuznetsova." The bitterness rolls out. She tries to backtrack. "I know what's best for you."

"Oh yeah, you make great decisions. Had me at sixteen. Married a spineless abuser."

"You have no idea."

"Tell me, then. Why keep so many secrets?" I wait for an answer.

"Because some things need burying. We've been over this." She throws her hands up in frustration.

I clip her as I roll by, struggling with opening the door. I'm not giving the door enough room and my knees block it. "Is it not tiring? Saying the same thing over and over?"

"Stop it, Genie." She slides between me and the door.

"He's not going to leave unless I tell him something." Kyle's determined; like any high-level athlete, he won't stop until he gets his intended result.

She rolls her eyes and hesitates. Her lips press together tightly, like she's afraid of what will come out if she opens her mouth. Mom's shoulders relent first, and then she steps to the side.

"Don't follow me," I tell her as I wait to hear the door close behind me.

A hopeful expression spreads across Kyle's face when he sees me. I struggle with the front door made of heavy glass, but Kyle wastes no time. "I—I—I was going to . . . s-s-stand here all day if I had to," he says.

"That's why I'm out here."

"W-w-we need to talk."

"Look, I'm sorry I thought we could be friends. It won't wo—"

"I—I—I know Nolan h-h-hurt you. I don't know fully what's going on with you a-a-and your mom." His eyes squeeze together as he tries to spit out the next bit. "B-b-but it's not a good enough reason for me."

My head collapses into my hands. "I can't get into everything now."

He looks wounded, and not because he's wobbly on his crutches. I've emotionally defeated him. I get a there's-more-to-this-story alert. This is deeper than me ignoring his calls.

"Everyone at the gym hates me . . . b-b-besides Chelsea . . . You're . . . my only friend now." He slumps back on the stair railing. Tears fall from his eyes. He doesn't bother to wipe them. "Y-y-you're braver th-th-than me . . . I—I—I was reminded."

I'm so grateful to still have Hannah, a link to my past life, but Kyle is my new life. Chelsea is his Hannah.

"I—" I what? I don't know. I don't want to know. Why can't I come right out with Mom's trust issues? Why can't I say I had feelings? Am I thinking like Mom? Some things need to be buried? She's wrong. I shouldn't have to hide being friends with Kyle. "I should've handled it differently."

Kyle doesn't look fully convinced.

"Kyle, I'm not sure why you even want to be friends with me. I—my mom's—difficult. I don't know why . . . there are things about me you probably shouldn't know." Now I look up to the sky. I'm not helping at all. "I like you, and I don't know how to just be with a guy who's nice to me without . . . sex. I'm afraid if I tell you my secrets, you'll use them against me." I sigh. I probably should go inside now.

His eyes close for a moment and he blinks them open. "I-I-I'm n-n-not like that. I want to be your friend . . . first."

If Mom's looking out one of the windows in the living room, she can see us, and I don't care. This isn't my over-the-top hugs or kisses I put on for her when Nolan was around. I'm not trying to shove anything in her face. This is me taking responsibility for my actions, caring about someone other than myself.

Kyle holds his hand out for me to grab, eyes locked on mine. I place my fingers lightly in his palm. For a moment I think he's going to kiss my hand the way he holds my fingers, but his hand goes limp in mine. *He doesn't care anymore. He just wanted to poke at your wounds.* Then he clasps his other hand over mine. He lifts his head up. "W-w-why'd you quit volunteering?"

I turn my head in shame. He doesn't pull back his hands, and I wouldn't dare let go. They're rough but comforting. "I'm sorry. I thought I was helping," I apologize. "And in the middle of what was happening between us I threw myself back into VAB because you reminded me that I really wanted to be there. I like being at St. Nick's with you, it's just VAB is my home, and then my mom got in my head about why I was volunteering in the first place and we got to fighting. I thought I was helping you by leaving you be and helping my friend by doing what I do best."

Mom's right. Kyle was a big part of the reason I went back to St. Nick's. The minute we fought, I didn't want to be there anymore.

"S-s-sorry I w-w-went all crazy on you."

He was going for gold in the Cray Olympics.

I pat my lap. "Have a seat, you can tell me all about it." I don't know how he'll react to me trying to lighten the situation, but he gives me a slight smile and it makes me feel a little better.

"F-f-for starters . . . m-m-my wish?"

"You still want to hang out with me? I thought the whole can't-feel-when-I'm-bleeding was enough to scare you away."

"I-I-I'm a gymnast. I-I-I'm not easily scared."

I know he's not. Even in my most embarrassing, sweat-faced, frizzy-haired times in therapy, he smiled at me. He sat in a germy ER with me.

"Clearly, you book smuggler. Dragged me into it. You're braver than you think."

I don't know how true this is for me, though; I can't even confront Mom about the abortion.

"W-w-what's wrong?" Kyle asks. I realize I haven't been looking at him and I've taken my hand back, rubbing my hands together nervously.

"I think I may have to disappoint my mom again." I was only thinking it, but I said it.

"H-h-how?"

Boy repellent in three, two, and one. "I kept—she doesn't know—I haven't told her about my abortion." My hands won't stop rubbing together.

He does his word-recall look to the sky, mouth making all kinds of shapes. I can't tell what he might say.

"W-w-wow," he finally says. "That's a h-h-hard s-s-secret to keep."

I nod. Saying it doesn't exactly feel easier, either. "I couldn't tell her because . . ."

"You thought it was best?"

"I don't know anymore." There's no moisture left in my mouth. "I haven't been a good daughter to her since the accident. Or before, really."

"S-s-start now."

"Yes, Dr. Phil." I squint my eyes. "It's not that easy."

"I know."

"So why tell me start now, then?" Really, why?

"B-b-because I'd d-d-do anything to see Dylan again. His family doesn't . . . want me visiting. Legally I can't. And even if I could, I'm too embarrassed to see him." His whole body seems to shrink. "D-d-do something. . . . Show her you still care."

Feels like I'm a balloon slowly letting out air. If I weren't anchored into my chair, I would float up to the sky.

"Y-y-you know how . . . d-d-don't you?"

"By being honest. I wish I could simply dance for her. Show her why I did it. Why I kept it secret."

"T-t-try not to think about it t-t-too hard." The innocence in his voice comes out again. He smirks, feeling himself. It's the best thing about today.

"What are you so happy about?"

"M-m-my friend's a Genie." He laughs. "Y-y-you can make . . . anything happen."

He does the *I Dream of Jeannie* head nod with matching hands but loses his balance, and I quickly catch him. Holding his waist to keep him steady, my heart nearly leaps out of my chest, but he laughs, and so do I.

I turn to the sound of the gate opening. Nolan stands at the bottom of the steps, still, like a stage manager has called "places." Before I can even say anything, Nolan knocks Kyle right out of my hands. Kyle slams into the ground, and the force pushes my chair into the railing. Nolan moves fast. A punch lands on Kyle's face—then another. His crutches fall away from him as he covers his head. It's not until Nolan's foot comes up that I'm able to react, grabbing anything on Nolan. I get ahold of his shirt and yank as hard as I can.

"Nolan, stop it! You're hurting him!" I pull some more. I'm useless.

"She's mine!" Nolan punches Kyle again. I yank at him over and over, but he pushes me hard. My chair almost goes down the steps. "Stay away from her!"

Kyle shouts some unintelligible words back at me. I don't try to decode it. I just keep trying to get Nolan off him. My arms aren't doing much to help. Even as I punch at Nolan, he keeps right on Kyle like I'm nothing but a butterfly kiss.

I look around for help. The few people around just stand there, not sure what to do. I'm used to audiences reacting.

Luckily, I manage to get one of Nolan's hands in my mouth and bite down. He's rotten inside and out. That gets his attention.

"Fucking bitch!" He draws in a sharp breath, shaking his fist like the pain will fall off.

"Leave him alone!" I shout. But it's scratchy and weak.

"Was I a game to you?" His hands are still clenched. "You were mad quick to get rid of me for him?"

Kyle moans, turning his head side to side, holding it like it'll fall apart if he lets go. He's bent over like a bad stomachache, not even our eyes can meet. I want to get on the floor to check him out, but I'm nervous it'll shift Nolan's attention. *If I keep him talking, he won't focus on Kyle.*

"Yes, Nolan, fuck it up just like the time at Broadway Junction."

"I did that for you."

Why is his skull so thick?

"I never wanted it! You did that for you. We were holding hands waiting for a train, Nolan, but you had to go puff your chest out, and for what? Not for me. For you to feel better about yourself. My dad did the same to my mom. She couldn't put up with it anymore, and neither can I."

He rummages through his bag and pulls out a paper. "Remember this? You invited me to watch you dance." Flaunting the invitation from last year's end-of-summer gala, he holds it high. "I just wanted that back. When we were just happy to see each other and sharing our love. When you wanted to be around me. Remember how excited you was to give it to me?" Nolan pants like an overheated dog. "Don't you want that too?"

I don't, but I'm afraid saying it will send him over the edge.

He drops his arms when I don't respond. "You don't even

look at me anymore—" He shoves the invitation back in his bag.

I must be competing for the Cray Olympics too, because I can hear how sorry he is. But it won't change anything.

"Why won't you get it?" I scream at him. "I hate you!"

I swear I see fire in Nolan's eyes. Not the passion kind I see when I look into a mirror before I dance, but one of hate, anger, and evil. He looks at Kyle with the same face he settled on me when I clung for life. He's going to punish him.

"Nolan, don't!" I shout. But it's too late, he kicks Kyle hard in his stomach. *Call for help.* "Mom, help! Mom!" I scream as loud as I can. I feel so helpless. With each kick I'm letting Kyle down.

Mom bursts through like the house is on fire. With a strength I've never seen before, she throws Nolan off Kyle, sending him sprawling on the pavement. "Stay away from here! Stay away from my daughter!"

Nolan gets up no problem. I think he's going to run at Mom, do to her what he's done to Kyle. But he doesn't. He just stands in place. "You fucking win, Ms. Davis. She chose that ballet over me and the baby."

"And you chose to let me fall instead of helping!" I yell back.

Nolan locks up and I look at Mom, who's hearing this for the first time. She wasn't supposed to ever know about either of these things—the abortion, details of the fall—and she finds out like this. She walks toward Nolan and I'm not sure what her plan is, if she has one. All I can see is her on the floor, her eyes swollen shut in a way that made it clear she wouldn't wake up. I remember that night too clearly. Nolan could push her to that again. I don't want the past to come back to light.

"Mom," I say. My *be careful* gets lost in my throat.

She holds her hand up at me, keeping her eyes on Nolan.

"Leave! And if you so much as think of calling this house again, I will end you." Mom pulls her phone out. Her chest is rising like it's going to explode.

Nolan and I stare each other down. I can see Mom in my peripheral vision, looking at me. Whatever she's thinking right now, I can't think about it. Kyle needs help, and he won't be safe until Nolan is gone. Nolan looks like he wants to say something cruel. Whatever the thought, it spreads across his face, contorting it, peeling his lips and scrunching his eyes dead at me before he runs up the block.

Mom gets on her knees beside Kyle. "We're going to get you some help, Kyle. Okay?" She uses her soft hands to take his from his face.

Her back blocks my view of Kyle. He must be bleeding. I saw those punches.

"Kyle, I'm sorry," I tell him.

I'm so sorry.

He doesn't respond.

CHAPTER TWENTY-SEVEN

Music Box

I follow behind the stretcher as the paramedics lift Kyle from the steaming hot concrete to its intended height, mimicking him as if I'm learning a routine. When he grunts, I grunt. He grimaces and so do I. Kyle's eyes follow the paramedics. His words sound like gargles, but he seems to understand what they're saying to him, and he blinks and gestures. The collar around his neck is meant to keep him safe, but it looks more like it's choking him.

"I think the collar is too tight," I tell the paramedic. "Don't forget his crutches."

The younger paramedic, a girl who looks like she's barely out of high school, picks them up off the ground and places them in the ambulance.

"Genie"—Mom touches my shoulders—"let them do their job." I shrug her hands off. "Where are you going?"

"I'm going with him."

"No, you're not."

"Yes. I. Am." They almost forgot his crutches. What else will they forget?

"How are you getting in the back of the ambulance?"

The clank of the paramedics lifting him into the back grabs my attention. I look at the distance from the ground to the rig. Too high for me. They close the doors and pull off, lights flashing. I should be with him. My face burns with anger as they turn the corner out of sight.

I spin around, knocking into Mom. "It's your fault!" Kyle hates me now, he has to. I can't imagine why he'll ever look at me again. There's a sharp pain in my stomach at the thought of not being friends with him again. Not being there if he ever has to go back to rehab.

"Let's go inside." She rubs her shins and looks at the onlookers who watched but didn't help. "You're not going anywhere until we talk. I mean it."

"No! If Kyle was welcome, he would've been inside. Nolan wouldn't have seen him."

"Like being welcome makes any difference to your boyfriends," she scoffs. "Don't think I didn't know Nolan was over here all those nights. I know that was him calling and hanging up. You're forgetting I had you at sixteen." Her eyes glow with embarrassment. All these years later, and it's like she's still sixteen and pregnant.

Why am I paying for it?

I find it hard to focus on just one thing. My eyes look in every direction. "Why not out me, then?" She could've stopped me before we got too deep. But she didn't.

"You would've pushed back harder. I'd rather have you here than over at his place. I guess in the end it didn't matter." She wrangles with her hair, trying to keep it out of her face. "Why didn't you tell me about the pregnancy? I've been there before."

"There was nothing to tell. I had an abortion. I was still going to keep dancing."

"Forget about ballet for a moment. It was an abortion, not a secret belly ring. I should've been told. There's no reason you had to go through that alone."

"I didn't think about anything else. It was my only option, Mom. I didn't want to make the same mistake." I was embarrassed.

"You are not a mistake! I chose to keep you, and I know I didn't do my best a lot of the time, but I've always wanted you."

Mom's inevitable disappointment weighed on me when I was about to have my abortion; sitting in that waiting room, hearing my name called, triggered all my parents' fights. I sensed a pattern with the ones I had with Nolan. Walking to that exam room, it felt like everyone knew about Mom keeping me. How Dad did her. The way Nolan and I were wrong for each other. All I remember thinking after it was done was that she was right about it all.

"But I didn't want this baby. And I didn't want you to give up on me like your mom did you."

"And that's fine, Genie. Whatever choice you wanted, I would've backed you up. There's nothing you could do that would make me ever treat you the way my mom treated me. Genie, I would die for you over and over again."

"When would you have had the time? Between the meetings and your duties at St. Nicholas?"

She shakes her head. "Nuh-uh. Don't even say that. I've always found the time. I got you to school in the mornings. Took you to every dance class. Never missed a performance. I didn't push ballet for me. Genie, I pushed because you were running for it. When you got into VAB and I saw how Kuznetsova took you under her wing, I knew you were safe there. That she would help you in ways I couldn't."

"How could you help me when you were still taking Dad's help after what he did to you?"

Her eyebrows meet and she frowns. "What are you talking about?"

"I know he paid for my tuition."

Mom's eye goes wide. "How?" She stops me before I can say anything. "Did he touch you?"

"No."

"He had no right to tell you anything." Her eyes flash some serious heat. Like when she was yelling at him to stop calling her.

"At least he told me something."

"Did he tell you he stole the money my mom left me in her will in one of his get-rich-quick schemes? That he beat me because I was going to use that money to get us out of there and he stole it? From you."

"I—"

"Stop. I'm not telling you because I want sympathy. You're right. You're old enough to know who your parents are. I never told you because I was afraid. I thought if he stayed away, you would forget him. For so long I thought he might come back. Try to take you out of spite, back when I wasn't sober. He held my drinking over me for so many years, Genie. When we were still in high school, he would buy me drinks, and I would just take them, knowing drinking was why I was in alternative school in the first place. I knew how manipulative he could be and I never wanted him to get custody of you, so I never went to the police. I never reported what he did to me. I just hid at home and drank some more, because I was so ashamed and scared and angry."

She's telling me it's not my fault, but I should've known. Should've figured it out and made my own better choices. Maybe if I knew about Dad or talked to Mom about what happened that night between them when I finally saw everything, I would've steered cleared of Nolan when things got too intense.

The block is too loud now, but not loud enough to drown out my thoughts. I thought I could fix everything myself. Grieve myself. Learn how to live in this chair myself—and I was so wrong. And here's Mom now finally telling me this. It feels too late.

"You think because you're finally being honest about everything, I'm going to tell you what happened on that roof? Like it'll change anything?

Mom pushes herself off the gate, her eyebrows touching. "I have never asked you anything about that night. I wanted you to tell me when you were ready. And it hurts me to think that you think I'm telling you about your father so you can tell me about your accident."

"You were right about Nolan. Not to trust him. Does that make you feel better?"

"No, it doesn't, Genie. If he let you fall, you need to be talking to the police."

"No!"

She crouches in front of me and looks me in the eyes. "Are you afraid he's going to hurt you?"

"I'm not you. Nolan didn't beat me. He never stole anything from me. I don't want to talk about him. I want to go see Kyle," I say, backing away from her hands, which are ready to touch me.

Mom sucks her teeth. "Don't do this, Genie. Please don't go back to hiding. I'm trying to help you!"

"Don't help me!"

I'm amazed no one's shouting, "WorldStar!" But we'd have to throw some punches for that. Mom bounces her leg and pulls her hair into a ponytail. If I back up any more, I'll hit the stairs.

"You can't ignore this. Genie, he wins if you don't speak up."

I shrug. "I'm back at VAB, I can help Hannah with Maya, I can possibly teach there. I cannot . . ." I don't know how to explain that I don't want to be dragged into Nolan's shit anymore. It's more people to talk to, more people that know what he did to me, what he let happen. When all I want is to forget about it and move on as best I can.

"And that's all good. VAB will always be there for you, but Genie, you're a victim too."

The way she says it so sure, so smooth. Like if she pretties it up, I'll nod and be okay with it.

"Don't call me that."

"There's no shame in it. You'll see. I was one too. *Listen* to me. There is nothing you could've done that would justify why he let you fall from that roof. Can't you see that?"

"You're blocking the gate and I'd like to leave," I deadpan.

"I'm not letting you leave. Not in this state."

"Move."

"Genie."

"Let me go!"

PLEASE. PLEASE. PLEASE.

The gate next door opens and the girl who got my ramp for me looks at both of us. She pulls her headphones down to her neck. "Hey," she says normally, like she probably hasn't been watching from her window and seen the shit show.

Mom waves to her. I turn away. When I look back, the disappointment on Mom's face is all too familiar. She doesn't even bother to wipe the sweat rolling down her forehead. I catch mine with my shirt. I use my shirt to wipe the taste of Nolan from my tongue.

"I don't want to be here right now," I tell her as kindly as I can, because I want to scream. "I'm not going to roll in front of a bus, if that's what you think."

I remember what Kuznetsova said about being so upset when her father died.

"I think you're scared and you're upset." She scratches her head and sighs. "But I can see you need space." She steps aside and opens the gate.

I push through before she can change her mind.

"Are you going to come back?"

"I don't know."

Before she can say anything, I'm at the end of the block, picking up enough speed that I create my own little wind. I wait until I'm around the corner in front of the laundromat to take out my phone. I can barely keep the phone steady as I hit Hannah's picture.

"She knows," I say as soon as I hear Hannah's sleepy voice.

"I'll come get you."

CHAPTER TWENTY-EIGHT

Black Swan

O n this episode of The Breaking Pointe, *Hannah pulls up in a minivan and still manages to slay.*

"Where are we going?" she asks me, stepping out of the car. Her lips are silver.

"Silver for the bullet we want to put in Nolan?" I ask.

"Sure, let's go with that." Hannah looks at my building. "You still have some stuff over at my place until everything blows over."

"Thanks."

"But really, where are we going?"

"I need to see Kyle, but right after I make Nolan swallow my caster." I hate that he's yet again taking priority. This is the last time, though.

Transferring into a minivan is new. Mom's car sits way lower, but I manage to get in without too much of a hiccup. I try to sit coolly like Hannah. She actually got her license while I was too busy wanting to be chauffeured everywhere. Now I'll never know what driving will be like with my legs. It's nice to see her finally driving after she swore never to drive the Odyssey. She scratches her curly hair with one hand and keeps the other on the wheel.

"Where do you think Nolan is?" she asks, beeping at a car who crosses into the lane without signaling.

"Probably trying to pretend nothing happened. My bet is the Y he works at."

"Plug it into Waze so we can get a shortcut."

I get Hannah to toss her hair at the guy at the front desk so I can go to the pool area and find Nolan. The smell of chlorine knocks me back a few feet. This isn't the pool we spent time in together, but memories rush at me. How he held me in the water, swaying on our toes in the deep end. The way he laughed at me when I jumped into the pool without my swim cap, letting my hair shrink under the weight of the water. "You're still cute," he told me.

That's not all I remember, though. I recall him sticking to me like a Post-it so no one could look at me in my bathing suit. Or how he told me he quit swimming to have more time to be with me.

It's so easy to push alongside a pool, it scares me. Not as easy for me to approach Nolan in his territory, though. I didn't fully think this through. He just beat the shit out of Kyle, pretty sure Mom was next on his hit list, and I have no one here to physically back me up in case he actually puts his hands on me or drowns me. I'm emotional and angry and scared. But this is more than him hurting Kyle. I have questions that need answering.

Nolan sits on one of the benches, surrounded by wet towels and flip-flops. He still has his street clothes on as he looks out at the pool like it's an ocean with waves and a tide and a sunset behind it.

It's like the AC isn't on, because even my ears go hot, and my stomach warms like I'm drinking tea. Seeing him just reheats the anger I have left over. But we have to do this. "Let's talk."

Nolan jumps in a startle, and I wish it made me feel better. "What are you doing here?" he asks. "You can't be here." He looks around like I might make a scene.

"You made it so I don't even want to be home. I got no place to be but here. You obviously came over to talk, so let's do it."

"Okay. Not here, though." He stands up and leads the way to a hallway.

It's great I'm nowhere near water right now, but the openness of the hallway is throwing me. Spotting the security cameras makes me feel better.

"Your mom ripped you a new one about the baby and now you need me?"

"Not even close." I try to keep my voice from shaking. "We can't keep doing this back-and-forth thing. Whatever we had is done. Over. Whatever you want us to be, it's not happening."

"I get vexed too easily, but I can get help." He folds his hands like he's praying. "Please, Genie. I'm sorry."

"You let me fall off a roof. That's more than anger issues." He's going to hurt someone more than me with whatever he has. "You hurt my friend Kyle for no reason." The list goes on.

"I got jealous. He's trying to take you from me. I saw the look—he can't have you." Spit flies out of his mouth like a rabid dog. "I won't allow it."

"I'm not your property, Nolan." I struggle not to shout. This isn't the best place to have this conversation, but neither was the roof. "All I see is hate when I look at you. All I feel is anger when I think of you. Any good thoughts are gone, and all because you didn't even try to help me."

"Stop bringing that up!" He turns away from me, pushing the wall with his fist.

"You still don't get it. I can't just stop. Do you know what it's like not to be able to see the mirror in your own bathroom anymore? I openly bled in an ice cream shop because I couldn't feel that my leg got sliced open. I wake up afraid that I peed the bed or shit on myself. I don't give a fuck if this makes you uncomfortable. I'm not comfortable, so why should you be?" I push him to respond. "Huh? Why shouldn't I remind you? If you want to be my friend, you have to deal with all of me." I wish he'd look at me, but he's too punk. "Too real, right? You don't care if I can't feel my legs so long as you can feel them up."

"I didn't want that to happen, but you got me so tight."

"What did you think was going to happen? Huh? I was barely hanging on and all I needed was a hand."

"It happened so fast. I thought . . ."

"I thought too. That you weren't going to leave me. That I didn't want to die."

"Stop!"

"Stop remembering? Stop stating the facts? Why? We wouldn't be here if you helped. So stop being scared and explain to me.

Because I tried to fill it in myself, but I can't." I never said anything because I couldn't figure it out. What if I did tell? They'd ask why and I wouldn't know what to tell them. I'd look even more stupid than I felt.

"You were going to leave me," he rushes out. "That wasn't supposed to happen. . . . I love you. Even like this." With a deep breath, he turns back around. "Now you need me. And I still need you. No one loves you like me. Not your mother. Not your father. Unlike him, I'm not leaving. I'm still here, but you're confused."

I can hear the pity in his voice, and it awakens something in me. "I'm not your victim, Nolan. You're just as wounded as me."

Nolan throws his head back against the wall. We both go quiet as people walk by. Kyle works his way into my head. His fuzzy, soft hair, the rich brown of his eyes, the way my body tingled when he rubbed circles on my hand, and the weight of his head on top of mine. How I wish I were with him now. When the hall clears, I speak first.

"Why didn't you help me?"

"Because you needed to suffer! Like how you made me feel! That was my baby, Genie!" He punches the wall. "We weren't going to be like our parents. We loved each other. All you wanted was that stupid ballet. And for what? Dance doesn't love you back. Dance can't kiss you, hold you, or tell you secrets. It never felt for you like I did the moment I saw you."

He whispers what sounds like counting to himself before addressing me again. "The more I loved you, the more I wasn't good enough for you. It was ballet this and Germany that. I was competing with all of that. You stopped looking at me. But you were looking at that boy—That baby was going to make you stay, and you would've come around. It would've been us again!"

Nothing like a confession to echo down a hallway. I knew it all along. He just wanted to trap me. All I want to do is punch him, beat on him, but I know it would never amount to the pain he's given me. That'll I'll live with forever.

"You can't trap people, Nolan. I'm not something you can keep to yourself." I never got to show myself to the world. Thanks to him. "I'm paralyzed, Nolan. Paralyzed!" I take in a breath. "I'll never dance again. And you aren't even sorry."

"You're not even sorry! Apologize to me! I meant it in the moment letting you fall but immediately regretted it. That's what I've been trying to show you, but you told me I was just sex to you!"

There's a rattling in me so hard, I grip my rims to hold steady. "I don't owe you shit! We can't talk without fighting. How was I supposed to tell you I didn't feel safe around you anymore? That I wasn't going to scale back my dreams because you weren't going for yours?"

"It's always going to be that stupid ballet, isn't it?"

"Nolan—I didn't want to end up like my mother! Alone. Unhappy. Stuck with someone because of a baby. Just one bad decision from becoming an alcoholic. I need someone stable and dependable to trust in."

In a way it's funny, ballet and I were in a relationship and it was far from stable.

"Did I not make you feel good? Can that other punk make you feel like I did?"

He doesn't know I feel so much more with Kyle. More than beautiful. I'm brave and funny.

"This has nothing to do with Kyle. I have my own life to live and I can't do it attached to you. There's no way I'm going to let you control me anymore." I pick at my rims, waiting for him to say anything.

"How am I going to tell Ma you don't care about me anymore? Dad is going to laugh at me." I can't even see his eyes, they're so low, matching his voice right now. But I hear him loud and clear.

I shake my head. "Honestly, that's not my problem. Do you see the way you look at water? I want you to swim again. Go get your life back! Remember how excited you were for me to go to a meet? You say you swam for me, but that was all for you." Regret is all over his face, but being sorry now doesn't help me. "Nolan, you need help, and I can't be it." I'm being a hypocrite preaching to him about help when I won't get any. But it's true. There's so much pain in his eyes, as he digs his nails into his arms. I pull his arms apart. "Be gentle with yourself."

"How . . ."

He doesn't need to finish for me to know what he's asking. "Some stuff you're just going to have to figure out for yourself," I tell him what Logan told me.

"Get out my face with that." He doesn't look at me but pulls his bag tighter on his shoulders and walks away from me.

I head back to meet up with Hannah, feeling lighter than I

have in a long time. I don't know if I'll ever not hate him, but I can't keep carrying it around. We both made our choices that night, and we're both paying for them. For me, it's whenever I sit in this chair and control it as easily as I used to walk. I may have named my chair Odile, but if I were a real black swan, I'd fly away.

CHAPTER TWENTY-NINE

Nightmares Sleep

O n this episode of The Breaking Pointe, *Genie lies in the dark in profound meditation.*

Hannah has stars on her ceiling. The kind that glow in the dark. I helped her put them up. We made a game out of who could jump the highest and stick the most stars. That explains why it looks so funky. My phone's glow touches the ceiling, still bright from texting Kyle. His last message telling me to let him know in the morning if I take him up on his invite to his house.

I look over at Hannah. She's asleep, her hair wrapped in a silk scarf to keep her curls from tangling. This isn't where I pictured myself tonight, but Mom knows I'm here, Hannah texted her, and that makes me feel somewhat better about what happened today. But not enough to go to bed. Sleep would be nice, but whenever I close my eyes, I remember that night. My fingers dig into my scalp as I hold my head to keep it from spinning any more. He only wanted to get back at me. That night just keeps pushing forward. I wish it away, squeezing my head harder, but I'll never forget and I don't have to be afraid of it. So I let it come.

The roof was like it always was since he started bringing me there when we were freshmen. There were the two chairs that Nolan kept up there; nothing was out of the ordinary. Nolan stood facing the only entrance to his roof, his hideout as he called it, waiting for me. If I had known then what I know now, I wouldn't have pushed open the creaky door and faced him.

But I did and he was quiet. Not rash and angry like his voice mails. For a moment I thought maybe it was me imagining him angry. My guilt over just breaking up with him without telling him about the abortion. I buried myself in the studio, staying at Hannah's for a bit. I danced through the cramps, thanked the heavens I only lightly spotted for a few days afterward, and I tried to forget. But Nolan knew what I'd done. I wasn't fooling him.

"Tell me you didn't do it," he said. His words reached. Hoped, even.

I couldn't say it, but I nodded. "I'm gonna go." I stepped toward the door.

"No," he called after me. "Why? You didn't even talk to me about it. Where was I in this decision? Where was I at all?"

Maybe it was the relief from telling him. Maybe it was his voice and how hurt he sounded. I never knew why I was so weak around him, and that was why I turned to face him, slumped shoulders and all. I had long since stopped feeling cramps from the procedure, but my stomach clenched at the sight of him—guilt.

"Nolan, I needed to be alone."

"So, you went by yourself?"

I walked past him, not wanting to sit and talk, took a spot against the brick siding, and peered down at the dumpster below. "I needed to do it alone. No distractions."

"I'm a distraction?" He didn't sound touchy, but it rubbed me the wrong way.

"I don't want to fight, Nolan."

"Clearly. You stopped fighting for us, killed my kid, and don't even tell me so I could've been there." He sucked his teeth. "I hope you end up miserable like your mother."

"Fuck you, Nolan. You know what? This is exactly why I did it. Because of shit like this, and the stuff you say. We can't only be good when we have sex." He hadn't even asked if I was okay or needed anything. "How about a 'can I help somehow?' No? Do you even want to know how I'm doing?"

He huffed. "Okay, fine, I'm sorry. I love you! I should've been there, though."

"Been there for what, Nolan? You would've tried to talk me out of it." I grabbed my head, frustrated by the circles we went through.

I couldn't picture Nolan holding my hand as my cervix was numbed. The whole way there he would've told me he loved me, begged for me to think it over. Told me it was wrong to do it. That I could be wifey and he'd take care of us. That's what he told me when I said I was pregnant out loud.

"You don't get to make these decisions without me."

"You're lucky I told you at all."

"What'd you say?" He balled his shirt between his fists.

"It's my body. You were right where you needed to be. It's over." I went to step around him, my eyes set on the door. He grabbed my arm. "Let go, Nolan."

"I know you love me. You made a mistake and we'll start over. Try again for another one."

I rolled my eyes at him.

We weren't trying at all. But we got caught up in a moment and took a risk. Sometimes I forgot a step of choreography, and instead of freezing I improvised. I made the earliest appointment I could.

"I'm not trying for anything. We're done." I yanked against his grasp.

"No!"

"I wouldn't be with you, let alone have your baby, even if it was a Misty Copeland–Nureyev love child." My teeth ground against each other. I tugged on his grip again.

I should've seen it coming.

The shove knocked me on my back. I was eight again, trying to get Dad off Mom. I felt small and weak and useless. My hands pressed on some tar rocks as I sat myself up—stunned. Nolan apologetically kicked the side of the roof, angry at himself, cursing under his breath. My heart yelled, but my mouth was empty. This wasn't one of his playful "throw me on the bed" shoves. Unlike the trials of being lifted by my arms, my shoulders thumped like a super bass. Being grabbed was one thing. But this was a shove to keep me down, whether he was sorry or not.

I fought the urge to lunge at him, or to stay down and let it come to a natural standstill. I decided to stand up slowly, a best of both worlds. Nolan couldn't think of me as weak. But I also wasn't going to strike at him when he was so angry, either. He was hurt.

If guilt was a company of dancers, I was the studio floor. My mind wanted to apologize and agree to be deserving of his aggression, but I didn't deserve that when I was only trying to keep myself safe.

"Now I look like the bad guy!" Nolan shouted. A gravel rock took flight at the trees behind me. Birds flew away at the sudden threat. "Why do you keep pulling away from me?"

"What the hell, Nolan!" I nurtured my shoulder, cradling it like a baby I wasn't having. "I have to dance tomorrow. How can I dance well with a bad shoulder?" The pain could be danced through, but I wanted to guilt him.

Miss Kuznetsova would not be so lenient about this injury. She would scold me for being careless and want to know what happened. My pride would get the better of me and I would lie. I would not be a victim.

"I don't care," he grumbled. "Stop making me out to be the bad guy. I'm sorry." He stepped toward me and I backed up. "Can I make sure you're good?"

"Offended" was stamped on his forehead.

"Don't come near me. You can't do anything but make it worse."

He batted his eyelashes. "Come to my room. I'll make you feel better."

"I'm not having sex with you ever again, Nolan."

The Olympic rings we were. Connecting circle after circle. Instead of breaking up, we just made new circles to burn. If I'd never fallen pregnant, when would I have taken a step back? I was done. Sex couldn't be the answer anymore.

It's like he took my comment as a challenge. His chest puffed out. "Oh yeah? That's a lie. You say the opposite when we're doing it." His eyebrows rose at me. "'Don't stop, Nolan. Keep going. Harder. Yes, yes, ye—'"

"Stop it!" We were alone, yet I still looked to see if anyone could hear or see us.

"Come downstairs and we'll talk about it!" He reached for me.

All I saw was his hands coming to grab me again. I didn't want his arms to hold me down, because I would give in, so I jumped back and bumped into the side of the roof railing. My balance rarely failed me. I wobbled trying to keep both feet planted at the same time. My arms flapped so much, I should've flown. Nothing kept me upright, this roof wasn't zoned for anyone to be on. The siding wasn't high enough and over I went.

I caught myself, hanging over the side of the railing. Looking down, all I could see was the empty lot. This was too high to drop from. "Nolan!" I shouted.

He peered over the edge and looked at me with bewilderment. For the first time he was speechless. Mouth open. There was a flash of panic over his face. I didn't have to see mine to know I sported a similar one. My shoulder was killing me and my hands were already beginning to cramp from the awkward angle I had to hold my frame up.

At that height a breeze was terrifying.

"I wasn't going to hurt you. I wanted you to come with me," he explained, his voice wavering.

"Just help me." I didn't care.

I looked down again. My sneakers clawed at the brick building, and I hoped they would turn into suction cups. When I looked back up, Nolan's face had changed from panic to icy, despite the fire in his eyes. So quick he changed tempers. From smiles to assaulting some boy at a train station. He was going to make me pay. *Because you needed to suffer!* Nothing I could've said would've changed his mind.

"Please, Nolan. Help me up! Nolan, please!"

My hands couldn't reach, but my eyes could. He was untouchable. His lips were tight together now. Was he literally going to leave me hanging? I hadn't even begun to fully think of answers before my hands slipped. I don't know what I was trying to get out, but it sounded like a scream.

I crashed through the top of the trees like a rock penetrating water. I heard cracks and snapping. At the time, I didn't know one of the snaps was my back. Somehow, I was alive. But I couldn't feel anything. Couldn't hear anything. Everything was still. I knew I would have a hell of a time in class with the way my head was spinning. If only I could get up. I tried but couldn't.

My spine broke, but I'm not broken. I'm better than alive: I'm living. I'm the girl in the wheelchair that has infinite dances in her head. That has to count for something. To drop all that way and remember these dances and what they feel like.

Finally I close my eyes, knowing that memory had controlled me for the last time. It doesn't scare me anymore. Nightmares sleep.

"Hannah, I'm taking the bus tomorrow," I whisper.

CHAPTER THIRTY

I, Genie Davis

Can I come right out and say I'm the shit? It is almost lunch time, but it's never too early to brag. I'm the awesome unstoppable Genie Davis, who has a studio in one of the top ballet schools in the United States named after her, who just got off a bus by herself. No Mom. No Hannah. No ride from anybody. This is so much cooler than locking the house door behind me. That's all baby stuff compared to bus hopping with nobody but me. Genie Davis.

I'm glad Kyle told me not to come by the hospital. That he had to do something afterward, and that I could come by the next day. I wouldn't have taken the bus otherwise. I spot his building on the corner and glide forward. An older doorman opens the door for me. "Hello, Genie," he says.

At first I'm annoyed. Why does he know my government? Was he told to look for the girl in the wheelchair? But then I think Kyle probably told him a beautiful girl by the name of Genie was coming by, and he made the connection. "Hi," I say.

He nods, and I practically slide across the old marble floor to the elevators. I roll out on the seventh floor, where the carpet slows me down, but I make it to the end of the hallway. Before I ring the doorbell, I tug on my T-shirt. I can hear the threads screaming at the pulling of my chest. Hannah shrank it in the wash a while back.

I give the bell a confident push. It takes a while, but Kyle opens the door.

Shirtless.

"I was going to say the ride didn't take as long as I thought it would, but I think 'damn' might be more appropriate." His stomach's a little bruised from Nolan, but he looks carved out of wood.

Kyle looks down at himself, then back up at me. "You r-really took the bus? I thought . . . you were g-going to call a cab or something." He steps back from the door to let me in.

"I told you I was taking the *bus*. You're not far from Hannah." I really do try to look at his face, but I can't. Not with his shirt off.

If there's a weakness I probably won't be able to overcome, it's a shirtless guy.

He snaps at me with his fingers, smiling. "M-m-my face is up here." Kyle waits for me to meet his eyes. They look swollen, and there's a purple bruise and butterfly bandage over his right eyebrow. "W-w-working out." He backs up, allowing me to take in his apartment, using the crutch to hold the door open. It's not as open as Hannah's, but there's a staircase going up.

"You walk up those every day?"

"N-n-no. I have a little . . . room down here. I o-only go up there when my . . . parents are around."

He walks confidently in his house. I guess having something within arm's reach for Kyle to hold on to is important. Still, it's an upgrade from Mom's place. Even when I do manage to go back, I don't think I'll ever be comfortable there again.

"You're alone?" I look around the cream-colored space. Everything seems to be beige here. It's mellow but not boring.

He faces me. "W-w-why do I feel like you're s-s-staring at my butt now?"

"I can't help it. I'm butt level. The bus was quite a ride, actually." That's not an excuse. It's my life now. One I'm having trouble adjusting to. "Have you any idea how many people wear ill-fitting pants? And don't get me started on how many crotches I turned my head into."

Kyle laughs. "S-s-sorry. Didn't think about that."

We head back to this little room. Looks like it used to be an office. I can see Kyle's parents threw it together for his needs until he masters the stairs by himself. There's a desk shoved in the corner and books stacked against each other, making their own bookcase.

Leaning his crutches up against the wall, Kyle pulls himself up onto a bar hanging from the doorframe. With ease, he pulls his weight up and down. I watch, in awe at his shoulder blades in action. That explains why he has such gladiator-like upper-body strength. He lowers himself back down. Not as smooth as he got up, however.

"Watch out now," I tease. "Shouldn't you be resting, though?"

"I—I—I got to f-feel macho again s-s-somehow after . . . getting my ass k-kicked." He gives me a bashful smile. "C-c-come in. D-d-don't be afraid."

"I was certain I could take you before. Now I don't know." I should be exercising. If I went out more, I'd get my arms going. Maybe I should break out my weights and get conditioned again. I roll in closer. "Mind if I lie on your bed? Stretch my legs out?"

"O-o-of course not." I transfer onto his bed, propping myself up on my side. Kyle straightens out next to me. "H-h-how was VAB? We never got to talk about it." He looks at me.

"Not how I thought it would be. I saw Chris, my partner. He cut his hair. Some of the girls saw me and that was hard, and I cried." I fill him in on the studio, the dance, and Kuznetsova's proposal for me. "I guess it went well. Been going well. I've been going back."

I try to leave it at that, but Kyle has the tendency to make me smile without even trying. I remember when he told me he felt the need to spill his guts, and I feel the same now.

"I feel so stupid now. For being afraid of being me. I stopped being myself. I can't control my legs anymore, but I can control how I treat people. I can still do a lot of the things I love. Choreograph, watch ballets, and hang out with my friends." I look back at Kyle. "I expected things to be so different, and they are, but it's not all bad."

"You're s-s-still the same Genie. M-m-mostly. Is that such a . . . bad thing?"

My eyes fall back down. "No, I guess not."

"Before, you didn't think you h-had a reason to go back. Now you do. You clearly still have f-f-friends there and the class your teacher wants you to be a part of," he says. "I wish I was . . . welcome when I t-t-tried to go back to my gym."

I feel for him. Going back to VAB was more or less a positive experience. I was afraid that no good would come from me going back there. That even all my friends would eventually say, *You know what? We thought wrong, stay where you are.* That didn't happen. I couldn't have done it without their patience. If Kuznetsova had given me the cold shoulder, I would be devastated. "Kyle, we all make mistakes. Give them time."

He gives me a half nod. "J-j-just think about your chance, though, and all the . . . kids who can see that they can b-b-be awesome just from looking at y-y-you." Kyle switches the conversation back to me. "A-a-and we both know you like attention."

"To be fair, the applicants for the job are pretty few. I'm not sure if I'll do it."

"I-I-I'm proud of you a-a-anyway, Genie."

"Thanks, Kyle." I smile at him. "Why'd you ask me to come here when your parents aren't around?" I'm not in the least bit uncomfortable, but I find it odd. I think maybe he doesn't want me to meet them, but they're doctors, so perhaps they're busy.

"B-b-because if I . . . waited for a d-d-day they both could be here, I—I—I wouldn't see you for a few days." His mouth twitches and his smile fades. "I—I pressed charges against Nolan. I—I—I thought y-y-you'd want to hear it in person."

I know Kyle will get his justice for what happened to him, but now I feel like I should find my own with Nolan too. If Kyle isn't afraid to put what happened out there, I shouldn't be either. It's not enough to forget him. He has to pay. Otherwise, it's like what Mom said. He wins. I clear my throat. "Oh. At least now he won't hurt anyone else." The news hits me more than I think, and I lose my balance holding me on my side and end up staring at the crown molding.

"O-o-or you." Kyle finds my hand. "M-m-most importantly."

My eyes drift to the bruises on Kyle's stomach. Shame smothers me. "He was hurting you and I couldn't do anything about it."

"B-b-but I'm okay." His hand brushes my arm. "D-d-don't punish yourself over what he did."

"I'm not . . . anymore. I don't want to cause more hurt for you. Between Dylan and calling you broken and not talking to you . . ." I stop to think. Kyle looks at me, waiting for me to continue. "You stood up for yourself and I took the bus."

"D-d-doesn't feel as simple as it sounds, r-r-right?"

If I hadn't dried myself up at VAB already, I'm sure I would cry. Feels like I want to. "Thanks, Kyle." I take in a deep breath. "I mean that."

"W-w-we're friends." He gives my hand a squeeze.

"Friends" is a weak word to describe us at this point. We're more than friends. Whatever Kyle and I have is deeper. I don't know if I love him. It's a mix of what I have for Hannah and used to have for Nolan. I have so much respect for Kyle. For standing up for himself and just going for it.

"If you hadn't spoken to me that day in therapy, I wouldn't have gotten the chance to know you."

"I—I—I was n-n-nervous. I heard the things you said to . . . Logan, and I was afraid you'd ch-ch-chew my head off."

I playfully punch him. "Was I that bad?"

Kyle nods. I was the whole cast of *Les Misérables* and hell-bent on being miserable, to Mom especially. I completely misread her my whole life. I thought she struggled because of me, when really, she struggled *for* me. I assumed she would handle the whole pregnancy/abortion thing differently. That she would hate me for falling into the life that wasn't easy for her. Mom is all that I have, and I was pushing her away. Still am, sadly. I don't know how to approach her and make things right.

Kyle could see how unhappy I was and he didn't mind. He didn't try to exploit my feelings to make himself feel better. I examine him. For everything that I find physically attractive, I pair it with something intellectually or emotionally attractive. The most attractive thing is I never get the feeling he wants something else.

"Do you get nightmares?" I ask him. I think back to the day I walked with Kyle down the hall at physical therapy. I wanted to ask him then.

"A-a-all the time." He moves closer to me. "I don't remember much, but I can hear the s-s-sound the car made when it hit the pole. I k-keep hearing it until I wake myself up." I don't know if he notices, but he's gripping my hand. I squeeze his hand back. He lets up on my fingers. "S-s-sorry."

"You're okay. I know what you're going through. I always hear my screams." Hollywood should run me my check for the new "Wilhelm scream." I turn back on my side. "Think we'll have them forever?"

Kyle twists himself on his side so we're face-to-face. Our noses almost touch, and I can feel his breath on my skin. He's blessed with the thickest eyelashes ever, and they curl prettier than any fake ones I've used for performances. He has the smallest collection of freckles I didn't know he had. I notice his lips don't touch fully, showing a little of his front tooth. When did I start to really look at people? Did crying clear my vision somehow?

"I—I don't know. B-but I read that . . . nightmares are good. M-m-means you still have . . . s-s-something worth fearing."

"Then what are dreams for?"

"T-t-to tell you things."

"If I dream about you, what does that tell me?"

He doesn't respond vocally, but tugs on my braid. If Kyle were anyone else, it would be annoying. But he doesn't stay on my hair for long, and his fingers slide up to my face. His rough fingers glide along my lips like they're a kind of braille, and he's reading what they want. Even Genies have wishes.

Our foreheads touch. His breathing is heavy, like he just finished walking. For a quick second I think of pulling back. If Kyle's not backing up, I certainly won't. Not when I'm so sure what he's about to do. I want to kiss him to get it started, but that was me a long time ago. I can be patient. Kyle can take his time.

Maybe he needs some encouragement. I gently run my hand over his bruises, taking in his firm but smooth skin. He tenses a little but relaxes as I bring my hands lower, following a trail of soft fur. My skin tingles like he's the one touching me. His breathing picks up and he nuzzles the side of my face. My fingers hit his waistband.

Kyle's hand stops mine. He comes in closer. His other hand spreads across my stomach. I can feel him. *Please don't go lower. I need to feel this.* So caught up in his touch, I almost don't register the kiss he puts on my forehead. I count ten inhales from him before I speak.

"Why'd you stop?" I ask.

"B-b-because if you went any f-f-further, I wouldn't know what to do."

I pull on my shirt, which is now twisted. "I'm okay with that. I don't care that you're a virgin."

I feel like one too. I haven't gone . . . *there* in a while, and adding my injury, I didn't think I'd ever want to again, but Kyle just proved to me that I can emotionally. I've been told that everything works. That with patience and time sex is possible, and I've always stopped those conversations before I blew a fuse, and now I wish I'd let them continue. I was feeling something. The urge was there. But that doesn't mean I could do it. What if it's not like riding a bike and I sucked? I don't even know what it would feel like anymore. He was right to stop me. Maybe we avoided a disaster we couldn't come back from.

"N-n-no, that's not i-i-it." Kyle shakes his head, like I have it all wrong.

"I'm sorry." I move back. Kyle follows.

"I—I—I do want to kiss you. R-r-really bad. I d-do. It's just . . . I know w-w-where this is . . . heading if I do kiss you. I c-c-can't think of anyone else I'd rather lose it to. B-b-but like you said, y-you have a hard time being in a . . . relationship that isn't just s-s-sex. I—I—I don't want to just have sex until I leave for college. I'd rather get to know y-you."

I can feel my face falling. Can't say I've ever been turned down for sex, let alone a kiss. But this is Kyle. He's got a really good point. There's nothing to be mad at.

"You're right. We should be friends first. And maybe I should talk to a professional about how this works with my paralysis. I legit don't know." My face flushes.

"M-m-maybe next time a c-c-condom, too."

I cringe. "Especially that." I offer my hand to him. "I don't know any friend that made me feel like you just did."

Kyle grabs my hand. "I—I—I think we both can . . . agree that 'friend' isn't the w-w-word for us, but it'll h-have to do for now." Rubbing circles on my hand, he continues. "I hope you know . . . I'll w-w-wait for you."

"Speaking from before, I'm worth the wait." I laugh at my own joke.

I'm not prepared for the kiss Kyle plants on my cheek. It's not pitying or uncomfortable. The confident smile left on his face says he's proud of himself. And he should be. It was strong and gentle at the same time. Like being lifted during a pas de deux. I'm speechless.

"I-I-I'm not much of a tease, b-b-but that's a taste of what's to come." He suddenly goes bashful. "Y-you can tell your friend I k-k-kissed you."

"I think I want to hold on to it for myself." I touch my cheek. "For a little bit."

We lie back down, only this time Kyle puts his arm around the top of my waist. "Is that o-o-okay?" he asks.

"It's comforting, actually." I feel his chin against my shoulder.

"W-w-what else do you have planned? J-j-just 'Magic'?"

I'm still not used to him asking questions out of curiosity and not to keep tabs on me. Kyle has his arm around my waist and keeps it there. No roaming hands or grinding against me. He really just wants to know what's up. It's amazing.

I groan. "I need to patch things up with my mom."

"W-w-why make it sound . . . impossible? Sh-sh-she loves you. I'm sure you two can make it work."

I find my fingers tap dancing on Kyle's. "Things were said. I don't know if they can be forgotten."

"M-m-maybe not. B-b-but they can be forgiven."

Mom might forgive me, but I feel like such a fool. I want to go home. I do, but I always seem to say the wrong things, or get so angry I can't hear anything but the flames dancing in my head. Hannah knows I'm struggling with this, and I haven't stopped talking to her about it since I asked her not to drop me off back home after the Y.

"How do you always know what to say? What are you studying at Stanford?"

"I-I-I've honestly just been l-l-lucky. I-I-I'm undeclared."

"You should be a psychology or philosophy major. That or play the lotto."

"Y-y-you know what to do. A-a-always have. I didn't . . . make you go to QUEST. You did that. S-s-same for going out with me. G-g-going back to your studio. You have the answers, Genie."

"Keep talking to me. Tell me things about you that I don't know." I snuggle against him.

Kyle begins to tell me about his favorite music. Surprisingly, he likes classical music but couldn't stand learning how to play any classical instrument. He snorts as he recounts his failed attempts at learning any kind of percussion, too.

"Private-school boy? I dig a guy in uniform."

"T-t-too bad I d-didn't have one. W-well, they did, but I always broke the code."

"Rebel. So, you're not a onetime bad boy."

Kyle keeps talking. I love his confidence, even with the stutter. His voice is just as comforting as his arm around me. I don't know what he sounded like before. I don't care to know. And I do want to get to know him. He tells me about how hard it's been for his parents to trust him again. That they had an awkward conversation about his weed stash the night before, which he initiated. He felt guilty lying about it. It's so interesting how he doesn't try to be perfect, though. Makes me think of Mom. I thought she wanted to be perfect to make up for everything before her sobriety, and that she wanted me to be perfect to help her image. But I realize she's never wanted that. Not for me or her. She just wants us both to be better.

"H-h-how long c-c-can you stay?" he asks, taking a break from telling me about some of his favorite places to eat nearby. "I—I—I have an idea."

Kyle's idea has us back at Brooklyn Bridge Park. Only this time we're by Jane's Carousel. I fall behind Kyle, watching it spin around and around. The East River and a ferry boat gleam behind him. I sigh. To turn without having to turn myself right now. Seeing as Kyle is walking away from the line, I'm guessing the carousel is not his idea.

"C-c-catch up, slowpoke. If you're nice, I'll buy lunch and dessert." He smiles back at me.

"Maybe I like you better from behind."

The front and both sides.

We settle at a bench looking out at the Manhattan skyline. Clouds are scarce, and I have to squint to look at anything, really. It's muggy and Kyle's curls are sticking to his neck.

He wipes his sweat away with his shirt. "L-l-let's make a list . . . of all the g-g-good things s-s-since our accident."

"Parking—easy!"

"N-no more r-r-random questions."

"I hardly have to deal with the bummy MTA anymore, plus I have my own personal roller coaster when blocks are hilly." I make an explosion noise.

"I—I—I can use m-my . . . crutches to knock things over . . . without r-r-reaching." Kyle spikes an imaginary football down.

"So we're turning this into something? I turn wheels, Kyle. You're gonna lose."

We laugh and Kyle waves his white shirt in surrender.

"It could've been a lot different for me. Like . . . You know I often think about that girl attached to the ventilator in PT."

"Samara. Sh-she was the one that the . . . scaffolding fell on. C-c-crushed her. I talked to her once."

"I thought she looked familiar." I remember seeing it on the news. Just three days later I fell from what felt like the top of the world. And what did Samara do to deserve her fate? There was a hole in her throat and she still managed to say, "Good morning."

"You know what? I'm tired of being mad all the time. Samara always seemed to be in a good mood despite it all. Fuck this shit."

Kyle sputters and even his hands mutter as he tries to get the words out. His eyes stretch wide excitedly and I lean in, waiting to hear it. "H-h-have an idea. O-o-on three, let's shout 'fuck this shit.'"

I waste no time. "Three!"

"Fuck this shit!"

Oh, we shout it. We scream so loud, people look at us like we escaped Bellevue's psych ward. Tourists point their cameras at us as we throw our heads back and yell it to Manhattan. It feels so good to let it out and not care about being looked at. I start talking to the people gawking at us.

"Fuck this shit, sir! Sometimes you just have to shout it, ma'am!" I roll up and down the promenade. Fuck the looks, fuck caring right now. *They see me rolling, they hating.*

Meanwhile Kyle sounds like George of the Jungle. He's not even shouting it. He's just plain yelling, smacking the banister with his crutch. And it sounds beautiful.

"I think you gave up too soon on percussion, Kyle!"

I can see the people on the boats waving at us. Some even shout back, and it's hilarious. Finally we calm down, my throat sore from the abuse of it all. Kyle sits down on the bench next to me, putting his arm around my shoulders. I lean my head into the crook of his arm, the Manhattan skyline turning in a circle before me. Or maybe I'm turning. It's most definitely me, because Kyle spins me to face him.

"Thank you." It's his adagio voice.

I take his hand and kiss it. "Come with me to the end-of-year gala."

"Of course. One request?"

"What's that?"

"W-w-wear something red."

Way ahead of him.

CHAPTER THIRTY-ONE

Finale

Backstage before any performance is hectic. Girls are fighting over the few mirrors there are. Costumes are swinging like ghosts are running sprints. Shrills of girls either laughing, crying, or both at the same time become louder than the music some chaperone put on to "calm" the environment. There is some order, even if it doesn't look it. There's the ABC track, meant to keep track of everything we need to do before getting onstage. *A* is makeup, *B* is hair, and *C* is costume. Hannah and I loved when we hit the *A* track, because we loved doing our best *Showgirls* clapbacks in the mirror without turning our heads to talk to each other.

Everyone has their thing they do before the show. The three odalisques like to stretch and warm up together. You can hear the ballet boys in their best frat-boy *rah-rah*. The little kids are usually singing and shaking their jitters out somewhere in the hallway. There's a moment where everything speeds up like end credits, but I know it's the beginning. Hearing the stage manager announce "places," it suddenly slows down. Hannah and I hold hands until we reach the stage and go to our correct side of the house. Nothing else matters as

I stare at the spot where I'm to be when the music calls me. I want to please the audience, but I have to do it for myself, too.

Hannah squeezes my right shoulder, bringing me out of my daydream. She's putting on a coat of yellow lipstick and I'm supposed to be doing the same, but I don't want to look like I ate Tweety Bird. "Where'd you just go?"

"Backstage. I felt like I was there again." I put down the tube of lipstick in the holder I got her. "Aren't you going to have to redo this at the theater anyway?"

Hannah's mirror's so big it feels like we're at a three-hundred-year-old theater in Italy. You can fit four ballerinas comfortably in the bulb-lighted frame. Pictures of old costumes, makeup guides, and us are taped to the old mirror. The bulb in the top right corner is dead and some glass is cracked, but that's why Hannah's cousin managed to scrape it from the Shubert Theatre a few years ago. Despite its worn look, we manage to look new in it, to me at least.

Without turning to look at me, Hannah stares at me through the mirror. "Well, you won't be backstage this year, will you? I've never not gotten ready without you, so we're doing it now." She blots her eyes with a paper towel. "Dammit, I just did my eyes."

I rub the small of her back. "Here I thought you were pitying me because I can't make a decision about going home." It's been four days since the blowup at my place.

"Speaking of home, is your mom coming? Has she ever missed a performance?"

I shrug. "Who knows? I'm not really performing, so technically her record is still clean."

Hannah turns on her stool to look at me for real. "This is just as important. 'Magic' is important and she knows that. Try calling her. You know, like you do Kyle in the middle of the night."

"That was one time since I've been here."

"You can add a zero to that."

"That snark is staining my good mood. Save it for your pointe shoes."

She smiles. "I'm sure she'll come. I'll leave it at that," Hannah says, walking to her bed and sliding on the yellow dress she put out last night. "Are you getting dressed now?"

"Hannah, we're leaving, come on," her mother shouts.

"Coming!" she shouts back. "My keys are on the table out there. I'll see you after the show." She stops. "Hey, it's gonna be all right. Don't forget to bring out Boss Genie." Hannah blows me a kiss before closing her bedroom door.

We're going to the same place, but it's not the same. My phone buzzes on Hannah's nightstand before I can get any deeper into my head. It's a text from Kyle.

Kyle: Should I meet you out front?

Me: Please and thank you.

Kyle: You okay?

Me: Nervous.

Kyle: I'll be there. We can be nervous together.

Kyle: I have something to tell you too.

Me: You're really forty with a wife and two kids?

Me: Jk jk

Me: I have a surprise as well.

We leave it at that, because I still have to do something about my hair. I've called on God a million times just to do it. I can't tell if I'm calling *the* God or just initializing my name, Genie Orchid Davis, because the saga continues with my edges. If I use any more gel, I'm going to look like those dolls with the plastic hair. Giving up, I drop my brush. Can't please everybody.

My fingers trace the ropy texture of my braids, making sure they're secured enough into my bun. It doesn't feel right to flat-out have a bun today, and yet, I've grown to really love my French braids. Hannah suggested having the best of both worlds and bringing two braids into a bun.

And I can't show up to the biggest night of the year at VAB and do any less than stun. Can't disappoint the fans. Not that I'm worried about "Magic" being seen, gazed at by some of the biggest people in the ballet world. Picked apart. Judged. Revered, maybe? A girl can dream. And I have been.

I dream all the way into the cab, wondering how many dressing rooms Miss Kuznetsova has blessed. She never stays longer than a glance, it seems, but I know she watches for longer than anyone realizes. Like a spirit, she drifts by the open doors, or you feel the softness of her drapey cardigan as she passes you on the stairs to the stage. If you listen closely, you can hear words of encouragement. *Make me proud. You look the part, now be the part.*

For the past couple of days, I've been changing up the choreography. Adding stuff. Moving things around. Picking things up. Slowing it down. Now I'm getting an idea. I unlock my phone to add to the insanely long group chat between Hannah, Maya, and me. The last thing Hannah wrote: Change anything else, and I might kill you. I text Break a leg instead. I bet no one ever told Alvin Ailey to stop. I doubt *Revelations* was a hit with him right away. I'm sure he wanted to make changes right up to the debut, like me.

But I don't want to stress Hannah or Maya out, so I won't. It is what it is. Same for seeing a psych. I don't want to go, but I figure a lot of great people see one sooner or later. Like Mom. Who also has been keeping tabs on me through Mrs. Hernandez (Hannah has spilled, but I won't spoil that I know), and I can tell she never knew how crazy my life at home was, but is now dropping hints about the therapy she and Mr. Hernandez have done just to keep the air clear. That got me thinking about how hard it is for me to keep my cool and speak freely without being disrespectful. Maybe someone can help make sure the fights stay clean.

Sometimes I need someone who isn't so close to the problem too. Kyle's more than willing to listen to me yap all night, but seeing how he comes up a lot in regular conversations, he's better for other things. Like making me laugh or trying out how much my sweet tooth can handle. I've been encouraging Kyle into the new wave of "shirtless therapy," where if I'm having a bad day or feel like the next day will be bad, he talks to me shirtless. He wants to see the studies on it. Apparently, he questions its validity and reliability, but I'm still looking for some publications. I've told him it works the other way too, and even then, he's set on taking things slow. I understand and respect his wishes, but it's fun to see his face whenever I lift my shirt, showing no more than a belly button, to put the therapy into action.

Once I'm out of the cab, I check myself over in a store's window. About now I'd be giving myself the glance-over in a full-length mirror. Making sure my costume was right, adjusting my pointe shoes if need be. Now I have on heels. Like my toe shoes at one time, it's a learning curve. My footplate has seen nothing but flat shoes until now.

I can see the theater and Kyle as I wait to cross the light. Somehow my chair isn't wobbling, but I shake. Even in this heat goose bumps spread across my skin. Kyle stands in front of the VAB poster that features Chris doing his famous cabriole in princely white tights.

Let's see if Kyle likes his surprise. He's too busy smoothing down his shirt to notice I've pulled up beside him. I pull on his pants leg. "Excuse me, mister, I'm looking for a fairly hot guy with wavy hair and the shiniest pair of crutches."

"Y-y-you scared me." He kisses me on the cheek. "Sh-sh-should we go in?"

I shrug. "What if no one likes the dance and I'm just the girl in the wheelchair?"

"N-n-not going to h-h-happen. You're Genie first. H-h-hey! R-r-red chair!" he shouts.

"Surprise!"

His eyes blink fast as he gets his words together. "W-w-when'd you do this?"

"Yesterday. Chris pimped out my ride." I turn a circle. "You did wish for me to wear something red." Sorry to anyone looking for red glitter washi tape at Michael's on Atlantic Avenue, but we pretty much bought out the inventory, and Chris's sister hooked us up with her employee discount, so now I look stunning while being economical.

"I—I—I was thinking red shoes or s-s-something."

"Everyone does red shoes. I guarantee you'll see somebody's little cousin in red ballet slippers or a dance bag with red pointe shoes on it." I pat him on the leg. "I do appreciate you trying to learn about ballet culture, though."

"I-i-is it that popular?"

"Let's just say it's been done to death. Like the dancer who put them on in the film. But no ballet dancer in the history of ballet dancers has ever, and I mean *ever*, had a red wheelchair."

"I—I—I have the . . . f-f-feeling it'll always be that way." He wiggles his eyebrows.

"It's blazing out here. Let's go inside."

VAB has used this theater for their recitals for years. It's not Lincoln Center or some three-hundred-year-old opera house, but you couldn't tell me that the first time I took the stage here. I wish there were a way Kyle could hold my hand as we make our way in. Kuznetsova invites everyone and their mama in the ballet world. Several people stop their conversations to follow Kyle and me as we maneuver through the small islands of people. I'm so used to being backstage during this, it's a little shocking to see the number of people in the lobby. I keep checking to make sure my legs aren't dragging or something.

I recognize some people as sponsors and onlookers in our classes. *All eyes are on you, Genie. Smile.* My smile has put the

Cheshire cat out of business. Kyle's focused on the slippery floors, and I almost veer off course to look at him. We manage to get by the mingling guests and enter the auditorium when a hand touches my shoulder.

"Genie!"

"Logan? What are you doing here?" I look him up and down. He's still wearing a polo shirt but has switched out the sweats for a pair of shorts.

"Did you think I'd miss seeing you in your natural habitat?" He elbows Kyle gently. "Somebody here told me about it. And seeing that you were my favorite client, I came."

I look at Kyle. That was sweet of him. "Oh, wow."

"I—I—I took a chance, b-b-but I talk too much. I see Logan when I go to QUEST still," Kyle explains.

Logan's eyes drift to the painted ceilings before settling back on me. "I'm sorry we had to meet under the circumstances. But I'm sure today will allow me to see the side of you that gave you great arms for your transfers," he says, putting his hands on my shoulders. "I saw you coming in. I'm proud of you."

"Thanks, Logan. I hope you enjoy the show."

"I'm going to take my seat, but so glad I got to see you." He has the same enthusiasm from our sessions and gives me a hug that makes me glad I'm buckled.

"See you around, Logan."

"Are you okay?" Kyle asks.

"Yeah," I exhale. "Let's go to our seats."

An usher hands us our program as we enter into the orchestra.

I have to clench my rims tight to keep from flying down the slope to our seats. There's the aisle seat for Kyle, and I pull up next to him. Technically it's a no-no, but I doubt there's going to be a fire. The accessible spots are in the back. Our spots are right in front of the stage. I cannot watch "Magic" from the rear. Not going to happen. I can't bring myself to open my program. Literally, my hands are too shaky to spread the pages.

I wonder if Mom is coming. I try my best to look around without too much movement.

"Th-th-think your mom is here?" Kyle whispers.

"I don't know. I was just stretching." I push my legs together.

"R-r-right," he says, practically making origami out of the booklet.

"Why so nervous?" I point to his program.

"C-c-cause you are. What's your *point*? B-b-but with an *e*," he says with a smile.

"Oh gosh, now you have puns?"

"G-g-got another one."

"Let me hear it," I feign little interest

"I would say this crowd's a nice t-t-turnout." His face has to hurt with that smile.

I shake my head at him. Kyle can be so corny sometimes. But I like it.

"W-w-what? That was a good one."

"Just keeping you on your toes," I tell him.

We both start laughing. I can barely hear us over the orchestra warming up. I'm glad my back is to most of the looks burning my neck. I peer into the wings as far as I can, to see if I spot Miss Kuznetsova. She's probably backstage, giving her speech to everyone. She rarely watches from the audience. I think she prefers the wings around her. After all this, she's still not a spectator.

Kyle turns my palm over into his hand. In a way it's better than any kiss I can wish up for us. I'm reminded I can still feel when he touches me. Maybe it's the delicacy with which he does it. Whenever Kyle lets go, I still feel like I belong to myself. We've started this game of writing in each other's hands and trying to decode it. His fingers begin to spell out something. It tickles me, though, and I squirm in my seat. He momentarily stops before continuing.

"T-O-N-I-G-H-T," I whisper. "What do you have in mind?"

Kyle's face turns redder than my chair. "N-n-not so loud." He looks at the woman sitting next to him.

"Ha ha. Okay, I'll be there."

I know he wants to spend some more time together, because he leaves at the end of next week. Maybe I've become Kyle-obsessed. I know the exact day he's leaving, what time his flight is, and have even joked about squeezing my way into a genie's lamp to go with him. Even through all my jokes, I know he can tell that I'm bummed.

"Excuse me, Genie, is it?" A woman with a little girl in front of her gets my attention.

"Yes, I'm Genie."

"I told you that was . . ."—the girl's voice trails off as she inspects my chair—"her."

Kyle lets go of my hand. "What can I do for you?" I ask, confused.

"Leilani here said you and a few other students did a performance at her school this spring." She looks down at Leilani. "She remembered your name and the school. Hasn't stopped talking about you or ballet since."

There's something familiar about this lady. Not that I think I've met her before, but she reminds me of the women in my Bushwick neighborhood. The cadence of her speech, the slight sass in her voice. Even sports the same twists like Mom.

I look from Leilani to her mother. I do remember. "P.S. 158? I picked you as a volunteer to learn the positions." I recall how shy she was at first, but she opened up in no time.

Leilani looks surprised that I remembered her, but a smile slips out. "Can you not dance anymore?" Her smile fades as she points to my chair.

"No. Bad accident—but that's okay. I can still enjoy dancing." I wait for her smile to return. It doesn't.

Her mother steps in. "I'm sorry to hear that. Leilani, tell her what you told me about that day."

Shifting from foot to foot, Leilani looks at me nervously. "Some girls in my class told me Black girls couldn't dance ballet. But when I asked them what you were, they didn't know what to say."

A knot forms in my stomach. I'm a good decade older than this girl and the foolishness still continues. Now more than ever I'm upset not to be on that stage tonight. Besides my own happiness on that stage, I wanted to inspire girls like Leilani to make the girls she goes to school with get dizzy from watching her turn. Looking around the auditorium, I can count the people of color in this room.

330

"I looked into VAB, but it seemed the school already had auditions for this coming year. So I got in contact with the woman who owns the school, Miss Kuznetsova, and told her that Leilani saw you dance. Miss Kuznetsova said you're her favorite student, and she invited us to come to the school and let Leilani try out with a class," Leilani's mom explains

"And I got in!" Leilani squeals, her cheeks flushed.

"That's awesome!" I high-five her with a smile. It is awesome. She should be excited. As I look at her smile, I'm reminded that I changed her life. Leilani wants to dance because she saw me. I inspired her. Passed on my magic. "Do you like magic?"

"Yes," she says, but I can see the question in her eyes.

"Good. Because you're magic. Don't ever stop for anyone."

I watch as she brings her other hand from behind her back and holds *Relevé* in front of her. "Can you sign this for me?" She pulls a marker out of her dress pocket.

I take the magazine in my hands for the first time since tossing my copy out the window. It requires all my concentration to keep my hands steady. The pages are cool to the touch. Even after all this time, I can't believe that's me on the cover. I finally pry my eyes off myself and up at Leilani, who looks like excitement is going to burst out of her. She holds the marker out to me and I manage to keep my hand still enough to write my name on the cover.

My first autograph!

"I'm gonna put it on my ceiling!"

She hugs the magazine to her as fiercely as I held on to the edge of the roof. The way I held my first pair of pointe shoes, competition trophy, and acceptance letter to VAB. I hope she holds on to her dream of being a ballerina just as tight, just as close. I have a good feeling about her, though.

The lights flicker, signaling everyone to settle down. Leilani's mother thanks me before leading her daughter back to their seats. Leilani wears a pair of red ballet flats. I make a mental note to tell Kyle when everything is over. As the lights go down, Kyle takes my hand again. He rubs circles on it, and I remember my breathing. *Slow it down.*

Kuznetsova takes the stage to talk about everything we're about to see. She walks so swiftly and lightly, it's like being in the presence of a spirit. I still can't believe she was injured by a car. It's more or less the same speech every year, but I always hold on to her voice when she says, *It's one thing to watch dancers who finish their training, but to witness the blossoming of talent is even more precious. You all are lucky. I am lucky to introduce them to you.* I think about all my classmates, how we practically grew up together. We would watch the seniors, wondering when it was our turn. Now they're doing steps we all dreamed about.

The orchestra starts, sending vibrations throughout my chair. I love how easy it would be for Kuznetsova to just play recorded music, but she thinks it's better for us to learn with a full orchestra. And like I know now, this could be the last chance for some of us to ever perform with real live accompaniment. You can see it in the dancing, how the music transforms a dancer when the screech of a string or the whistle of a flute is as real as you are.

When youngest students start the gala, I can't help but gush and "aww" with the rest of the audience. By the time it gets to the preprofessional year I feel a change in my mood I'm not proud of. I realize how effortless it is for me to be jealous of these thirteen-year-old pointe babies, leaping themselves to the stars and turning magic with every pirouette. I can only assume their flight is powered by butterflies I would be feeling. Should be feeling. Envy takes hold of me. I have to look down. *They deserve their time*, I tell myself. Even though mine was cut short.

Everything from my stomach to my heart hurts.

I remember the first piece I ever learned on pointe, as though it were only yesterday. It was new choreography for *Sleeping Beauty*. I wish there were a way I could tell them it only gets harder from here on out. But it gets better, too.

Chris leads a coda after a special piece Mr. Balandin created for the boys. Is this how mothers feel watching their children? I'm equally excited and proud to see Chris commanding the stage. He could definitely leave here tonight with a soft offer from a company. The stage is his. No wonder Kuznetsova chose him for the posters.

There are a few more performances. I get to watch Maya and Chris partnering. Seeing them together makes me miss him and the jokes I'd hurl at him. A prince in and out of character, he'd simply hug me before partnering. They've been working hard together. It shows. Maya looks great with him. They seem to be dancing in a snow globe with all the glitter swirling around them.

"...Genie!"

I blink in surprise, so far into my own head I didn't realize it was time for "Magic" next. Hearing my name through a mic makes me feel like I'm onstage again.

Logan shouts, "You got this, Genie!" Everyone laughs in response, but it doesn't feel harmful as if I'm the butt of a joke. Still, I squeeze Kyle's hand when the curtain reopens and Maya stands center stage.

Wearing a red, silky, slip-like dress, she has her back to the audience. Instead of a bun, she wears a braided ponytail. The murmurs circulating throughout the theater about her hip-length hair make me smile. They have no idea what's about to happen, and Maya hasn't even begun anything yet.

The first zing of the violin starts.

She's been holding out on me. Maya's showing off. She's loose, yet in control. Her jumps are higher than in rehearsals, and her chaînés are *almost* as good as mine. I look over to see Kyle's white teeth glowing in the dark, he's cheesing so hard. Too bad the gymnastic life chose him instead of ballet.

Hannah enters on a grand jeté. Her sass turned all the way up. Not that anyone would be paying attention, because Hannah and Maya execute perfect grands pas de chat in unison, so flawlessly that it took now for me to really see it from this distance. I wasn't far back enough to appreciate it from the Genie Davis Studio.

Damn, I'm good.

I'm practically eating out of my own hand with this choreography. Hannah doesn't wear a bun or braid. Her black curls hang freely, and it's outright badass. When she does entrechats six, her hair knows nothing about gravity, and I love it! *That's my best friend!* I want to shout. I've probably elbowed Kyle no less than ten times by now, but he doesn't seem to mind.

I wish it were me up there with her. The sadness creeps back in when they fouetté until the music finishes and the curtain drops again. As everyone claps and whoops and whistles, I can't help but remember that the applause should've been for me and Hannah together. I'm both impressed and proud of Maya, but I didn't get to do it. I never got to perform "Magic" in front of an audience. I'll never get the chance to either. I allow myself a short minute to be upset and it goes by fast, because the applause is booming. Maybe I'm used to hearing it from backstage, but it's so incredibly loud out here.

Miss Kuznetsova comes back out again. I find myself bowing out of respect like after every class.

"That is the end of the show, but we are not done," she says. "We have a very special guest tonight. As most of you may know, VAB lost a student, but not a dancer, to a bad accident. The last piece you saw was created entirely by our very own Genie Davis." She gestures to me.

The house lights are up and everyone stares at me. My eyes drift to see heads turn in my direction, followed by claps. Miss Kuznetsova has to quiet the audience down. I don't let Kyle's hand go.

"Now, we had flowers ready for you, but your friend sent some too."

I look at Kyle, who shrugs like he has no idea what she's talking about.

Hannah, Maya, and Chris come out, each with two bouquets in their hands. They hop off the stage to hand me red roses and orchids. They all talk at the same time: "That was awesome!" "I told you it was worth it." "What do you think, you're some kind of legend?" It looks like wind is blowing through me the way the flowers shake in my arms. Hannah is ugly-crying.

"One thing more." Kuznetsova waves to the wings at stage right. Everyone that took the stage tonight comes back out again. They all have a magazine in their hand. "We all have a copy we want you to sign."

And I lose it. The tears start rushing out of me like they have someplace to be. The only way this moment could get better is if Mom were here to see it. I know seeing "Magic" would've made her happy, even just for a little bit. I did it all from this chair.

"O-o-open your eyes. S-s-see them standing for y-y-you," Kyles says into my ear.

I open them slowly and look around to see the house on their feet. Hannah, Maya, and Chris clap too. "Is this really happening?" I don't think Kyle can hear me, but he somehow does.

"D-d-don't tell me you're shy now," he shouts over the noise.

"Genie, would you like to say something?" Miss Kuznetsova asks as she smiles wide.

I shake my head no. There's no words. Kuznetsova closes it out, ending the gala, and a bunch of people line up to shake my hand and congratulate me. I'll never have to work on my signature again, that's for sure. When the place finally clears out and Hannah, Maya, and Chris head backstage to get out of their costumes. Hannah points to Kyle and mouths, "He's cute." I just about die from that alone as Kyle witnesses it. Miss Kuznetsova comes down from the stage. She has a copy of *Relevé* in her hands. When she gives it to me, I see that it's signed by pretty much everyone at VAB. Front and back. I notice Miss Kuznetsova's starlike *A* and her bold *Z* in the corner. This magazine doesn't feel like mine, though.

Not just this magazine, but this moment. Mom has never missed a performance. I shook all these hands and smiled at all these people, and she isn't here to insert that I get it all from her. Even though I hate when she does that, I know she's proud of me. I don't even know where she is now. Maybe she's at St. Nick's with people that actually appreciate all that she does. I know it's selfish of me to think, but I wish she were here.

Relevé belongs to Mom, for her to add to that box in her closet. Only maybe I can convince her to keep it out on display.

I introduce Miss Kuznetsova to Kyle and she gives me a devilish grin before pinching my nose.

"No mom?" Miss Kuznetsova asks.

"No, not this time." Hearing it out loud chokes out the good I've been feeling.

"N-n-nice meeting you. I'm a f-fan of ballet t-truly now," Kyle gushes. He gives me a quick smile before heading back to the lobby.

I have to plan what I want to say. I'm afraid it'll come out as mush if I don't. Miss Kuznetsova waits patiently as I start over and over with each attempt to shove it out.

"Thank you, Miss Kuznetsova. I don't deserve it at all," I finally say.

"Still distracted by your own light, I see." She takes the seat where Kyle was. "I am surprised not to see your mother. She is well?"

"I hope so. Will there be a recording?" Maybe I can give her that.

"Yes, of course. I'm sure the photographer got several pictures of you crying, too."

I blot my eyes with the back of my hands. "There was a camera?"

"Yes, definitely distracted!" She pulls me in for a hug. "So. It is the end of summer. I need an answer."

I take a deep breath. "I've thought about it. I really have. I'm not sure how great of a teacher I'll be, but I'm willing to try. You've done so much for me, even when I wanted nothing to do with ballet because I couldn't dance anymore."

"Bolshoe spasibo! Thank you very much, Genie! This will be very good for both of us. I am very proud of the lady you have become. When you started here, your head was so big, full of attitude and arrogance, it threw off your pirouette." She pinches me on the nose again. "Still arrogant with attitude, but you give yourself to ballet and let you friends shine. You always have a place here. You are why I teach. Actually, I see now you still will be my student. You have a lot to learn."

She gives me a kiss on both cheeks before standing up.

"Thank you, Miss Kuznetsova."

"I don't think you will need video for your mother," she says, pointing her chin behind me.

I turn to see Mom walking down the aisle. Miss Kuznetsova touches her arm as she passes by.

"I couldn't leave without letting you know I was here," Mom says, stopping just a few feet in front of me.

I try to be mad. But I'm happy more than anything to see her. "I didn't—I thought you weren't coming."

She steps forward. "I've never missed a performance." I can hear a tear hit the magazine. Mom rushes for me. "No, no. Why are you crying? You should be nothing but happy today."

I feel small as she wipes my tears away. "I'm happy. Mostly. It's just that I should've been up there." I look to the stage. "I should be meeting you with my dance bag on my shoulder."

"Aww, Genie." Mom hugs me, rocking me slightly. "It won't feel okay for a while." She speaks with the confidence of experience, but the softness of being a mother. "You are everything. The stagehands are going to have a bunch of magic to clean up."

I laugh and wrap my arms around her tight. "Mom, I have something for you." She releases me and I hold out *Relevé* for her. "I want to give you this since I lost the other one."

Her hands cover her mouth. "Oh no, Genie. That's clearly for you."

"And I can do what I want with it. I want you to have it." I keep it out in front of me.

She takes it and holds it to her the same way Leilani held hers. "Thank you, Genie." She sits in the seat next to me. "How have you been?" She smooths the top of my head.

"No more hospital visits, but I'm sure Mrs. Hernandez told you that."

"You know I had to check up on my only baby." I see her fiddle with the magazine, and a smile comes across her face. "I think I'll frame this."

"I would hope so. No one can see it in the box in your closet."

She rolls her eyes. "Speaking of boxes, look at this." Mom dangles my red ribbon in my face. "Turn around, let me put it on you."

I do as I'm told. "Matches my chair."

"I can see that. It's more you, too." She runs her hands over the sparkly tape. "You know what else I saw? I saw Hannah's family up front." There's that cautious tone of hers. "I was invited to go out to eat with you. I told them I would ask you first."

"Of course. I've missed you . . . but Kyle's coming too."

"I'm glad you've found a friend through everything. Think he'd mind being introduced to me?"

"Not at all."

Kyle has wanted to thank Mom personally since the whole stoop incident.

"What's the name of this place that Hannah found somehow?"

I smile. Hannah chose the restaurant Le Magie. Definitely trying too hard with the whole magic theme, but how else would I describe everyone together? That's the thing about magic. It doesn't always work when you want it to, but it's there when you need it.

Grande reverence.

ACKNOWLEDGMENTS

First, I want to thank my family. Cherish, my bosom buddy, friend, sister, and pal: thanks for always rocking with me on this writing and publishing journey since we were kids. You're next, no doubt. And to Mom, too, for being you and sacrificing a lot for me. For always saying I could do anything I put my mind to. Anthony, cousin, as you can see, Genie never needed your math lessons. I don't miss those days! And to my godmothers, Brenda, Karen, and Sharon, and my godfathers Dwayne and Sam: thank you for being the village I needed then and now.

My super agent, Saba: thank you for seeing in me what could be. We did it! And to Denene, for truly getting the story I was trying to tell and being an editorial genius. How my voice blossomed under your direction. And to Lisa Moraleda, Milena Giunca, Justin Chanda, Alyza Liu, Krista Vossen, and Talia Skyles, the *Turning* team at SSBFYR/Denene Millner Books—I literally couldn't have done it without you all.

Big ups to Beth Phelan for starting #DVPit and using the platform to uplift marginalized voices; it put me on the path toward meeting Saba. Same to Despina Karras and Vilissa Thompson for all their insight on living with a disability, which helped make Genie come to life more authentically. You both are literal lifesavers, and I truly appreciate your honest words.

Where would I be on this journey without my writing buddies in the Villa Villekulla? Sue, Susan, Sara, Michele, Em, Kathleen, and Lauren: thank you for being my first fans and great companions in doing this thing we all love called writing!

Here's to Mr. Greer, my English teacher for three out of my four years of high school at BCAM, for being the first one to call me a writer, and for helping me find the way to Girls Write Now, which, without a question, is the reason I'm published. How lucky was I to have Radha Blank, Ibi Zoboi, and Emma Straub as mentors as a teenager? Also, hey, Ms. Gardiner!

Thanks to all my early readers of *Turning*: Claudia Clarke, Renee Frey, and Erica Caldari-Roberts! Erica, you went the extra mile to physically show me the ballet steps that I could never do! Thanks for bringing the words to life.

And lastly but not least, the many casts of *Waitress*, who kept me going through this publishing journey! With the release of *Turning*, we were both born today! And to Lexie! Tea Cleves Gang Gang! A true queen both on and off the stage, thank you for the never-ending encouragement, laughs, and wisdom. My life has changed for the better knowing you.